Praise f

"When you read a Robin Jones Gunn book, you know you're going to receive a tender lesson and you'll be blessed for it."

Francine Rivers, *New York Times* bestselling author

"Robin's storytelling is a breath of fresh air. Her tender heart and wisdom make every one of her books poignant and unforgettable."

Karen Kingsbury, *New York Times* bestselling author

"Robin Jones Gunn writes about everyday women with truth, tenderness, heart, and soul . . . while taking me on an adventure."

Rachel Hauck, *New York Times* and
USA Today bestselling author

"Both poignant and fun, Gunn delivers a story that is like a warm hug from a good friend in this first installment of the Suitcase Sisters series."

Library Journal

"Robin's stories always make me feel as if I've actually visited another amazing part of the world."

Tricia Goyer, *USA Today* bestselling author

"Gunn premiers her Suitcase Sisters series with a heartwarming story of sisterhood, international travel, and Christian faith in times of uncertainty."

Booklist

"Only a well-seasoned traveler like Robin could pen such a lovely tale of two kindred spirits exploring a beautiful slice of Africa. . . . Well done, Robin!"

Melody Carlson, award-winning author of
Welcome to the Honey B&B

"Gunn is adept at denuding light fiction of its usual tics and imbuing it with the hallmarks of literary fiction. The characters are multidimensional and ring true at nearly every turn."

Publishers Weekly

"Robin Jones Gunn brings the ravishing wilderness of Africa to life in *Tea with Elephants*. This gentle, beautifully written story laps around you like the warm waves of the sea, soothing away the day's stress, whispering a soft promise of hope and lasting friendship. An altogether delightful read."

Tessa Afshar, *Publishers Weekly* bestselling author of *The Queen's Cook*

"It is a widely acknowledged fact that Robin Jones Gunn has a knack for creating unforgettable characters. . . . As I read the story of these charming characters, I couldn't help but smile at their joys, grieve for their hardships, and wish that I could go on adventures with them."

Susie Finkbeiner, author of *The All-American* and *The Nature of Small Birds*

"Readers will be swept off their feet by this faith-forward celebration of friendship."

Amanda Cox, Christy Award–winning author of *Between the Sound and Sea*

"Through the lens of faith, friendship, and the majestic wonders of nature, *Tea with Elephants* is a testament to the enduring power of love and the divine beauty that awaits those who seek it."

Sara Brunsvold, Christy Award–winning author

Gelato at the Villa

Books by Robin Jones Gunn

Victim of Grace

Suitcase Sisters Series

Tea with Elephants

Gelato at the Villa

Christy Miller Series

Sierra Jensen Series

Katie Weldon Series

Haven Maker Series

Sisterchicks Series

Glenbrooke Series

Father Christmas Series

SUITCASE SISTERS #2

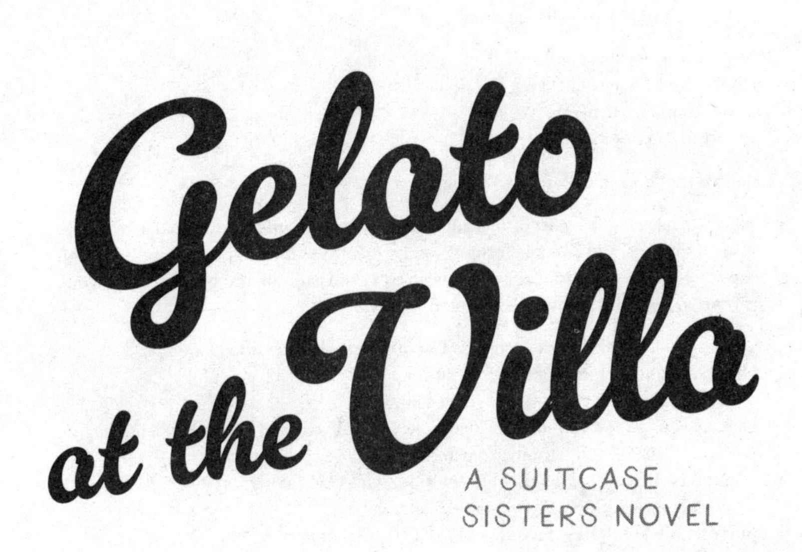

Gelato at the Villa

A SUITCASE SISTERS NOVEL

ROBIN JONES GUNN

a division of Baker Publishing Group
Grand Rapids, Michigan

Published by Revell
a division of Baker Publishing Group
Grand Rapids, Michigan
RevellBooks.com

Printed in the United States of America

Library of Congress Cataloging-in-Publication Data
Names: Gunn, Robin Jones, 1955– author.
Title: Gelato at the villa / Robin Jones Gunn.
Description: Grand Rapids, Michigan : Revell, a division of Baker Publishing Group, 2025. | Series: Suitcase sisters ; 2
Identifiers: LCCN 2024053717 | ISBN 9780800744830 (paper) | ISBN 9780800747114 (casebound) | ISBN 9781493450626 (ebook)
Subjects: LCSH: Italy—Fiction. | LCGFT: Christian fiction. | Novels.
Classification: LCC PS3557.U4866 G45 2025 | DDC 813/.54—dc22/eng/20241122
LC record available at https://lccn.loc.gov/2024053717

This book is a work of fiction. Names, characters, places, and incidents are the product of the author's imagination or are used fictitiously. Any resemblance to actual events, locales, or persons, living or dead, is coincidental.

Cover art by Art of Nora

Cover design by Laura Klynstra

Published in association with Books & Such Literary Management, BooksAndSuch.com.

Baker Publishing Group publications use paper produced from sustainable forestry practices and postconsumer waste whenever possible.

25 26 27 28 29 30 31 7 6 5 4 3 2 1

For Paula,
my Suitcase Sister and favorite Pilgrim.

Prologue

Chi trova un amico, trova un tesoro.
Whoever finds a friend finds a treasure.
Italian saying

We didn't expect to love her.

Admire her beauty? Of course. Enjoy her traditional recipes? Absolutely. Appreciate the accomplishments of her many children? No question.

But fall in love with Italy? Become irresistibly smitten with her voice, fragrance, and unforgettable personality so much that we cried when we left her?

No, Claire and I didn't anticipate that. Nor did we expect that the stories of our lives would be forever altered under the ancient Tuscan night sky. Beauty and chaos, truth and understanding melded in ways I don't think would have happened for us back home in Redlands, California.

We had to go to Italy.

The possibility of our adventure began as a daydream eight months before we boarded the plane. Claire got the bug while watching a travel show about Italy and proposed the idea of a trip the next time we met for coffee.

"Did you know that we can take a cooking class and stay in a real Italian villa?" she asked. "I did some research and there's one just outside of Florence that looks amazing. Can you imagine making our own pasta?"

"That sounds like your best dream come true," I said. "Are you and Jared thinking of going?"

"No, I was thinking you and I should go," Claire said. "I know you're not obsessed with cooking the way I am, but don't you think it would be fun to go to Florence? And maybe Venice?"

"Ooh. Venice." I let the possibility settle on me and answered in a faraway voice, "I always wanted to go to Venice."

"Then let's do it," Claire said decisively. "Let's go to Florence and Venice. But not Rome."

"What's wrong with Rome?"

"I went there in high school for a school choir trip and . . ." Claire's chin dipped.

"I didn't know you went to Rome."

"Bad memories," she said.

"What happened?"

"There was this guy . . ."

"In Rome?"

"No. From my school. He was in the choir, and he told me a week before the trip that he liked me. I was so excited and thought he was going to be my first boyfriend. I really liked him too. Then on the plane he ignored me and avoided me the whole trip."

"That's brutal."

"I know. It's hard to get excited about the Colosseum or the Vatican when you're sixteen and walking around with a broken heart."

I reached across the table at the coffee shop and gave her arm a comforting squeeze. "Rome is off our list," I said with the tone of a solidarity sister. "And that's fine with me because my memories of Rome aren't that great either. I was twelve when my family went. It was our first trip on my dad's airline passes, and my mom was determined to see everything. All I remember is that my brother and my dad got into an argument in a nice restaurant and my mom was mortified."

"With all the trips you took with your family, why didn't you ever go to Venice?"

"I don't know. Maybe my mom had bad memories of Rome too. The only other place my mom and dad went to in Italy was Bellagio. They loved it. I think they went there twice."

Claire leaned forward and brushed her bangs back so she could look me in the eye. "I need to do this, Grace. We need to do this. Venice and Florence and let's add Bellagio. Perfect. Done."

I knew she was worn out emotionally after losing both her parents in the last year. The weeks she'd spent closing up their home and settling their affairs in another state had sparked a restlessness, and my best friend seemed to be on the hunt for an unnamed piece of her life that had gone missing.

"I'm not the only one who needs to get into an escape pod right now," Claire said, giving me a stern look. "Your stress levels at work have been too high for too long. What's that saying about how you need to come apart before you come apart?"

In the same way that I knew about Claire's emotional exhaustion after the passing of her parents, she knew about my boss, a high-strung ophthalmologist in his late seventies. His health was declining, and every week at random intervals, he would walk past my receptionist desk without a word and leave the office with no indication of when he'd return. Dealing with irritated patients for months and trying to reschedule them and provide an adequate apology is more draining than it sounds.

Claire's proposal of a trip to Italy felt like an open window. I longed to fly out that window and go far away, where I would not have to deal with another incomplete insurance form or misplaced patient file. It would be wonderful to spend a whole week without having another patient take out their frustration on me.

I told my husband, Nathan, about Claire's idea, and to my surprise, he agreed we should go. His exact words were "Claire's right. You need to do this."

He reminded me that his mom had gone to Venice with her sister-in-law about twenty years ago. I called her for advice, and Sue had only praise for her adventure.

"Grace," she said, "you and Claire will be so glad you went. I might be able to arrange a place for you to stay in Venice. Would you like me to reach out to the people I know?"

When Claire and I met again for coffee a few days later, I felt like I was twenty and not almost forty. Dreaming of the possibility of the trip was cathartic. Even if we weren't able to pull it off, just having something else to think about and dream about did my heart a world of good.

I presented Claire with possible dates, a tentative confirmation from my mother-in-law for a place to stay in Venice, and the promise of flight vouchers from my dad, a retired airline pilot. I also had lots of advice from my mom on what to see and do in the Lake District of Northern Italy around the chic town of Bellagio.

"Looks like all we need are new suitcases!" A sparkle lit

up Claire's pale blue eyes. I could always tell her mood by her eyes. Over the last few years, she had grown her bangs out and they'd become like curtains she could pull down and hide behind on her worst days. That day, I had an unobstructed view of her expression, and it was clear that something important was happening. We were about to turn the page and start a new chapter in the book of "us."

One of the things I loved about our decade-long friendship was that it began because of a book. Claire had been nestled on the cushioned bench by the door of the coffee shop I frequently stopped at on my way to work. One morning, as I was leaving with my latte, I noticed the cover of the novel she was reading. The book wasn't a new release, nor had it been a bestseller or the top pick of some famous person. The surprise was that I had just finished reading the same book the night before.

Claire glanced up. I introduced myself politely and nodded at the book. Five minutes later we were friends. It was that easy.

Now, is that odd? Or is that God? I'll tell you the answer. It's God. It's always God when the coincidence is too much of a . . . well, coincidence.

It's poetic, really, that God used a book to connect us, because Claire once said that some books made her feel as if she belonged at the same table with her favorite imaginary friends. I love that thought because I've felt the same way with certain books too. But until Claire said it, I didn't know how to name the sense of being invited into the story.

When I was young, my mom read Bible stories to me every night. My tender little heart embraced Jesus when I was eight, and I never doubted that I had been invited into God's story and belonged at the table along with the many real people He wrote about.

Claire, however, had walked away from that table, so to speak. When you hear why, it will make sense. But what I witnessed in Italy was that the Author and Finisher of her faith was about to add an astonishing twist to her story. I'm so glad I got to share that chapter with her.

It's been only a few months since our trip, and just the other day I was thinking about how different we would be if we hadn't made the trek, or, as we learned to call it, the pilgrimage. We discovered that a tourist travels to seek something new and curiosity-satisfying in a faraway place. A pilgrim travels to seek a sense of belonging and something soul-satisfying in a faraway place.

Claire and I planned our trip as tourists. We returned home as pilgrims.

Yes, we needed to go to Italy. We needed to gaze at works of art that are without equal anywhere in the world. We needed to meet some remarkable people who elevated our limited concepts of hospitality, kindness, and love. We needed to indulge in every variety of pasta we could find.

Most of all, Claire and I needed the luxury of long, uninterrupted conversations. We needed to sit under a trellis dripping with wisteria and talk about things we'd never shared with each other. We needed to laugh hard and give way to a river of tears.

And yes, we needed to close our eyes and dream new dreams as we savored fresh strawberry gelato at the villa.

It is not down on any map; true places never are.
Herman Melville

Even though Claire and I spent months researching, planning, and organizing every detail for our trip to Italy, from the moment we arrived in Venice, I wondered if we'd made a big mistake.

The doubts crept in as thick as the heavy fog that enshrouded us when we boarded the water bus outside the Santa Lucia train station. The inside cabin of our vaporetto was full, so Claire and I had to stand in the open space at the front of the large craft. We braced ourselves, shoulder to shoulder, leaning on the railing, and could barely see ten feet in any direction as we floated down the Grand Canal.

"This is not what I expected." My voice quickly dispersed into the mist.

Claire pulled up the hood of her jacket. "It's creepy, isn't it? All the buildings seem to have vanished."

"I pictured us arriving just in time to see a blistering orange sunset like the ones we saw in all those pictures."

"I didn't expect it to be this cold."

A horn sounded.

We couldn't tell which direction it was coming from. Claire and I turned toward the captain at the helm inside the crowded vessel. He quickly looked right then left and did not appear confident at all.

Another horn sounded.

"Hey!" Claire pointed straight ahead and waved her arms.

The nose of a sleek wooden boat emerged from the haze, heading directly toward us. Our captain veered to the right. Claire and I gripped the cold metal railing and steadied ourselves as the smaller craft passed with only a few feet separating our hulls. I looked down into the cabin of the passing boat, where the passengers looked up at us with wide eyes and unmoving lips.

Our craft bobbed and tilted. Claire grabbed her suitcase and tucked it between her legs to keep it from rolling away. She looked like a nervous hen who had just laid a big rectangular egg. I gripped the handle of my suitcase and tried to keep my posture straight and steady.

"Claire," I said, "I think we should have spent the money to have a private boat pick us up."

"Too late now. Besides, don't you think it would be more dangerous to be in a small boat right now, like the one that just passed us?"

"You're right." I drew in a deep draft of the moist air. "We should be fine."

I tried to appear confident because I was the one who had worked out the details for this part of our trip. I had every reason to trust my mother-in-law, who had set up the accommodation for our three nights in Venice. She even surprised us and paid for our room.

However, when Claire and I tried to look up the lodgings

online, the place didn't seem to exist. We had only a few details about the room from the confirmation email and hadn't seen any pictures. All I had was an address that I'd marked on my phone app before we left California. That didn't seem like enough now that we were here on the other side of the world and adrift in an eerie, blinding fog.

"Two more stops before we get off, right?" Claire asked.

I nodded and checked my phone to be certain.

Claire remained uncomfortably quiet as our vaporetto pulled up at the next dock. I tried to think of how we could go about finding a different place to stay if our plan A turned out horribly wrong. The good thing about Claire was that she was efficient and resourceful. She'd planned the details for the rest of our trip, and I was confident that if my contribution to our journey was a disaster, she would be able to come up with a plan B.

I didn't want my plans to fail, though. This was Venice! We wanted to love Venice. We had placed so many hopes in this being a fun and restful getaway.

Our large vaporetto motored on until it made a bumpy arrival at the dock where we needed to get off. A dozen other passengers exited along with us, but nearly all of them went in the opposite direction from where the map indicated we should go. We pulled our suitcases behind us on the uneven path as if they were belligerent old dogs that didn't want to go for a walk. At the moment, I kind of didn't blame their reluctance.

I checked my map again and followed the arrow. Within a hundred yards of the dock, we were alone, headed down a shadowy, narrow passageway.

"Grace?" Claire didn't have to finish her sentence. I knew what she was thinking. I was thinking the same thing.

I charged ahead, walking at a quick pace. The passageway

soon opened to a plaza area labeled on my app as a campo. We crossed the broad space that was void of any other humans and headed for a narrow bridge over one of the many small waterways. The old buildings on every side of us were easier to see now that we were away from the thick fog over the water. They looked menacing with their darkened windows.

Once we were over the bridge, I told Claire, "Look for a sign over a door that says 'Trattoria da Tommaso.' It will be on the left side."

We went about a hundred feet before Claire said, "Is that it? It looks like a restaurant."

I double-checked my phone. "The confirmation email said this is where we pick up our key."

I went first, cautiously entering the softly lit café. The tables were empty, but the scent of the food cooking prompted us to exchange slightly hopeful looks. At least we could eat well before having to venture out in the fog to find a real hotel that would take us in.

As per the instructions, I went over to the bar and politely cleared my throat, waiting for the bartender to notice us. Claire pushed the hood of her jacket off her wispy blond hair and suddenly looked like a dandelion.

The bartender came over with a towel over his shoulder and an unruffled expression.

"Hello. Good evening. I'm Grace. We have a reservation. We were told to come here for the key."

He gave a single nod, his posture making it clear that he had done this so many times he had stopped trying to be charming about it. After reaching into a drawer behind him, he pulled out a fob with the number 4 on it. He handed it to me and walked away, saying, "Benvenuta."

"Excuse me," I said. "Can you tell us which direction we should go?"

He nodded toward the back of the restaurant. Claire gave me a wary look, but I did my best to ignore it. After all, we had a key. A modern key. A fob. We had a room number. The check-in guy knew we were coming. It all seemed legit.

Trying once again to appear more self-assured than I felt, I led the way past the tables covered with white cloths and folded cloth napkins. The local time was a little after seven o'clock. Apparently, Venetians ate later than seven. At least I hoped that was why the tables were vacant and the eating area felt strangely quiet.

We entered a narrow hall with a bathroom on the left. The opening to the kitchen was on the right. Delicious scents wafted from the slightly open door, causing us to slow down and breathe in deeply.

"Now that is how onions sautéing in olive oil are supposed to smell," Claire said in a mellow voice.

I started dreaming of lasagna. A big, fat serving of true Italian lasagna with sauce made of fresh herbs and vine-ripened tomatoes. My taste buds made a silent promise to the dinner that would inevitably find its way to my empty belly. *I'll be back. Wait for me.*

We continued past stacked boxes to the open door at the end of the hall. Claire reached for my arm and we stopped at the same moment, frozen in place.

Before us was an enchanting courtyard. Lanterns hung from curved shepherds' hooks placed at intervals along the stone path. Raised garden boxes symmetrically radiated from the center like sunbeams. At the heart was a fountain welcoming us with the gentle sound of the water flowing over the top.

The fog that enshrouded Venice was barely a whisper in this enclosed space. Only a thin, slightly hazy touch of the vaporous clouds settled here. They only added to the dreamlike feeling. In the far corner, a large tree sheltered two chairs, and from the tree's limbs hung softly glowing lanterns, flickering like chubby fireflies.

We entered the hidden garden slowly, as if we'd been transported to another world. A fairy-tale kingdom. The meeting place of Romeo and Juliet.

I loved gardens and kept a small one at home. It thrilled me to find a garden in the middle of the dense jungle of Venetian structures that had dominated this small island for centuries.

"Did your mother-in-law tell you it was like this?" Claire asked.

"No. I don't think Sue came here. She stayed someplace else, and she never said anything about a garden. I would have remembered the garden."

I trailed my fingers across the edge of the fountain and slid them under the gentle cascade of cool water. It was difficult to tell what was growing in the raised garden beds under the fairy lights. I'd take a closer look in the morning.

"I think that's our room." Claire pointed to a door by the tree and led the way across the stone walkway. "Number four, right?"

The wooden door looked old, and the metal door knocker in the shape of a lion's face looked even older. What an unconventional thing it was to then press the fob against the installed box by the metal door latch and hear it click.

We pushed the door open together, and as soon as the lights came on, Claire and I halted once again.

"It's like a storybook," Claire said as she ventured inside. "Look at the details on the woodwork. This room is so big."

My gaze had fixed on an exquisite chandelier that hung from a main exposed wooden beam in the ceiling. The chandelier had five curved arms from which blue and amber glass dripped like large frozen raindrops. The colors blended with the rich brocade upholstery on the sofa and the matching roll pillows at the arms. Next to the sofa was an ornate writing desk with built-in boxes just begging to be opened.

"Look. We have everything we need to make coffee." Claire pointed to the mini nook next to the door. The space was too compact to be called a kitchenette, but it looked well equipped for some simple hot beverage prep.

"I love this little round table." I lowered into one of the plush chairs by the small table, where two crystal drinking glasses and a matching carafe filled with water awaited us. I carefully removed the crystal stopper and poured the water, and we raised our glasses. Neither of us came up with words for a toast, so we drank the welcome gift in silence and a sense of relief.

Claire strode across the tile floor, checking out the two twin beds with matching ornate headboards and the tall dresser with a large, gold-frame mirror above it. On the edge of the dresser sat a vase filled with red roses. Claire picked up the card at the base of the flowers. Instead of reading it aloud, she came over and sat in the other chair and handed me the card.

Benvenuta, Grace and Claire.
May you know Peace.
Rest well, Pilgrims.
Paulina

"Who is Paulina?" Claire asked.

"I'm not sure. Sue's friend, maybe?"

"This is all just . . ." Claire looked up at the chandelier. "Wow."

"I know. Big wow. I did not expect this."

"It makes sense why they don't post pictures or list this as a vacation rental. It's too special."

"This space has been well loved," I said. "I feel privileged to be able to stay here."

"Do you think that's a closet or a bathroom?" Claire popped up and turned the door handle. "You won't believe this. It's a bathroom and it's marble. All marble. The floor, walls, shower."

"I would believe anything right now."

She turned to me. "Grace, I'm sorry I was skeptical about this place. I should have trusted you."

"You have no reason to apologize. I didn't know what we were getting into either. I was more nervous than you about all the unknowns."

Claire stepped into the bathroom and laughed. "Grace, why didn't you tell me?"

"Tell you what? That I was nervous?"

"No. Tell me what my hair looked like! The moisture here is going to be my nemesis." She trotted over to her suitcase and began playfully singing, "Oh, where is my hairbrush?"

I smiled and decided to stay settled in the chair, sipping the refreshing water. I wasn't ready to look in the mirror. I was pretty sure that my attempt at the end of our flight to pull my long, dark brown hair up into a smooth twist had been pointless. The twist had unraveled into a loose cluster, and I knew the dense moisture had enticed oodles of wayward strands to curl and come out in every direction in a free-for-all. I was just glad we were here and that the room far exceeded our expectations.

I pushed up the sleeves of the merino wool sweater my mom had purchased for me in preparation for this trip. She insisted that layering would be essential since the weather in May would vary. I was already thankful for the warmth and the quality of the finely knit sweater. I liked being comfortable, and at the moment, I was quite comfortable.

While Claire was in the bathroom, I glanced around at the touches of elegance in our room and thought about the trips I'd taken with my mom during high school and college. If she were here, she would have diplomatically suggested that I shower, fix my hair properly, and change into a crisp white blouse with fresh "slacks" before going out for dinner. Her wealthy upbringing, etiquette, and expectations had governed my life until I met Nathan.

He and I were a case of "opposites attract," and I loved the way we still balanced each other. We started married life with china dinner service for sixteen from my side of the family and camping gear from his side. I hoped that traveling with Claire would be more like camping with Nathan and our daughter, Emma, than the elaborate trips I'd taken with my mom.

"What do you think?" Claire asked, exiting the bathroom. "Do you want to rest a little, or should we go find something to eat?"

"Food, please."

"Good. Because I just happen to know a place that looks pretty good," Claire said. "Or at least it smells good."

I grinned. "Is it within walking distance?"

"Yes, just a tiptoe through the garden."

"Sounds good to me."

"I should warn you that the bartender isn't especially friendly," she said with a grin. "But if we ignore him and focus on the pasta options, we should be fine."

I thought of how I had told her on the vaporetto that "we should be fine," and here we were—more than fine. I caught her eye and said, "Claire?"

"Grace?"

"Guess what?"

"What?"

"We're in Italy."

2

As soon as I saw you, I knew an adventure was about to happen.

A. A. Milne

Nearly every table was taken when we returned to the restaurant. True, the place was small, but the transformation in less than an hour from our first introduction was surprising.

We entered through the back door and waited in the hallway until two waiters had passed in and out of the kitchen before making a quick dash into the now-vibrant hub of conversations and laughter. I found it hard to remember how peaceful the space felt when we first entered. The added high notes of silverware tapping against plates and clinking of glassware in toasts accompanied by the words "cin cin" invited us to be part of the liveliness.

Claire navigated her way through the maze of tables and held up two fingers to the nicely dressed man by the front door. He returned the peace sign as if it were a joke.

"Due," I said, attempting to use the limited Italian Claire

and I had quizzed each other on during our long flight. "Two. Table for two."

The man gave a courteous tuck of his chin and escorted us to what was now the last open table in the restaurant. It was also the smallest table and was wedged in between two other parties gathered around tables that should have hosted four people but were accommodating five. The bartender we'd interacted with earlier was now taking orders, and a younger man was pouring wine behind the bar. A third waiter delivered plates of pasta to the table beside us and then turned and spoke to us in Italian. We hesitated.

"Do you speak English?" Claire asked.

"Of course. What would you like?"

"Menus?" Claire ventured.

He studied us for a moment. "Are you Paulina's friends?"

"Yes," Claire said.

"We're staying here," I added with a nod to the back of the restaurant. "My mother-in-law made the reservation for us, but we don't actually know Paulina."

He nodded. A pleasant smile lifted the corners of his mouth. "No menus. I will bring you the best." He turned and was gone.

I hoped his idea of the "best" was the lasagna my palate longed for. I let my shoulders relax and tried to adjust to the proximity of our dinner companions at the other tables.

Claire leaned across our small table. Her hair was pulled back in a low ponytail, and the sleek style made her eyes look especially large and expectant. "Don't look so worried. I have a feeling that whatever they bring us will be delicious." She drew in a slow breath and closed her eyes.

I did the same and noticed that the air was laced with a variety of fragrances now. Aromatic food was only one of the scents. I also detected smoke and fish.

Two glasses of red wine were placed in front of us, followed by two plates with a modest serving of tiny fish popping out of a mound of sautéed onions and topped with pine nuts and raisins.

"Would it be terrible to say that I was hoping for lasagna?" I whispered.

"This is only the starter. The antipasti." Claire took a bite and nodded her approval. "Sardines. This is nice. A little olive oil, onions, and maybe a dash of vinegar."

"It amazes me the way you can deconstruct food like that," I said. "All my palate tells me is if I think it tastes good or not."

I didn't tell Claire, but my taste buds weren't excited about the antipasti. The flavors launched my appetite, though, and I wondered if that was the intention.

Claire reached for her glass of wine, then drew in a slow breath like a connoisseur before taking a sip and swallowing slowly. She looked at me without blinking. "I think I'm in love."

I followed her actions of lifting my glass to my nose and then my lips. I didn't have wine very often, so my first taste fell into the same category as the sardines. The sensation on my taste buds was a bit startling, but then the aftertaste of the wine blended with the sardines seemed to be satisfying.

"What do you think?" Claire asked. "Nice, isn't it?"

I nodded and confessed, "You know how my parents are adamantly against drinking, so wine with meals was not one of the charm school courses I received from my mom."

Claire took another sip.

"Nathan and I don't know the first thing about how to select wine or how to pair it with a meal."

"I don't know much either," Claire said. "But I decided that if I was given the opportunity on this trip to drink wine that was ordered by someone who knew about such things, I was going to enjoy it all." She raised her glass, and I did the same before letting another taste linger on my tongue.

The next dish was a plate of rice and peas in a creamy sauce. The delicious and satisfying flavors had the effect of comfort food, and I finally felt I could lean back and stop being hesitant about everything.

"You know what feels strange?" I said. "No one is staring at us."

"Why should they?"

"We're the outsiders. Tourists. When I traveled with my mom and dad, I could feel people staring at us."

"Your mom tends to draw attention," Claire said. "Not in a bad way. She just has an air about her."

"I know. She does, doesn't she?"

"I hope it didn't sound like I was saying that your mom is aloof. She's not. She's classy. And kind and generous. I love your mom. Did I tell you she gave me some money last week so I'd have extra souvenir funds?" Claire asked.

I smiled. "She gave me some too."

"You know what?" Claire leaned in closer and looked serious. "We decided that this trip was going to be a chance for us to try new things."

"True."

"So let's be brave and try new things. If someone stares at us because we have no idea what we're doing, so what? Everything is new to us."

"You're right."

Our server placed a dish in front of us with layers of pasta stacked up. I hoped it was lasagna. Then I took a closer look. "Claire, why is the sauce black?"

"That must be the squid ink."

"The what?"

Claire took a hearty first bite. "Oh, that's good. I was hoping we'd have something tonight made from local scampi. Look at all the little curly shrimp in there. And the Parmesan cheese is amazing." Claire dove in for a second bite.

When I hesitated, she grinned and said, "Bravery, remember? Try new things."

I took a bite and was surprised. She was right. It was nice and tasted even nicer with a sip of wine. If squid ink had a distinct taste, I couldn't detect it.

The final course was served, and we could see by the layers in the glass dessert bowls that it was tiramisu. However, this was unlike any tiramisu I'd ever had. I scraped the sides of the glass with my spoon, trying to nab every bit of it.

"What a great dinner," Claire said after we paid the bill.

"I don't think I would have ordered any of those dishes if I had seen a menu in English, but it was all good."

"I loved it. Did you have a lot of meals like that when you traveled with your family?"

I thought for a moment. "I'll never forget the drinking chocolate we had at Angelina's on the Rue de Rivoli in Paris. Oh, and the orange blossom macarons at Ladurée on the Champs-Élysées. Those were so good."

"Sounds decadent."

"I also loved the fruit scones with clotted cream we had at afternoon tea at the Ritz in London. That was memorable. And we had some sort of cherry pastry in a village in Denmark that was so good I ordered a second one." I smiled at the memory and added, "Funny how all my food memories are of desserts."

"You know what always amazes me about you?" Claire said.

"My sweet tooth?"

"No. It's how down-to-earth you are. I never knew you'd

traveled so much until we started planning for this trip. In all the years I've known you, you've never acted like a rich girl or bragged about all your first-class experiences."

"The rich girl days were back in my childhood. My life is nothing like that now."

"I know. But I love that you don't act like you're from money."

I thought about her comment when we returned to our room and while I took a shower. Once we were in our beds and about to go to sleep, I said, "You know what I realized? I've been married to Nathan longer than I lived under my parents' roof. My mom taught me the finer things in life, but Nathan has taught me the simple things and that's how I want to live. I mean, I'm grateful for all the experiences my parents gave me, but I don't miss that life. There were always so many expectations."

"Kind of like how things have been at work for you this past year?" Claire asked. "The way your boss keeps handing all the extra jobs over to you ever since his wife passed away?"

"It's not too bad," I said.

"Grace, he has you picking up his dry cleaning and scheduling his lawn maintenance. I've told you this before. I know he's paying you extra, but I think he's taking advantage of you and your kindness to him."

"I know. But I've been working for him since before Emma was born. How can I resign?"

"Like this. You say, 'I resign.'"

I didn't reply.

The sisterly-advice tone in Claire's voice lowered. "I am not trying to be insensitive. I know it's a complicated situation. But didn't you tell me that you and Nathan are the most stable you've ever been financially? Didn't he say that if you didn't work for a year you'd be okay?"

"Yes. That's because of the inheritance from my grandfather."

"Well, just think about that. And don't worry about what your boss will think of you if you resign. You've been caught up in the whirlpool of his life and have gone above and beyond to make things easier and better for him."

"I know."

"All I'm saying is that you're not responsible for keeping his practice afloat." Claire reached over and turned out the light. "Now, to change the subject and give us something to dream about, I need to tell you about the promise I made to Jared."

"Okay. What did you promise?"

"Remember how you were saying your mom introduced you to the finer things in life? Well, my parents pinched every penny, and I tend to be more like them. As you also know, my husband likes to splurge every now and then, and he made me promise I would splurge on our trip."

"I can help you with that," I said. "We'll start by ordering two tiramisus next time."

"Actually, I was thinking gelato should be our first big splurge. Did I tell you I made a list of all the gelaterias in Venice?"

I laughed. "How many are there?"

"I don't know. The list is long. One of them opens at nine tomorrow morning."

"With that to look forward to, I believe we are going to have sweet dreams tonight."

"Yes. Gelato dreams," Claire said.

"Gelato dreams," I echoed. "Love you, Claire."

"Love you, Grace."

Sleep came in two pieces. The first three hours were immediate and deep. Then I woke up and felt like I should check my phone. That was a mistake.

I soon fell into the trap of scrolling, even though I told myself I wasn't going to be phone dependent while we were traveling. I'd already let Nathan know we had arrived in Italy. He'd replied, and all was well at home. No messages were waiting for me from work. I didn't need to check anything else like the weather or how many steps I had taken that day. But I did.

Forcing myself to put my phone back on the nightstand, I tried to fall back asleep. My thoughts tumbled into a deep hole as I ruminated on Claire's comments about work. Even though it was financially feasible, resigning before our trip hadn't felt right. I hoped Mary, who was filling in, was keeping up with everything. I tried to let it all go and dozed off and on for a few more hours.

I finally gave up trying to sleep when I saw the morning light shyly slinking into the room through the edges of the front door, creating faint lines on the tile floor. I stood and tiptoed around our room, gathering my clothes. I felt like I had a weight on my head. Claire was having no problem staying in dreamland. She didn't even stir when I opened the bathroom door and it creaked loudly.

My eyes were puffy, so I pulled out all the aids in my makeup bag and began a futile effort to look fresh and friendly. I was surprised that my hair combed out nicely after washing it last night. I let it fall over my shoulders, and once I was dressed, I decided to go outside and visit the garden.

"Morning," Claire said in a groggy voice as I exited the bathroom. "How did you sleep?"

"Okay. Not great. How about you?"

"I slept deep. This bed is so comfy."

"Hope I didn't wake you."

"You didn't," she said with a yawn.

"I'm going to step outside and have a look at the garden.

I'll make some coffee when I come back." The cool morning air scurried into the room as I opened the door.

"I can make the coffee." Claire pulled the thick comforter up to her chin. "Just give me one more minute in this perfect cocoon."

I left her to her bliss and stepped into mine.

The pale morning sunlight illuminated the garden in the cool morning air. Two small birds flew to the edge of the fountain, where the water glistened like silver. I watched as they shimmied and dipped and then fluttered off to start their day with drip-dry wings.

Taking slow steps, I rounded each garden bed, admiring the healthy-looking tomato plants along with the eggplant, carrots, celery, onions, scallions, and zucchini. I spotted what looked like the start of a few pumpkins. In one of the beds, nasturtiums tumbled over the sides, brightening the corner of the wooden box with their orange and yellow flowers. The final box held stunning rosebushes. I smiled, thinking of how the bouquet in our room must have come from this well-tended garden.

The door of room number two opened, and a woman wearing a simple blue dress with a wide belt stepped out into the garden. Her white hair was carefully pulled up in an elegant chignon. I noticed her flat shoes because they were floral.

She smiled at me and said, "Buongiorno!"

I repeated the "good day" greeting and hoped she didn't say anything else in Italian that I might not understand. Blessedly, she tilted her head slightly and said a single word that I understood and welcomed.

"Cappuccino?"

3

The traveller sees what he sees; the tripper sees what he has come to see.

G. K. Chesterton

Holding my finger up to let the woman know I would be right back, I scooted to our room and was surprised to see that Claire was up and dressed and ready to go. We grabbed our cross-body bags that contained everything we'd need for the day and exchanged glances that reflected how excited we were to seize the day.

Following the woman along a side path that bordered the restaurant, we discovered an exit that took us through a gate. I noticed that a fob was required to return through the clandestine passageway. Exiting and knowing we held the key that would let us back in made me feel like we were Venetian insiders. I loved our little hideaway.

The world beyond the garden and over the short bridge was a different scene than what we had experienced on our arrival in the fog. Sunlight transformed the open space of the campo. Last night, the same area had felt medieval. This morning, people walked about, starting the new day. Nearly every balcony on the buildings had flower boxes from which long strands of green foliage cascaded. In the doorways were clay pots with bright red and pink geraniums.

A shop owner rolled up a metal garage door, exposing gleaming shop windows where shanks of preserved meat hung. Against the wall next to his shop, a woman set up a table and was arranging signs in front of baskets of various fruits. The two of them carried on a lively conversation as if they were longtime friends. To the right of the butcher shop was a café with small round tables set up in front. We moved as one toward the open door of the café. The gorgeous scent of coffee encircled us.

Until this moment, the only two words the older woman had said to us were "Buongiorno" and "cappuccino." I realized how odd it was that I trusted her, followed her here, and hadn't asked any questions. She seemed to know us, or at least know that we were welcome guests in her corner of the world. This was a strange and lovely sort of hospitality.

We took seats around an outdoor table. Claire leaned forward and in an uneasy-sounding voice said, "I'm Claire. Did you meet Grace?"

The woman gave a calm nod of hello.

"Is it okay if we speak English?" I asked. "We have translator apps on our phones if that would be better."

"No. English is preferred." The woman smoothed back the sides of her white hair. "I'm Paulina."

"Oh!" Claire and I remarked in unison. My twinges of apprehension dissipated. Claire leaned back and her shoulders relaxed.

"Thank you for the roses and the card," I said.

"Prego. You're welcome."

I didn't detect an accent in any of her words.

"I trust you had everything you needed last night?" Paulina asked.

"Yes. The room is beautiful, and we slept very well," Claire said. "Or, at least I slept well."

A nicely dressed man approached us and greeted Paulina warmly. They chatted a moment, and then she turned to us and asked, "May I order for us?"

We both nodded.

A plodding pigeon sauntered over to peruse our area for crumbs. The man at the table next to us shooed it away. Sunlight broke through a space between the buildings and spread a glow over our table. I wanted to take a picture so I could remember this fresh morning and the charm of the plaza. But I didn't want to dig for my phone. I preferred taking the time to just drink it in with my eyes and capture our surroundings the way someone who lived here would.

"I'm glad you've come to Venice," Paulina said. "One of you has a mother who came here some time ago. Is that right?"

"Yes," I said. "My mother-in-law, Sue, came with her sister-in-law, Jenna."

"I didn't meet them," Paulina said. "But I know they stayed in a place one of my relatives used to rent to special guests."

"She loved her visit. She said it changed her life. We appreciate you letting us stay at your place. We feel like special guests."

"It is our privilege to have you. My husband's family has a quiet ministry of caring for pilgrims. It started long before I first came to Venice."

"When did you come here?" Claire asked.

"I was eighteen. Some girlfriends and I were backpacking

around Europe for the summer. We were on a vaporetto on our way to the youth hostel, and that's where I met Nico." She paused and smiled softly. "We were a love-at-first-sight couple. He invited my friends and me to have dinner with his family that night. Within minutes, I knew I had found my new family and my new home. That was forty-seven years ago. I have only been back to Missouri four times."

"You're from Missouri?" Claire sounded as surprised as I was. Paulina appeared distinctively Venetian from her nicely tailored clothes, elegant expression, and skin that looked remarkably smooth for her age.

Our waiter returned with our cappuccinos served in small white cups on saucers. A cube of sugar was balanced on the edge of the saucer along with a small spoon. He also served a pastry to each of us on a plate.

"Perfect way to start the day," Claire said. "I love croissants."

"Cornetti," Paulina corrected her. "We improved on the French by adding eggs. Ours are better. You'll see."

She was right. The flavor was sweeter than a typical croissant. I followed Paulina's example and took a small bite of cornetto followed by a sip of cappuccino. Her bites and sips were as refined and dainty as she was. I tried to imitate her pace.

Claire may have been incorrect about the croissant, but she was right about how this was an enjoyable way to start the day. We chatted comfortably about where we were from and our families. I was sad when Paulina told us that Nico had passed away three years ago. It was evident that their love for each other had been unwavering, in spite of the differences in culture.

Changing the subject, Paulina asked, "What have you come to Venice to see?"

Claire pulled out her phone and read our list of the main points of interest. We had prepaid passes for the vaporetto, downloaded maps of Venice, and a list of the times when museums and churches were open. A gondola ride was on our list along with seven options for highly recommended places to eat. I noticed that Claire didn't recite the names of the gelaterias on her list.

Paulina made no comments on our itinerary. Instead, she motioned for the waiter to bring the check. "I am going to the Frari this morning," she said. "Would you like to come with me?"

Claire and I exchanged questioning glances. Neither of us knew what a Frari was, nor did we know why Paulina was inviting us to go there with her.

"We have time," I told Claire. We'd gotten an earlier start than we expected, and none of the places we planned to visit were open yet. It would be nice to have a fellow American who had lived in Venice for forty-seven years take us to a place she was familiar with, even if it was a big unknown.

"Okay," Claire answered for both of us. "Sure."

"I was hoping you would want to come."

Paulina insisted on paying for our breakfast and led the way at an impressively brisk pace. Claire and I had to pick up our usual stride to keep up with her as we turned down curved walkways and trotted over several footbridges. We wandered through a forest of three-story buildings, and I soon lost all sense of direction. Anxiety started to creep into my thoughts. I hoped we would be able to navigate our way out of wherever she was taking us.

We crossed another bridge over a narrow canal, and in front of us stood a huge building with an imposing entrance. Above the door and on both sides were life-size statues.

"What is this?" Claire asked.

"This is the Basilica di Santa Maria Gloriosa dei Frari," Paulina said.

"Frari?" Claire repeated. "This is where you wanted to take us? To a church?"

"My family worships here," Paulina said. "It's the largest basilica in Venice." She checked her watch. "They will be nearing the end of the morning meditation. We want to be seated before the Office of Readings."

Claire gave my sweater a discreet tug. I was pretty sure that if she had known we were going to a church and were now being ushered into a service, she probably would have declined the offer to accompany Paulina.

"What would you like to do?" I whispered. "I'd like to go with her, but if you don't want to, we can bow out."

Paulina had moved on ahead of us, making her way along the side of the church rather than going through the front door.

Claire paused. She seemed to be sorting through the options of what we could do this early in the day. With a slight twitch of her mouth she said, "It's okay. Let's go with her. We're trying new things, right?"

Paulina led us through a side entrance. I remembered that when we were in Rome, my mother and I had to cover our heads, shoulders, and knees before we could enter the churches. Paulina didn't put on a scarf, and all three of us had our shoulders and knees covered, so I guessed we were dressed modestly enough to enter.

The scent of lingering incense, beeswax candles, and old, musty wood was the first impression that hit me. Next was the way sounds seemed to rise and somehow evaporate before bouncing off the immensely high ceilings. The interior was enormous and ornate in every direction.

Paulina led us to an alcove where a dozen or so older

people sat scattered in the first few rows of the narrow wooden pews. If these were the original pews, worshipers must have been much smaller when it was built.

In front of us, to the side of the altar, stood a robed priest with his head bowed. I knew little about the traditions of a church like this. The church our family had been part of all my life was a traditional Protestant denomination. Our church building had been constructed in the 1950s and shared no resemblance to the space we had entered.

Paulina led us to the second row, halfway in. I had a feeling she'd sat in this exact spot on this well-worn wooden bench for decades. She was at home here in her family church, and once again, she was welcoming us into her world, her routine. That thought warmed me. This, too, was her world and there was a place for us here.

The three of us sat close, absorbed in the defining calm and stillness that encircled us.

I bowed my head and prayed silent words of gratitude for everything about the trip so far. I heard faint shuffling and peeked to see that Paulina was standing. We stood with her. The officiant, who was now positioned in front of the altar, read in Italian from a worn book. Even though we couldn't understand the words, I felt in rhythm with the reverence and solemnity of the service. When the small congregation responded at certain places in the reading, I felt something well established inside me joining silently.

I wanted to glance over at Claire and see how she was feeling about all this. Instead, my gaze fixed on the alcove behind the priest and the tall, narrow windows that stretched up to the domed ceiling. The altar reminded me of a long table because it was covered with an intricately designed lace cloth. Behind the altar was a breathtaking altarpiece in ornately designed gold. In the center was a painting that had unusual depth and vivid colors. The subject of the grand work was a Madonna in a long blue covering holding a rather pale baby Jesus with two cherubs on each side.

The size of the altarpiece amazed me. The humans in the painting were life-size. On either side of them were four more figures of men. Disciples, I assumed. The detail and the depth of the work were mesmerizing and seemed as if they were in 3D. I knew it had to be old. I wanted to pull out my phone and search for details about the artist and when it was painted. I knew we were going to see a lot of incredibly old art while we were in Italy, but this was our first glimpse, and the details captivated me.

When the reading ended, Paulina lowered herself to the kneeling bench with agility. I followed her lead, thinking about how many women over how many centuries had knelt in this same spot and offered up a prayer. The thought thrilled me.

Claire chose to sit on the pew and lean back against the narrow piece of rigid wood. The space around us fell into a hush as silent prayers were offered. For the first time in weeks, I felt a sense of peace. I was so glad we'd come to the Frari. My jet-lagged body and still-on-high-alert mind needed this saturating calm to cover me the way it did.

A moment later, Paulina rose, and I did the same. The priest was gone. The others had shuffled out. Claire looked at me with wide eyes as if asking what we were going to do next.

I had no idea. But the truth was, I wasn't eager to leave. I loved this. All of it. I knew Claire wouldn't mind being here if she understood how much it meant to me.

Paulina gave a reverent nod to the altarpiece I had been studying during the reading. With the authority of a tour guide mixed with low-voiced reverence, she said, "The *Pesaro Triptych* is my favorite of all of Giovanni Bellini's works.

He finished it a few years before Columbus sailed across the Atlantic."

"That was painted in the 1400s?" Claire asked. Her awe was evident.

Paulina nodded.

"Do you know who the men on the sides of the painting represent?" I whispered.

"Yes. You've probably heard of them. They have rich life stories," Paulina said with the hint of reverence lingering in her voice. "On the left is St. Nicholas of Bari. Behind him is St. Peter."

"St. Nicholas?" Claire asked. "As in jolly ole St. Nick?"

Paulina nodded. "I don't know about the 'jolly' part. The stories of his generosity and giving in secret are well known. But the accounts of how he was persecuted and imprisoned for his faith in the third century are not often told. Some of his bones are enshrined here in Venice. At the San Nicolò al Lido."

I tried to grasp her casual mention of bones from the third century.

"On the right," Paulina said softly, "is St. Benedict in the front, and behind him is St. Mark, the patron saint of Venice."

"I read that Mark's bones are buried here too," Claire whispered. "Is that true?"

"Yes. At the Basilica di San Marco."

"We plan to go there this afternoon. It's on our list. We bought tickets ahead of time so we wouldn't have to wait in line."

Claire's comment somehow shifted me out of the mindset that I was a worshiper in this solemn space. True, I was a visiting worshiper, but one who had been welcomed in and was caught up in the swirling mystery of past and present, eternal and temporal. Admitting that we had paid for tickets to look inside a church sent me back to feeling like an outsider peering in. An observer. A tourist.

Paulina paused for a moment. I wondered if she was trying to gauge our true interest in seeing and hearing the details she was sharing with us. I hoped Claire would be okay with seeing a few more pieces in this enormous, ancient church. The space was filled to overflowing with art and sculptures. Curiously, this church wasn't one of the ones I'd researched.

"What are your other favorites?" I asked Paulina.

She led us to an intricate altarpiece covered with gold. The precious metal caught the faint light, giving the extraordinary piece an ethereal glow. In the center was a life-size statue of a man draped in a tattered robe with a dark gold shawl over his shoulders. He was holding what looked like an unfurled scroll.

"This is Donatello's statue of John the Baptist," Paulina said. "He carved it in wood and then painted it. I've always been moved by John's woeful expression. Byzantine art did not capture this level of realism. You'll see the difference when you go to the San Marco Basilica. This style of humanity as it appears in nature is one of the hallmarks of St. Francis's influence and why some say he created a bridge into the Italian Renaissance."

I wished I knew more about the differences between the medieval, Byzantine, and Renaissance periods of history. We were going to be surrounded by variations of art created during all those eras. I hoped I would learn more along the way.

"When was this church built?" Claire asked. "In the 1400s?"

"No. It was built by followers of St. Francis of Assisi not long after he died in the early 1200s. The art is inspired by his approach to telling the stories of the gospel artistically and using the language of the common people. The church in his time used only Latin. He taught in Italian because how could people know the Word of God if it wasn't in a language they understood?"

"I can relate," Claire said.

We turned to look at her.

"Like the service this morning," Claire said. "It was all in Italian. I didn't understand a word of it."

"True," Paulina said. "You can see the value St. Francis brought to the church when he ushered in a more naturalistic style and an accessible way of telling God's stories."

"Kind of like using a cucumber and a tomato," Claire said more to herself than us.

"Pardon me?" Paulina asked.

"Oh. I was just remembering my childhood."

"Your childhood?"

"I was raised by singing vegetables."

Paulina didn't catch the reference, but I did.

As we continued on, I felt like a little girl misbehaving in church when I leaned closer to Claire and whispered, "Tomatoes are actually a fruit, you know. Not a vegetable."

Without turning to look at me she whispered back, "And guess what? Cucumbers can't sing."

4

Chi si somiglia si piglia.
Whoever is similar gets along.
Italian saying

Paulina concluded our tour of the Frari by leading us past a number of remarkable statues and paintings. She paused in front of the burial place of Titian, who she said was the greatest painter in sixteenth-century Venice. I counted nine life-size marble statues at the front of the staggeringly large dimensional relief. They looked dwarfed by the columns and detailed carvings in the marble behind the statues. At the top of the great work was a winged lion that was larger than any of the humans represented.

I tried to take it all in, but it was overwhelming in its size and details.

We headed to the center of the wide-open cathedral, where the red brick and white limestone tiles created a pattern across the floor that seemed as much a work of art as the many paintings on the walls. As I was looking down, admiring the floor, Claire was looking up at the soaring ceiling above us and the intricately carved wooden beams.

"Is it safe in here?" she asked Paulina, pointing to the support beams. "You said this was built like eight hundred years ago, right?"

"Yes. The beams have provided support for a long time," Paulina said. "Everything in Venice is always shifting because we're resting on wooden poles."

"What do you mean by 'wooden poles'?" I asked.

Paulina seemed surprised that we didn't know that Venice was built on millions of logs driven into the marshy lagoon, with layers of wooden platforms laid across the top of the timber.

"The Veneti tribe wanted a place to live where they could defend themselves against invaders," Paulina said. "That's why they fortified and expanded the swampy islands to create Venice. They started during the collapse of the Roman Empire in the fifth century."

It was difficult to grasp the age of everything we'd seen. I especially couldn't imagine how a city could be built on a colossal stack of logs. How had Venice been able to endure for so many centuries?

"I remember when I first came to Venice," Paulina said. "I was continually amazed. Not only because of the abundance of art and the fact that so much gold had been used everywhere. I was caught off guard by how ancient everything is. That applies to the traditions and family lines. They run deeper than you can imagine."

"Where we live, in California," Claire said, "if a house is a hundred years old and still standing we think it should be turned into a museum. That's what they did with Grace's great-grandparents' first house."

"It was actually my great-great-grandparents' home," I

said. "They were early ranchers and had a large orange grove. I live in an eighty-year-old house my grandparents built on the land."

"They had a lot of renovations done," Claire added.

"You said earlier that you're a project manager for a construction company," Paulina said to her. "Did you have a hand in the renovations?"

"Yes. Our company did. One of the things I do is hunt down old blueprints. Everyone wants to have walls torn out when they renovate, but the contractors have to know which walls are load bearing. They end up using a lot of support beams. That's why I was curious about these beams. They're huge."

"And they seem to be doing their job," Paulina said.

We made our way to the tall front doors and stepped outside. The sun was now shining on the campo and had dispersed the early morning shadows. I quickly hunted for my sunglasses while Claire checked her phone.

"Thanks for the tour," Claire said to Paulina. "We should find a vaporetto dock. The bookstore we want to go to opens soon. Could you get us headed in the right direction?"

Our shepherdess clearly knew every narrow walkway and bridge in this part of Venice. We came out at a dock on the Grand Canal and boarded the vaporetto with several passengers. I wondered if this was a morning commute to work for some of them.

It had been embedded in me to never speak on public transportation because as soon as the people heard us speaking English, they would know we were tourists. My mom had said it put us at a higher risk of being mugged.

Claire didn't seem to have the same self-conscious qualms about chatting or about being robbed. We hadn't gone far before she said, "It doesn't seem possible that this is the same canal we were on last night. It's gorgeous. Just like I imagined it would be."

I nodded but kept my thoughts to myself and took in the views. We could clearly see in all directions. Other boats passed us with room to spare. The tattered but still grand edifices on both sides of us cast wavy reflections in the calm water. What stories these once-grand palaces had to tell! I tried to imagine all the possible tales of wealthy owners and generations of families raised on the other side of the many arched windows that faced the canal.

Leaning close to Claire, I whispered, "For the next book we read together, let's find one about Venice. Old Venice."

"We could always read Shakespeare's *Merchant of Venice*."

I nodded and glanced around, making sure no one was listening to us.

A gondola appeared from a smaller canal, and I smiled. The gondolier was wearing the traditional uniform of long, dark pants and a blue-and-white-striped shirt. He had on a straw hat encircled with a blue ribbon and tails that fluttered down his neck. He guided his beautiful craft into a dock marked with quintessential red-and-white-striped poles. The sight was the embodiment of everything I hoped we'd see on the Grand Canal.

The Rialto Bridge came into view, and once again, the real thing eclipsed the many flat images I had studied before our trip. I wished I was outside the cabin as we approached because it was difficult to see the whole bridge from inside. I was only catching glimpses of how the morning light had given the marble and stone of the old bridge the gleaming look of a freshly washed face.

If I wasn't so locked into the way my mother had taught me to not draw attention to myself on the international trips she and I took together, I would have joined the young man who stood at the helm with his camera. I would have zoomed in to capture the details embedded into the arched sides of the bridge and especially the sculpted face of the lion at the center.

We were at the dock before I realized the moment was gone. I hadn't even tried to take a picture, and that made me sad. As we disembarked, I told myself that if I was going to get the most out of this once-in-a-lifetime experience, I needed to make a few changes.

"I think we go this way." Claire started walking before I was able to pull out my phone and look at a map. Her hair was pulled up into a high ponytail, so following her was like being behind a fluffy blond machete. I lost track of how many times her hair swished back and forth, slicing a trail for us.

She led us to the renowned bookstore, where a sign out front said "Welcome to the Most Beautiful Bookshop in the World." At first glance, I wasn't sure about the accuracy of that statement. Out front was a table laden with prints and postcards and a large tree that seemed to have sprung up through the well-worn stone pathway. A wheelbarrow filled with books was positioned next to a rustic-looking painting easel, and a sturdy chair sat vacant, ready for a reader to stop and peruse their choice of the offerings in the wheelbarrow.

It wasn't necessarily beautiful compared to the sort of intricate art we had been immersed in half an hour earlier, but for two readers like Claire and me, it was enchanting.

We knew there could be a line for this popular destination, which was why we'd wanted to arrive at the start of their business day. Our plan worked. The door was open, and inside only a few people were browsing in the narrow spaces between the exuberance of books. And I do mean exuberance.

Books were double stacked on the shelves in every direction. They were brimming over the top of an old barrel and filled a porcelain bathtub to the brim. In the center of the main room was a weathered black gondola bursting with picture books in several languages, all facing out.

"I could spend the whole day here," Claire said. She already had two books in her hands. One was a hardback vintage tour book of Venice. She turned the spine of the other book so I could see what she had found. The title was in Italian.

"What's it about?" I asked.

"I have no idea, but I love the binding. Look at the gold letters on the cover. I wish they still made books like this. Little works of art."

"We'll have to ask Paulina," I said. "And by the way, thanks for going along with the unexpected visit to the church this morning."

"I didn't mind. Paulina is adorable. I would love to return to her café for cappuccinos again tomorrow morning," Claire said.

"Me too."

More people had entered the tight room where we were standing. Two of them began taking pictures. I wandered to the back and stepped outside, where three people were waiting their turn to take a picture on the clever stairs that were made of hundreds of large hardback books. What could be done with encyclopedias that had been damaged by the high waters of Venice? Instead of throwing them out, the owner had created an outdoor stairway against a wall. Planks of wood covered the books, helping to create secure-looking steps. Brave climbers could scale the steps to look over the wall and see the canal below.

The high waters that flooded Venice regularly during

various seasons and tides had inspired the name of the book shop, Libreria Acqua Alta—high waters. It was easy to see how the shop would flood easily. It made sense that the books should be kept in boats and barrels and bathtubs. That way they could float when the acqua alta crept in.

Claire joined me outside and took pictures of the steps even though other visitors were setting up their ideal social media poses. She had me take pictures of her as she carefully climbed the book stairs, and when she reached the top, she stood with both arms up in a starfish pose. I felt nervous just watching her. Heights of any sort were not my thing.

"Your turn," she said, reaching for her phone. Instead of going to the top, where I envisioned a misstep causing me to topple into the canal, I sat on the third step and turned to the side, trying to create a more slimming pose.

"Do something," Claire said.

"I am." I was aware of a gathering audience behind her and said, "Just go ahead." I tilted my head and held my closed-lip smile.

We moved inside and found a green delivery door that opened onto the canal. The name of the shop was painted on the door, which was held open by an upholstered chair. Less than a foot away from the legs of the chair, the canal water touched the floor of the bookstore. It seemed as precarious to me as the outdoor platform created from books.

We slid into the informal line of people waiting to take pictures, and Claire placed a hand on my shoulder. "Grace, relax."

"I am relaxed," I whispered back.

"Are you sure?"

I turned, ready to defend myself, but saw by Claire's expression that her suggestion to "relax" was her way of saying, "Grace, guess what? We're in Italy. Enjoy it."

She was right. I was breathing rapidly. The sense of peace I'd felt during the morning service was quickly escaping as my mind opened the doors to all kinds of possible mishaps. I drew in a deep breath and turned my attention to the books on the shelves next to where we were waiting in line. In a catawampus stack I found a book of jokes. The copyright was only four years earlier, and it had been published in London.

I showed the small book to Claire. "For Nathan." My physical therapist husband had distinguished himself as the "Dad Joke Guy" because he was always showing up with a new groaner of a joke to keep his patients relaxed and not focused on the pain he was inflicting on them.

"Good choice," she said. "And look!" She held up a hardback version of Jane Austen's novel *Emma*. Perfect for my Emma. It had been printed in England eighty years ago. As I fanned through it, I saw dot-size marks on some of the pages. I imagined they were droplets of tea spilled from a china cup in the hand of the original reader who had lived in a manor. In the Cotswolds. And rode a beautiful horse and excelled at archery. And—

"Here's another good one," Claire said, bringing me back to reality. She showed me a worn copy of *Treasure Island*. "Would Emma like this too?"

I decided that one was too tattered and seemed to be missing pages. Another book caught my eye. It was a small hardback in English. A quick flip through revealed that it was about St. Francis of Assisi. After hearing about him from Paulina, I wanted to learn more.

"Here we go." Claire moved in and took her seat on the chair by the delivery door. She crossed her legs and pretended to be reading her pretty Italian book with the ornamental cover. Her second pose was casual. She stacked her books in her lap and leaned back with her arm over the back of the chair.

When it was my turn, I positioned myself with my ankles crossed, shoulders back, and hands folded in my lap. I realized I'd gone into a default formal pose from my childhood, so in an attempt to look relaxed, I lifted my chin and gazed out at the canal. That was when I remembered photos I'd seen online of a gondola docked outside this door. The gondola was set up so that visitors could step inside the iconic craft, get comfy on the cushioned seats, and indulge in reading a new book while bobbing on the canal.

Leaning out the open door, I looked in both directions to see if the gondola was tethered nearby. Sadly, it wasn't.

"Are you trying to look like you're going to jump into the canal?" Claire asked. "Because if you are, I want to get closer so I can take a video when you fall in."

I pulled back, and to play off her teasing comment, I pressed my palms together and posed in a mock diving position. The line behind Claire had grown, and judging by the many expressions, my attempt to look like I was having fun was about as humorous as one of my husband's dad jokes.

I gladly relinquished the coveted photo spot and went back to looking for another book or two to take home. Maybe I'd find something about how to reinvent yourself when you're traveling with your closest friend and all your flaws and foibles rise to the surface and you're aware that you're entirely too self-conscious about everything.

Like the missing gondola, the book on my needed topic was not to be found.

What we did find was a cookbook in English that featured Italian dishes. Claire was elated. I moved to the next grouping of stacked books and was greeted by the piercing eyes of a black-and-white cat nestled in a snug space between two fanned-out assortments of books.

"Hello," I said, giving the furry charmer a smile. "Would you mind if I had a look at the book you're sitting on?"

Claire looked at me. "Who are you talking to?"

5

Venice . . . its temples and palaces did seem
Like fabrics of enchantment pil'd to heaven.

Percy Bysshe Shelley

The bookstore mascot meowed at Claire. I gently wiggled an old book out from under the cat's front paws. The book was in surprisingly good shape and had sketches of pressed flowers accompanied by short poems. Any book about flowers was a treasure to me.

We browsed for a few more minutes, but the shop was getting crowded. We reminded each other that anything we bought had to fit in our carry-on luggage. While splurging was our agreed-upon goal, maybe an excess of heavy books wasn't something we should splurge on.

After making our purchases, we stepped outside, and Claire showed me a small brown case she'd picked up last minute at the checkout. "Did you see this?"

"No. What did you get? Is there a tiny book inside?"

She lifted the lid to show me a vintage set of watercolors.

The green had been used, but the other primary colors appeared to be untouched in the small squares of the old set.

"For Brooke?" I guessed. Her daughter was eight, and I wasn't sure she would appreciate a box of used watercolor paint.

"No, it's not for Brooke. It's for me. Remember when we read *The Enchanted April*? The older woman in the story brought her poetry books with her on their trip to Italy and planned to sit inside and read them all day at the villa."

"Yes, I remember. I loved the movie."

"Me too. And when she opened a drawer in her room she found an old tin of watercolors. Remember? She went outside and started painting what she saw. The flowers and the trees. The paints transformed her life."

I wasn't sure I agreed with that assessment, but clearly the watercolor set was bringing Claire as much joy as the discovery had brought the woman in the story. "Does it come with a paintbrush?" I asked.

"No. But I'm happy just to find a little antique paint set in Italy."

I loved seeing Claire so happy. The joy continued as she navigated our way to a nearby gelateria that, she reminded me, opened sooner than almost any other gelato shop in Venice.

Eight people were ahead of us in a haphazard line. We weren't able to see the flavors until we were right up against the case and could look in. I quickly chose stracciatella, which looked like chocolate chip. Claire went for the lamponi, which we were pretty sure was raspberry.

When we tried to pay with an app on our phones, the young man who scooped our treat started talking loudly in Italian. His tone was sharp, and we had no idea what he was saying. Finally, he said, "Euros!" and we understood that he only accepted cash. The bookstore had been the same. No credit cards or apps. Only cash. I was glad we'd thought to exchange money before arriving in Italy. I just didn't think we'd go through it so quickly.

I wasn't sure what we paid for the small cups of our first taste of real gelato because that would have required a bit of calculating of euros to dollars. At the moment, we didn't care.

Once we were outside, Claire took her first taste. "You have to try this. It's so good."

I dipped my plastic spoon into her pink mound and immediately agreed. She had chosen wisely. Mine was good. Rich and creamy. But hers was better.

"Is there such a thing as gelato envy?" I asked.

Claire chuckled and held out her cup for me to take another taste.

"No, I'll wait until we come to our next gelateria and try something more adventurous, like you did. Mine is vanilla with bits of chocolate. It's good, but it doesn't wake up all my taste buds the way yours does."

"I want to try pistachio at our next gelato stop," Claire declared. She scraped the sides of her cup. "Why didn't we get doubles? That went too quickly."

"Do you want to go back for seconds?"

She thought for a moment. "No, let's wait until we come across another gelato place. We know there are lots to choose from."

Claire was right. On our way to St. Mark's Square, we saw two gelaterias. We also saw a dress shop, a leather goods shop, a candle shop, and several restaurants that weren't open. We came upon another small campo with an equally small church and kept following the route. We must have been on a main thoroughfare because more of the street-level doors and windows were renovated and had become specialty shops rather than front doors to dwelling places.

We popped into one of the small shops just for fun because they had books in the display window. Another customer told us in halting English that we were standing in the oldest paper store in Venice and that this was the third time she had come here. She said they rebound old books.

"What do you buy when you come here?" I asked her. "What keeps bringing you back?"

"These." She held up what looked like a custom-made book. As she flipped through the blank pages, I saw that it was a journal with crisp white paper and a one-of-a-kind cover.

"That's lovely."

Claire perused the colorful journals lined up in a neat fashion on the shelves. I was captivated by what looked like long sheets of wrapping paper that hung like drying towels on wooden racks. The racks were above what appeared to be the owner's worktable, complete with glass pots of glue, rulers, tape, and box knives. The orderliness was the opposite of what we had experienced at the first bookstore, and yet this one held as much fascination.

"Do you have small paintbrushes for sale?" I asked the shopkeeper. "For watercolors."

He stepped across the room and reached for an item in the front window display. It turned out to be colored pencils tied with a ribbon like a bouquet. Using a string of Italian words, he went to a drawer and pulled out a small pencil sharpener, indicating that the sharpener came with the bouquet of pencils.

It wasn't exactly what I'd hoped to find for Claire to go with her watercolor set. But the man and the bouquet of pencils were so endearing, I had to buy them for her.

Claire had the same idea of blessing me with a gift. She and I had done this often in our long friendship. Both of us had a hard time buying anything for ourselves, but we had no problem spending money on our friends and family.

Every woman should have a friend who gives her the gift she hesitates to get for herself.

Claire held up two journals. "What do you think?"

"They're beautiful."

"I'm going to get that one." She used her chin to point to a sketchbook sort of journal she had placed to the side. The cover had a very "Claire" floral pattern of tiny white and pink flowers. "I'm asking for you. Which do you like? I want to get one for you too."

"You don't have to."

"I know. But I am. Just tell me. Which one?"

I studied the two leather-bound journals more closely. "I love that one. It feels Venetian." The one on the right had an old-world feel, and the gold-embossed design shimmered as Claire held it up.

With a gratifying grin, she said, "That's what I thought you would say. Just wanted to make sure."

She bought the journals, I bought the pencils, and we felt sweetly touched as we watched the shop owner carefully wrap each item as if he were preparing them as a special gift. He walked us to the door and warmly sent us on our way.

"You know what I just realized?" Claire said. "This is what we came for."

"Pencils and journals?" I teased. "And books? Because you and I have a shortage of those at home."

"No, I mean the people here. The unexpected moments. The little places that don't have a website because they're truly local. I hoped we would find a place like this. Can you imagine taking a beloved old book to that shop and having it restored? Where do you even find places like that in our modern world?"

"True." I linked my arm in Claire's as we walked, feeling lavishly content.

On our stroll to St. Mark's Square, Claire and I came upon a small campo with a sidewalk café. A dozen tables with chairs were tightly arranged under several large outdoor umbrellas. From the other end of the square, classical music floated toward us.

"Come on." I nudged Claire off our main path and meandered closer to the musicians. A young man playing a cello and a young woman with a violin had just finished a piece. Their stage was a small rug that looked well-worn. Listeners tossed coins into a blue and yellow ceramic bowl at their feet.

The young woman straightened her shoulders and tucked her violin under her chin. Her companion tapped his foot four times and began playing a piece I recognized because it was one of Nathan's favorites. His mom had taught piano lessons at home while he was growing up, and he was better educated in classical music than I was. I had learned much from him over the years.

The couple beside me recognized the piece too. An older man said, "Bach. Prelude to Cello Suite No. 1 in G major."

I turned to him with a smile and a nod, but his eyes were closed and he seemed to be breathing in each note. The acoustics on this corner of the campo were ideal. I wondered if it was okay to film the musicians. No one else was.

The violin came in, and the two instruments did what they were created to do with perfect rhythm and harmony. The beauty of the moment brought tears to my eyes. I had to share this with Nathan. I tried not to be too noticeable as I pulled out my phone and held it at chest level, capturing the last few exultant bars of the beautiful duet.

They held out the last note. When it vanished, a lingering hum seemed to quiver in the air around us. Claire and I pulled out some coins to add to their tip bowl.

Sadly, that was their last performance. They quickly packed up and returned their instruments to the cases. I walked away with the same sort of sadness I'd felt when the morning service ended at the church and when the last bit of gelato melted on my tongue. The mini concert, like the other touches of Venice we had experienced that morning, was unexpected and gorgeous. The distinct moments taunted me when they were over as if to say, "Did you enjoy that? Good. Because you'll never experience anything exactly like that again."

I wanted more.

Claire was feeling the same way, at least about the gelato. She peered at her phone and was making a plan. "If we change our route, we can stop by another gelateria before we start our tours at St. Mark's Square. It only adds a few more minutes to our walk."

"You don't need to ask me twice if it involves more gelato!"

The gelateria was small and the line was long. When we reached the counter, Claire and I said, "Pistachio" at the same time.

"Our best," said the woman. She used a flat metal spatula to scoop and pat the pale green treat into two paper cups. After inserting tiny pink plastic spoons, she added a sprinkling of pistachios on top.

This time the first taste of pistachio gelato produced closed eyes and lingering "mmm's" from both of us. We took our time enjoying every last taste of our two-thumbs-up flavor.

Claire rattled her spoon around in her empty cup when she finished hers. "More, please."

"We really need to get over this habit of only ordering a single scoop," I said. "Didn't you tell me last night that Jared told you to splurge on this trip?"

"Are you saying that two scoops of gelato before lunch isn't a splurge?" Claire asked.

"Not even close. Trust me. I'm the one who only remembers the sweets from my trips to London and Paris, remember?"

"And Denmark."

"Yes. And Denmark. So believe me when I tell you that the requirement for gelato on the International Splurging Chart is a four-scoop minimum before noon. Sadly, you and I are underachievers this morning."

"We will have to do something about that." Claire pulled out her phone to check the time. "But first, the Doge's Palace."

We had another "we're in Venice" moment when Claire and I entered St. Mark's Square. Visitors brushed past us, bumped into us, their voices filling the air with a stirring blend of languages. A couple stopped and stood in front of us to capture pictures of the elaborately designed ninth-century Basilica di San Marco in all its golden glory. The balance of the curves and great domes made a striking contrast to the regimented buildings that enclosed the huge plaza.

We moved with the crowd as if we were in a school of fish, and the closer we got to St. Mark's Basilica, the more majestic the church became. It appeared established and unmovable as if it were anchored. Quite a feat in Venice, where everything, including this great square, rested on tree trunks driven into the mud eons ago.

I was beginning to understand the unspoken urgency of people around the world to visit Venice so they could see it before it was gone. In the same way that I'd felt sad about the unique moments of our morning coming to an end, I couldn't bear the thought that one day Venice could be over. I didn't want this unstable, often flooded fairy-tale place to ever be gone.

Claire stopped to take a picture of the tall bell tower at the end of the plaza by the lagoon. The structure reminded me of a rocket made of red bricks with a pointed green cap.

"Did I tell you that Galileo demonstrated his telescope up there, at the top of the campanile?" Claire asked.

"Are you still thinking you want to go to the top?" I asked.

"Yes. And like I said before, I'm fine going up by myself if you don't want to go."

Part of me wanted to declare that I would go with her. I had agreed to try new things, so why not climb to the top and see whatever it was that held such fascination for her? It was a once-in-a-lifetime opportunity.

Another part of me felt certain I would be just fine if I went my whole life without ever seeing a bird's-eye view of anything that required me to climb three hundred and something steps inside what had to be a claustrophobic tube of bricks. The canals and buildings held plenty of once-in-a-lifetime fascination for me. Best of all, I could see those sights while remaining at sea level. Or, in some cases, a few feet below sea level.

I would decide about the bell tower later. For now, I wanted to see the opulent rooms in the Doge's Palace, where Marco Polo had presented his gifts when he returned from the Far East. I'd read a novel years ago with memorable scenes set in the Great Council Chamber. It felt unreal that we were here, about to enter the place that had mesmerized me and remained in my memory.

6

Chi fa sbaglia.
He who does, makes mistakes.

Italian saying

Before we started climbing the grand staircase inside the palace and pioneering our way along, Claire pulled up a list she had made of the highlights to look for since we had opted not to pay for a tour. We entered the cavernous room I'd been so eager to see.

"This is one of the largest rooms in Europe," Claire read from her notes. "The painting at the end of the room is considered the largest painting on canvas in the world. It's by Tintoretto and is called *The Paradise*."

The greatness of the painting was in the immense amount of details. It felt like too much to take in from where we stood, so I turned my gaze toward the ceiling. Painted scenes covered every inch of open space. Ornate gold moldings separated each scene like frames. It would take hours and a comprehensive key to decipher the stories being told in each section.

"It's over the top," Claire said. "Literally."

I tried to figure out why I wasn't having the strong emotional reaction I'd expected. This was the Great Council Chamber. In the novel, twelve hundred members of the Venetian parliament filled this space, and decisions were made that affected the course of history. Today, the space felt hollow. The aura of power had vacated long ago, leaving an enormous, gilded shell where visitors trampled across the ancient floors and paused to take pictures of the glory that once influenced the known world. The room felt sad to me.

"It says here that Venice was a republic for more than a thousand years until Napoleon conquered it in 1797," Claire said. "Can you imagine a political system lasting for a thousand years? And for more than five hundred years, with all the trade that came through here, Venice was among the wealthiest societies in the world. No wonder they covered everything in gold, the way our generation used to cover everything in shiplap."

I was too caught up in my emotional letdown to comment on Claire's shiplap statement.

We continued our self-guided tour through more rooms that were equally ornate. Each had been used for hundreds of years for some branch of the government. I tried to picture what it must have been like when Marco Polo returned from his travels to China seven hundred years ago. Did he walk on these same tile floors? I wished we had signed up for a paid tour so I could ask the guide my questions and hear new stories that would revive my long-held image of the Doge's Palace.

"This is what I was looking forward to seeing," Claire said as we moved from the palace onto the covered bridge that led into the adjacent prison.

We stopped midway and waited our turn to get closer to the small window carved in the sandstone wall of the bridge. Tourists with a different sense of personal space than what

I preferred leaned in behind us. Below us was a canal and in front of us were people walking over a low footbridge. Beyond that was the lagoon and the nearby island of San Giorgio Maggiore.

"This view is what the prisoners saw," Claire said. "Their final glimpse of Venice from the Bridge of Sighs."

"No wonder they sighed," I said.

"Exactly. Casanova was one of those prisoners," Claire said. "But he escaped."

I wanted to escape as well, so I picked up the pace as we moved quickly into the narrow hallway of the prison and only glanced into the small, dark cells where prisoners were once kept. I didn't want to linger and gaze inside, trying to imagine what incarceration would be like in such a place.

We wound our way along to the exit and came back out into the open main square. "What did you think?" I asked.

"Would I be revealing how uncultured I am if I said I liked our visit to the bookstore more?" Claire asked. "I mean, I want to see these main places of interest, but I'm glad we didn't take a tour. This place has an ominous vibe, doesn't it? What did you think?"

"It wasn't what I expected."

I wasn't sure what else to say. Our time inside Paulina's church had felt more awe-inspiring.

We walked through the crowds and instinctively headed for the water, where we stood by a gondola dock and gazed at the lagoon. It was such a pretty day. Chilly, but the sky was clear and the air felt crisp. Our view had a different sort of magnificence, and I felt a sense of calm returning.

"Grace, I like the way you and I go at about the same pace and our level of interest is pretty equal. I appreciate that," Claire said. "I'm guessing the pace was different when you went on your mother-daughter trips with your mom."

"Quite different. She always hired a personal guide to lead us around for the whole day. Every tour would be long, and she would be curious about every historical detail. Her mind holds dates and facts like no one I've ever met. I don't have the same curiosity, I guess. I like the ambience of a place, and I love the stories."

"Me too. I'm curious about how Casanova managed to escape."

A pigeon fluttered up from where we were walking, and Claire waved her hand to shoo it away. No need. The bird was already flying across the water.

"I wish we could feed the pigeons," I said. "I know there's a law against it now, but Sue said that when she was here they bought packets of corn from vendors here on the square, and the pigeons came and ate out of her hand."

"No thank you," Claire said. "I would not want to be here among thousands of disease-carrying, aggressive, land-on-your-head-and-peck-out-your-brain pigeons." She gave a shiver. "There is no way I would want to encourage a bird to come near me."

I chuckled at her dramatics. "I never knew you carried such animosity toward birds."

"It's because of the Bird Lady," Claire said. "When I was in elementary school we had a neighbor who was bird crazy. She had feeders everywhere in her yard. I thought of her this morning because this lady had a statue of a monk with birds eating out of his hands and she called him St. Francis. I never wanted to leave the house because I was afraid I would get dive-bombed by one of her overfed birds."

"I hope you never saw Alfred Hitchcock's movie about birds."

"I did! I saw it when I was eleven and had nightmares for a month."

"Your childhood was more traumatic than I realized," I teased.

Claire caught my eye. Her expression sobered. "It was."

I couldn't tell if she was still being playfully dramatic or not.

"Let's not talk about this anymore," Claire said decisively. "I think we should go get some lunch."

"Lunch instead of gelato?"

"Yes. Lunch, please. I can live with being an underachiever on the gelato splurge-o-meter," Claire said. "Come on."

We headed for one of the nearby restaurants on her list. The crowded deli-style eatery had only a few small tables and all of them were occupied. We stood at the counter, observing what the people in front of us did. When it was our turn we pointed to what we wanted from the assortment of small, open-faced sandwiches in the closed display case.

"Six cicchetti?" the woman asked before taking my credit card.

I gave her a puzzled look because I hadn't heard of a money system that had the word "cicchetti" in it. "Do you mean six euros?" I asked.

The man behind us said, "She's not talking about money." He appeared exasperated but was gracious enough to explain. "She means you are getting a total of six cicchetti. These small bites. They're called cicchetti. And don't ever call them tapas."

"Oh. Thank you. Grazie."

Once again, I was embarrassed for drawing attention to myself and being culturally clueless. A weakly offered "grazie" wasn't going to help, but that was the best I could come up with for the gentleman at the moment.

A table opened up and Claire scooted over to it, welcoming

the chance to sit. At the same moment we realized we had forgotten to buy something to drink.

"I'll be right back," Claire offered.

I waited for her to return before I started eating. Again, my manners were showing. I wondered what it would feel like if I slouched and took a big bite before she came back. Funny how in my mind that was about the rudest and most irresponsible thing I could think of doing.

Looking around at the other people in the café, I thought about how I'd tried to emulate the way Paulina sat and ate her cornetto that morning and how I felt like I couldn't speak English in public on the vaporetto. I remembered how warm my face felt when the man explained that cicchetti referred to food and not a monetary system.

Why was I so worried about what people thought of me? I was surrounded by strangers. They would never see me again. Why did it matter how I drank my cappuccino or that I didn't know the proper name for Venetian tapas? Who cared?

Apparently, I did.

Claire was grinning as if she had a secret when she returned to the table with two bottles of water in the crook of her arm and two small glasses of red wine. "You are going to love this."

I felt a nervous twinge. Should I feel guilty about drinking wine again? In the middle of the day?

"I think I have a problem," I said.

Claire stopped, holding both glasses of wine in mid-delivery position. "What's wrong? Did you lose your phone? Please don't tell me you lost your passport."

"No, I didn't lose anything." I reached for the water bottles and placed them on the table. "It would help if I *could* lose something, though."

"Don't say 'lose weight,' because we agreed we were going to enjoy everything we eat on this trip and not count carbs or calories."

I lowered my voice. "It's not weight. It's the way I become self-conscious so easily."

"Oh, that." She looked relieved and sat down across from me, placing the wine glasses on the table.

"What do you mean, 'Oh, that'?"

She shrugged. "Sometimes you get embarrassed about things that aren't a big deal."

I didn't respond because I didn't want another mini intervention like we'd had last night about my job. I especially didn't want to put the topic of my personality flaws on the table when we had much nicer things on the table at the moment.

Claire left her statement as it was, without further encouragement or counseling, and lifted her wine glass. "Ombra!"

I picked up my glass and tapped the side of hers. "I thought in Italy you're supposed to say 'cin cin' or 'salute' or something like that."

Claire shook her head and slowly took a sip. "I learned something from a guy at the counter. He said they call this wine ombra because it means 'under.' The story is that when Venetian workers like fishermen and gondoliers gathered at St. Mark's Square for lunchtime, vendors lined up to sell wine. The merchants moved their carts along with the shadow of the tower because everyone wanted to be under the shade of the campanile. Do you see? Ombra. Under the shadow of the bell tower. Don't you love that?"

I nodded and took a sip of the red wine, allowing it to float on my tongue before I swallowed. A hint of sweet cherries and a touch of almonds lingered. "This is nice."

Claire had already bitten into her first cicchetti. She

nodded as she chewed. I had chosen the same one. The small, open-faced appetizer was a slice of a baguette-type of bread and was spread with a creamy white paste with a thin slice of cucumber. On top was half of a green olive with a red pimento.

"I wonder what this is," I said. "It's good."

"I don't know the name, but I think it's cod. They slow-cook the fish until it becomes a paste. I like the added parsley."

My next cicchetti had two different kinds of thinly sliced meats that looked like ham with a bit of white cheese and two short sprigs of asparagus tips. With a sip of wine, it was an amazing taste sensation. Claire evaluated the ingredients of the third cicchetti to be pumpkin puree, sliced egg with a thin sliver of a truffle, and edible tiny flowers on top. Whether she guessed correctly didn't matter. It was delicious. I could have eaten three more of that one.

Claire took her last sip of wine and twirled the stem of the small glass between her fingers. "I'm surprised how full I am. I thought we'd need to go back for at least one more round."

"Maybe it's because the bites were so good. I feel satisfied too."

"But are you too full to improve our splurge score?" Claire gave me a mischievous grin. "If we hurry, we can get to a gelateria near here before noon."

"Oh, if we must." I mimicked the preteen roll of the eyes that my daughter had been perfecting lately.

Claire wedged her way through the lunch crowd to the door. My morning purchases were in a lightweight backpack that I opted to wear in front due to the crowds. My cross-body bag was also in front of me for safety. I felt like an oddly pregnant woman as I tried to move through the people and catch up with Claire. I finally understood why my mom had been so insistent on these specific travel items. It would be so easy to lose something or be pickpocketed in the swarms we moved in.

It struck me that my mom had contributed a lot to our trip with travel gear, clothing, money, and advice. But she did those things out of kindness, not expectation. I was the one reverting to standards from previous trips that had happened twenty years ago. Standards of how to behave in front of other people and how to present myself.

But this wasn't her trip. It was ours. Mine and Claire's, and we could do whatever we wanted. I needed to hold on to that thought the next time I slid back into thinking I wasn't doing things correctly.

Gelato, I decided at that moment, was useful for clearing the palate as well as clearing out old ways of thinking. So when it was my turn to order at the gelateria, I selected two scoops of limoncello gelato. My first taste was so tart, I could barely stop squinting. I hadn't expected the vibrancy or the lingering tingle on my tongue.

"Not your favorite?" Claire asked as she spooned her choice of cherries and almonds into her mouth by playfully turning the tiny plastic spoon upside down. She closed her eyes and dramatized how she savored her gelato with drawn-out satisfaction. Opening one eye to see if I was catching her performance, she added, "You know that limoncello is a liquor, right?"

"It is? I thought it was Italian for lemon flavor. I expected it to taste like your famous lemon bars." I took a second taste. "It's better after the first jolt."

Claire didn't look convinced. She also didn't offer a taste of her winner. My gelato envy was growing.

A moment later she showed me her empty cup. "Eleven bites and it's gone. And that was two scoops. The portions at this spot are the smallest yet. I think it's because we're so close to the hub of everything. But this was a good one."

As we walked, the sound of bells filled the air. Claire paused, her chin toward the clear sky as she counted. Twelve bells.

"Noon!" she said triumphantly.

"No slackers on our splurge team," I said.

On our return to St. Mark's Square, we discussed which sight we would we see first: St. Mark's Basilica or the three-hundred-foot-high campanile? More importantly, was I going to wait "ombra," under the shadow of the bell tower, while Claire went to the top? Or would I be brave and accompany her?

A third option I didn't mention to her was that I wouldn't mind staying behind and returning to the gelateria on my own for a different flavor.

Then Claire added a significant piece of information about the bell tower, and I made my choice.

The world is but canvas to our imaginations.

Henry David Thoreau

While I stood in line with Claire waiting to go to the top of the bell tower, I quietly asked her, "Why didn't you tell me they had an elevator?"

"I thought you knew. They don't open the stairs to the public. Besides, I thought the height was what you wanted to avoid. Not the stairs."

I didn't reply, so she leaned closer. "Think of this as a chance to try something new."

"I am. That's why I decided to go with you. But be honest with me. Aren't you a little hesitant about the stability of the tower? You were questioning the beams at the Frari. What about this structure?"

Claire shook her head. "The original bell tower collapsed."

"It collapsed?"

"This tower replaced it, and this one is only a hundred years old, so we're good."

I felt anything but "good" on our way to the top and even

more queasy when the elevator door opened to the observation area. True, a hundred-year-old bell tower was better than one that was a thousand years old. But it was still very high.

I let the other visitors exit first. They probably thought I was being polite. I wasn't. I was trying to convince myself that this moment was important. This was my opportunity to face my fear. Where did that fear come from, anyway? My childhood? I wasn't a child anymore.

I drew in a deep breath, whispered a little prayer, and stepped out into the enclosed area. Claire went directly to the windows around the edge of the tower. The view straight ahead was of sky. Sky and one long, wispy cloud. I took a few steps closer to Claire to see what she was looking at. My eyes stayed on my feet as I walked across the tile floor. It had the same red-and-white-checkered pattern as in the Frari.

These two elements, red bricks and ivory-colored limestone, were the building materials of Venice. Strangely, my brain told me it was okay. I was walking on tiles I had experienced before. This was just another sight to see in Venice.

I looked up. The observatory felt spacious and airy. The openness was unexpected. With the high ceiling and large windows that stretched from floor to ceiling, the space almost felt modern compared to the other buildings we had been in. Huge, round support columns rose from thick stands and were positioned between each of the grand windows. I stopped walking halfway between the elevator and the window where Claire was leaning forward, drinking in her bird's-eye view of the great city.

I decided that if I could get to one of the pillars, I would be good. I'd be stable.

With another long inhale and a slightly wobbly exhale, I moved my feet across the checkered tile and kept going until

I reached a pillar. There, I calmly rested my hand on the waist-high rim of the base that supported the column. I was sure someone who knew about such things would explain that I had just extended a hand of friendship to my potential nemesis by making friendly contact with the cool stone base. Whatever science or psychology might be at play, I didn't know. All I knew was that I felt grounded. I lifted my chin to look out the window and felt only slightly off-balance.

"Are you seeing this, Grace?" Claire turned and beamed at me. "Isn't it amazing?"

I nodded, and when I did, I felt as if something in my head was slightly sloshing.

"The roofs are so striking," Claire said. "Red roofs in every direction. I love that you can see so far. So many churches. Weren't you the one who told me more than a hundred churches are in Venice? Or did I read that?"

I had no recollection of any such detail. My objective at the moment was to continue to breathe in and out and hopefully do nothing to draw attention to myself.

"I'm going to go look over on that side." Claire brushed past me and then stopped. It must have dawned on her what a big deal it was that I was standing there and hadn't broken into a panic attack. She smiled slowly and gently touched my arm. "Look at you," she said softly. "Well done, my friend. This is significant."

I nodded and immediately remembered that any head movement brought on a low-level slosh. "I'm going to stay right here. You take your time. Enjoy it all. If I need to leave before you, I'll meet you down in the shade."

"Ombra," Claire said with a grin. "I just love that word. Okay. Got it."

In the same way I had learned to focus on an image on the horizon to calm my stomach when we went out on my grandfather's boat, I now focused on a single, fixed image out the window to soothe my mind. My visual target was the clock tower that was part of a building to the left of the basilica. Aside from the large winged lion statue that stood out against a deep blue tile background above the clock, the most interesting thing to stare at was at the very top, where two male statues held hammers, poised to strike against the huge bell. It would have been difficult to see the unique figures from the ground. The details were more defined from this elevated view.

My breathing continued, calm and steady, as I moved my gaze from the clock tower, past the red rooftops, all the way to the blue water of the lagoon that stretched out past where the island ended. A smile lifted the corners of my lips. I felt balanced. Steady. This was a victory.

I was aware of someone standing a little too close but told myself I needed to get used to the proximity issues we kept encountering.

A man spoke in a low tone with a thick accent, "You are very beautiful, you know."

I assumed he was speaking to the person he was with and turned my head slightly to take a quick, guarded glance. To my surprise, the man was alone, and he was staring at me. I didn't shriek, but inwardly I was yelling at my feet to move away from him. They didn't obey.

"I am a painter," he said with a sense of authority. "You will be my *La Fornarina*."

My anxiety meter peaked. I wished Claire would notice and come back over.

"I am Raphael." He lowered his voice. "For obvious reasons."

My throat began to close. I'd never been in a situation like this before in my life.

"Tell me your name," he said, moving closer.

I spouted the first words that came to mind. "Go away! Leave me alone, you sleazy, creepy creep!"

Unfortunately for me, my pinched voice sounded like Minnie Mouse's.

Unfortunately for him, my words came with a spray of lingering lemon gelato essence.

My feet finally got the message I'd sent them, and they took me to the elevator with brisk, unhindered steps. I rudely pushed into the already full elevator and the door closed. With my lips pressed together, I counted silently. How long did it take to descend three hundred feet?

Come on, come on.

This time I was the first one out of the elevator and didn't show any manners as I made my way into a spacious part of the plaza, where I stopped in the shade of the bell tower. My gaze was fixed on the exit, watching for Claire and hoping she would appear before the guy emerged. I sent her a quick text while a squiggle of perspiration slid down my back. The afternoon was warming up, and I had on too many layers for comfort. Removing my sweater didn't seem like a good idea. I also felt the urge to find a bathroom and looked around for signs.

Fortunately, Claire had taken the next elevator car down. We met each other halfway. "What happened? I saw you rushing to the elevator. Are you okay?"

I nodded, feeling the unwelcome slosh returning. "Did Raphael say anything to you?"

"Who?"

"I'll tell you later. Could we find a restroom?"

"Sure, let me check my app."

The bell tower rang a single chime. So did the clock tower. Another bell echoed a solitary stroke from another corner of Venice. I was glad I wasn't standing in the tower at that moment. I was also glad that Claire had voluntarily taken on the role of trailblazer for us.

After a stop in a not-so-bad public restroom, we agreed to trek the short distance back to our room and take a rest before our next round of sightseeing. Less than fifteen minutes later, with the help of a quick-paced walk guided by the map on Claire's phone, we entered the peaceful courtyard of our hidden apartment through the side gate. The garden looked inviting. Our room felt cool, and a faint scent of roses graced the air.

"Home sweet home." I dropped my bag with the books onto the sofa.

"I think I have a blister," Claire said.

"I think I understand why afternoon naps became a tradition here."

"Do you want some water?" Claire kicked off her shoes and filled two glasses from the refilled carafe on the table. "Did you see this? There's a bowl of cherry tomatoes here and two apricots."

"How nice. And another note." I read it aloud.

Travel offers two gifts to the simple pilgrim:
Unrivaled wonders on display in the wild.
The unveiling of wishes on hold in your heart.

Claire and I exchanged perplexed looks. I read it again and said, "What do you think that means?"

She shrugged.

"It's not signed by Paulina like the other note was, but I'm guessing it's from her." I put it on the table and we nestled into the comfortable chairs, sipping the water and enjoying the fresh fruit.

"Why did you rush out of the campanile? Did the height get to you?" Claire asked. "When you were up there by the pillar, you looked like you were fine. But when I saw you outside, you seemed rattled."

"I was rattled. Not from the height. I was doing okay up there. I really was. The reason I had to rush out was because I was being harassed."

"Harassed?" Claire looked like she didn't believe me.

"Yes. By this . . . guy."

Claire leaned forward in her chair. Her expression turned serious. "Grace, what happened?"

"I was standing there, a little spacey but calm and feeling like I'd conquered my fear."

"Yes, yes. And well done, my friend."

"Thanks. But then I heard this man saying something like, 'Do you know you're beautiful?' I glanced over and he was this close." I held up my palm next to my face to demonstrate. "He was talking to me."

"Did he touch you?"

"No. He just kept talking. He said I was his 'formarina' or something like that, and he wanted to paint me."

"What's a formarina?"

"I have no idea. He said his name was Raphael." I attempted to imitate his sultry voice and added, "For obvious reasons."

"So that's why you asked if Raphael said something to me too." Claire picked up her phone and started tapping. "Raphael was a painter."

"Yes, that's what he said. He was a painter."

"No, Raphael was an Italian Renaissance painter. Grace, look." She handed me her phone. "This is a painting by Raphael of a woman, and it's titled *La Fornarina*."

I looked at the image and frowned. "Why does she barely have any clothes on?"

Claire covered her mouth. I couldn't tell if she was hiding a grin because of the ridiculousness of it all or because she felt the incident was as much of an affront as I thought it was.

She stood, leaving me with her phone, and walked across the room to get her travel first aid kit for her blister. "Do you think his pickup line has ever worked on a tourist?"

"I don't see how it could."

On her way back to the chair, she playfully dramatized the scenario. "Raphael scopes out a classy woman on vacation. She's all alone. He saunters over and casually compares her to a famous painting. She's smitten, and he lures her to his gondola."

"Stop." I felt my shoulders ease. "If I hadn't been so focused on my equilibrium, I probably would have reacted differently."

"Differently than what? What did you do?"

"I wasn't very nice."

"Grace, you do realize that you never have to be nice to weirdos and scumballs."

"I know."

"So, what did you do?"

"I said, 'Go away, you sleazy, creepy creep!'"

Claire's eyebrows rose and she pressed her lips together.

"Or something like that."

"Creepy creep?" Claire looked down and pressed a Band-Aid over her forming blister. This time I knew she was trying hard not to laugh. "That's the best you could come up with? 'Sleazy, creepy creep'?"

I realized how ridiculous I must have looked and sounded.

"Grace, you are so refined, even when you try to throw an insult at a stalker, it sounds like a line from a children's book!"

"There's more," I said, beginning to see the humor in it all.

"More?"

"I was so nervous, my voice sounded like this." I demonstrated my high, squeaky, Minnie Mouse voice and repeated, "Hey! Go away, you sleazy, creepy creep!"

Claire burst out laughing. She laughed so hard, she unexpectedly snorted. I couldn't help but break into side-splitting laughter with her. Once we started, we couldn't stop.

When I finally caught my breath and wiped the laughter tears away, I said, "It really was the rudest thing I've ever said to anyone in my life."

"I believe it!" Claire leaned back, still chuckling. "I always wondered how classy girls acted in a catfight. Now I know."

"Hey." I leaned forward and gave her my best fierce face. "Don't you make me take off my earrings and come over there!"

Claire burst into laughter again. "Listen." She caught her breath. "If any more creepy Casanovas find you irresistible, you just say to them . . ." She mouthed a phrase I would never repeat.

"Claire!" I acted shocked, even though I wasn't. "You certainly did not learn *that* from a singing tomato."

8

La vita è bella.
Life is beautiful.

Italian saying

Our belly-laugh endorphins proved to be an afternoon reboot for both of us. Instead of flopping on our beds and giving in to our jet lag, as I had envisioned while we were tromping back to our room, we agreed to go back out into the wild.

It was after three o'clock when Claire and I headed out again to see more of Venice. We only made it as far as the courtyard, where we stopped to talk with Paulina, who was pulling up carrots and layering them in a flat basket. She wore an apron, gloves, and an adorable straw hat.

"Ah!" Paulina said. "I noticed you had returned. I thought you might be taking a riposo."

"Is that what you call an afternoon nap?" Claire asked.

"Yes."

"That was our original plan," Claire said. "But we ended up discussing . . . art."

"Not art, exactly," I added, repressing a grin.

Paulina extended the basket to us. "Would you like some?"

"No thanks," I said. "We appreciated the cherry tomatoes and the apricots, though. They were delicious."

"We're off to go see . . ." Claire looked at me. "What did the note say? 'Unrivaled wonders on display in the wild.'"

Paulina gave us a Mona Lisa smile. "Keep your eyes open for 'the unveiling of wishes on hold in your heart.'"

"Is that an Italian saying?" Claire asked.

"Yes and no. It was said by a Venetian I know. Nico's grandfather. He used to say it to certain pilgrims who stayed with us. I thought of it today and wanted to share it with you."

"Sounds like you've been taking in visitors for many years," Claire said.

Paulina nodded.

"May I ask how long?"

"At least three hundred."

"Three hundred guests?" I asked, thinking she had misunderstood Claire's question.

"No, three hundred years. Probably longer. I told you the traditions run deep in our family." Paulina shifted her basket to her other arm. "A long time ago, my husband's relatives took on a family motto to remind each next generation to show ospitalità. Hospitality. You may have seen the motto on the menus."

"We didn't see a menu last night," I said.

Claire added, "Our server asked if we were your friends, and then he said he was bringing us the best. And it was the best. Dinner last night was delicious."

"What is your family motto?" I asked.

"A tavola non si invecchia," Paulina said. "It means, 'You don't get old at the table.'"

"I love that," Claire said.

I wanted to add a comment like, "You must spend a lot of time at the table because you're so youthful," but I caught myself and was glad I did. I didn't think it would have come out sounding the way I meant it, judging by the way my brain and my words were intersecting lately.

"Do you have plans for dinner tonight?" Paulina asked.

"We don't know yet," Claire said.

"You are always welcome here."

We thanked Paulina, and she waved us off on our next adventure. After exiting by the side gate, we retraced our steps to St. Mark's Square. We strolled through another whirl of fellow tourists, chatting as we went. As we got closer to St. Mark's Square, I realized we'd been talking openly around other people and I hadn't felt the need to hush. Perhaps the incident with Raphael had somehow helped me overcome my self-consciousness. Laughing about it with Claire had certainly lightened the moment.

When we arrived at the tour entrance to St. Mark's Basilica, I felt eager to go inside. After the roller coaster of emotions I'd gone through already that day, I was hoping to feel a return of the calming peace I'd felt at the Frari. I also hoped the basilica had a different "vibe," as Claire called it, than what we felt at the palace.

Inside the great basilica the light was dimmed, giving the church a sense of hallowed quiet. My first impression was that the large interior was as crowded and overwhelming as the Doge's Palace had been, except the basilica was more beautiful and more ornate. Jewels were used to accentuate crosses. The rounded archways, walls, and ceilings were covered in works of art created with tiny tiles. Gold was added to the walls and ceilings, giving an otherworldly shimmer to this place where people had worshiped for more than a thousand years.

Closing my eyes, I listened to the rolling sound of lowered voices speaking in various languages around me. With a slow breath, I drew in the scent of the burning candles and felt something like a pulsing solemnity flowing through this space.

I opened my eyes and noticed the floor for the first time. It was nothing like the red and white checkers of the Frari and the bell tower. The well-worn flooring was composed of a dizzying design of tiles no larger than my thumbnail. The colors were white, black, rust, and gray, and the multiple and varying patterns were inside blocks spread out the way a quilter would design a crazy quilt.

I caught up with Claire, who was standing under a magnificent dome, looking up and tilting her head. "Here's a Bible story I recognize," she said. "Adam and Eve. The naked couple and the apple gave it away."

The story of creation depicted at the center of the dome was overflowing with gorgeous details of the fish of the sea and the birds of the air, followed by the creation of all kinds of animals. Adam and Eve were featured in the widest ring. Their saga was in storyboard style, each frame depicting what happened next and every inch used. The dome was so high above us, I wished we could get closer to examine all the details.

"You know," Claire said as we kept strolling, "I never understood why God didn't end everything after the Adam and Eve debacle. How do you forgive people who turn on you and betray you like that?"

I stopped in front of a nearby scene of the crucifixion, contemplating an answer for Claire.

"Again," she said, nodding at the crucifix, "why did He forgive the people who betrayed Him? Why doesn't God hold people accountable for the horrible things they do?"

"He does. He will. Justice is coming at the end of all things." I moved on and gazed up at a stunning painting on a gold-inlay alcove. Christ the risen Lord was seated on an elaborate Byzantine throne. He balanced a large book on his thigh. I pointed up and said to Claire, "One day everyone will have to answer to the King of Kings and Lord of all. Nothing is hidden. It's all recorded."

"Love the big journal," Claire said in a way that sounded like she wanted to change the subject. "Gorgeous cover. That whole image is stunning, isn't it?"

I smiled at Claire calling the Book of Life a "journal." I guess it was, in a way. God keeps notes. He knows. At the last judgment all would be revealed. I lingered a little longer, staring at the remarkable image.

Claire had stepped away and paused to nonchalantly listen in as a guide a few feet away was answering questions for her small group. I joined her and hoped we wouldn't be asked to move along.

"Yes, the winged lion represents the strength and dominance of Venice. It is also recognized as representing Saint Mark, who is entombed in the crypt below us here in the basilica."

"Is he really?" a woman asked. "I mean, why isn't he buried in the Holy Land?"

"Venetians love a good story, and many exist about how the remains of the author of the Gospel of Mark were stolen from Alexandria, Egypt. Remember, this was a time in history when relics were highly prized. The two Venetian merchants who returned with the bones of Saint Mark knew they would obtain a high standing with the Doge. They smuggled the remains into Venice by hiding them under layers of pork in barrels because the Muslim guards wouldn't touch the pork."

"Is that true?" a man asked.

"First, I will tell you that it happened more than a thousand years ago. Next, I will remind you that I am from a Venetian family with a long lineage, so yes. Of course it is true."

"Can you take us into the crypt?" the man asked.

"Sadly, no. The crypt has flooded in the past and remains under repair. I have been down there and have seen where Mark is entombed. It's well maintained, and a lovely cross made of beautiful sea-colored Murano glass marks the tomb. I feel it is a sacred place."

The guide directed her group to follow her onward to one of the cupolas, and Claire and I continued our stroll in the opposite direction under the archways that gleamed with their gold covering in the light. Like the tour guide, I felt the sacredness of the space, and I felt privileged to see it. I asked Claire what she thought about all of it.

"I don't know. It's stunning, and I appreciate all the years of work put in by the artisans, but I can see why Paulina's guy wanted all this to be simple and boiled down to just the stories and not all the opulence."

"By Paulina's guy, do you mean St. Francis?"

"Yes. Francis. I don't think I can bring myself to refer to anyone as a saint."

"Did you see that one of the books I got this morning is about his life?" I asked.

"That could be interesting. Let me know if you find anything in it about him feeding birds, because that could be a friendship breaker for us."

"Us, us? You and me?"

"No. Francis and me. I figure it's my turn to break up with a guy in Italy."

I gave a courtesy grin at her quip. I wondered if Rome was where she "broke up" her relationship with Jesus. I wanted to make a plea for her to give Him another chance and get back together with Christ here in Italy. Why wouldn't she want to? His story was everywhere. His open invitation was accessible to all.

But, unlike Claire, I rarely could come up with the right thing to say at the right moment.

The opportunity passed as we took our time strolling across St. Mark's Square. The space felt different in the lull of the late afternoon than it had midmorning. On both sides of the plaza, outdoor tables were set up in orderly clusters in front of the restaurants. It seemed as if a sense of anticipation was in the air. Preparations were being made for the dinner crowd. A string quartet was setting up outside one of the restaurants on a small stage. Waiters in formal black jackets and bow ties were bobbing between the tables, checking to make sure they were set properly.

"Were you the one who told me that Napoleon called this area 'the drawing room of Europe'?" I asked Claire.

"No, I hadn't heard that."

"I must have read it. His declaration appears to still be true two hundred years later. It seems like at some point every tourist in Venice finds their way here."

We headed for the walkway under a beautiful arched portico and stopped to look in the windows of some of the numerous high-end stores.

"Do you think we need reservations to eat at one of the restaurants here?" I asked.

"I don't know, but I'm sure they're the most expensive places to eat. Is that something you'd like to do? I mean, we have some extra spending money, if it is. I'm sure the food would be amazing."

"I'd rather walk around some more and find a gondola that will take us for a ride."

Claire agreed and our objective became threefold: Walk across the Rialto Bridge, take a leisurely gondola ride, and find a fabulous little hideaway restaurant for dinner.

In keeping with how the first part of our day had gone, I had a feeling our plans would be shuffled once again, and I was right. Before we had even reached the Rialto, we crossed a campo by a canal and Claire spotted a gondolier.

"Look. He's dropping someone off. Let's see if he's available." She waved to the gondolier and asked, "Are you open?"

He smiled warmly, dipped his chin, and extended his arm in invitation. The attractive young man certainly knew what he was doing because his gesture had a Cinderella effect on us. I felt as if we were late to the Doge's ball and he had been sent to collect us. The rates were standard and our budget was for a half-hour ride, so we settled with him before agreeing to slip into the boat.

When he asked, "Do you wish to see the Grand Canal?" I asked if he had a preferred route on the Rii Rii. I don't know why I remembered the term used for the many small canals that ran through Venice. Once again, words were coming out of my mouth that I hadn't premeditated.

My question seemed to humor him. Or impress him. I couldn't tell which.

He nodded, still smiling, and expertly steadied the gondola so we could step into the hull and nestle into the beautifully upholstered and cushioned seats.

I took the bench seat in front of where he stood and leaned against the plush back of the wide seat. Claire went for a seat on the side. We hadn't even pulled away from the stand before she started taking pictures. She didn't have to tell me to smile for her carefully lined-up photos because at the moment, smiling was all I could do.

I soon lost all sense of direction as we floated down a

narrow canal and slid under a short bridge. The buildings on both sides of us had splotches of peeling siding and looked weary with age. Sounds of a dog barking and the sight of laundry strung on a line above us made it seem as if we had entered a different Venice, where families lived and tourists didn't crowd the walkways.

Claire leaned back in her seat and stopped taking photos. I adjusted my posture so that I wasn't sitting up quite so prim and proper and photo ready. Neither of us spoke. The rhythmic sound of the gondolier's steady strokes through the water became calming music to my ears. I loved the sense that we were gliding so effortlessly through Venice. After a day of navigating one new sensation and sight after another, this time to simply float felt like a gift.

The only thing that would have made it better would be my husband beside me with his arm around me and my head resting on his shoulder. *Maybe one day . . .*

My romantic notion of one day taking a gondola ride with Nathan met its equal when we came out of one of the smaller canals and entered what had to be the Grand Canal. A sleek, private boat came surprisingly close to us. The tawny-brown wood shone in the late afternoon sun. At the back of the boat a bride and groom cuddled together with her veil fluttering in the breeze.

Claire quickly snapped a photo as the couple kissed when the boat slowly passed us. I thought it might be an invasion of their privacy. But then I realized the couple would have reserved a covered boat if they'd wanted privacy. They seemed to want to parade their love for their special day.

This was the Venice I had hoped to see. A novel come to life. I wanted to believe that the legendary tales of romance and beauty still existed here. I loved that we were seeing it and feeling it.

As quickly as we had entered the Grand Canal, we turned down another narrow canal. A few minutes later, we were back at the stand where we had started. Our enchanting thirty minutes were over, but I knew I would never forget them.

"Grazie," I said to our gentle captain when he offered his hand to steady my departure. I looked him in the eye. "You gave us the perfect experience. It was exactly what I had hoped for. Thank you."

He smiled and dipped his chin again. "My pleasure."

I still felt floaty as Claire and I stepped back onto the open campo. The waning sunlight cast a mellow blush across the umbrellas that sheltered the tables of the outdoor café. All the tables were occupied. If one had been available, I would have persuaded Claire to sit and order something with me so my happy heart could marinate a little longer in what had been an introvert's dream come true on our serene float down the hidden canals of Venice.

Clearly Claire was still enchanted as well. We'd reverted to our goal of seeing the Rialto Bridge and found that the closer we came, the more difficult it was to continue at our leisurely pace. I had hoped the crowds would have dispersed in that area because the open market had closed for the day. But we soon found ourselves immersed in another shoulder-to-shoulder experience, tromping along at a brisk pace.

I felt as if we were being swept along by the rising human tide, especially when we were halfway across the bridge and were bumped each time we stopped to take photos. Admiring the view of the Grand Canal or any of the architectural details of the bridge was difficult. With another swell of pedestrians, we rode the wave to the broad walkway on the other side of the bridge.

"Where are we headed?" I asked Claire.

"I pulled up a restaurant near here, but you know what? There's a takeout place that serves pasta. It's closer to our room."

"Let's go there instead. Do they have lasagna?"

"Possibly."

"Without squid ink?"

"I'm afraid I can't guarantee that."

9

L'amico è quello che ti prende per mano quando tutto il resto del mondo ti ha voltato le spalle.
A friend is the one who takes your hand when the rest of the world has turned its back on you.

Italian saying

Forty minutes later, Claire and I entered through the side gate into our courtyard garden with dinner in tow. The amber light from the evening hour cast a warm glow over our favorite hideaway. As soon as I heard the faint splashing sound of the fountain and some birds twittering in the branches of the tree by our room, I felt my pulse slow down.

"Let's eat outside," I suggested. "In the chairs under the tree."

"I was thinking the same thing." Claire was the first to settle into one of the waiting chairs. She immediately pulled off her shoes.

"How's your blister?"

"Grateful to be able to breathe again. I am definitely going to wear my other shoes tomorrow."

Our to-go pasta came in containers that resembled Chinese food takeout boxes. We'd ordered more than we needed because the prices were low and everything sounded good. Sadly, they didn't offer lasagna, but at this point, I was eager to dig my plastic fork into the spiral pasta and creamy white sauce with mushrooms. So satisfying.

Claire started in on the one with wide, flat noodles and special sauce made with minced duck, onion, carrots, and olive oil. By the look on her face, it was divine. I would let her enjoy that carton all by herself.

The third container for us to share was basic spaghetti with tomato sauce. I tried it first. "This is not basic spaghetti. I have no idea how they managed to elevate it, but it has so much flavor."

Between the two of us, we polished off all three containers. As we watched the evening light wane, two butterflies with bright blue wings checked on us. Like the street musicians of Venice, they provided us with free entertainment. Theirs was in the form of an elegant evening dance.

The scent of dinner being prepared in the restaurant wafted our way. I stretched out my legs and gazed up through the branches of our sheltering tree. The sky had turned to a muted periwinkle shade of blue. Hints of sunset oranges stained the underside of the thin clouds that scuttled by.

"You know what we should do?" Claire had joined me in tilting her head back and viewing the evening sky.

"If you say go find another gelato place right now . . ."

"How did you know? Come on. The scoops are little."

Her mischievous smile let me know she was kidding.

Paulina stepped out into the garden and turned on each of the lights in the hanging lanterns. "Buona sera."

"Buona sera," we repeated.

"How was your afternoon?" she asked.

"Full," Claire said, patting her tummy.

"Dreamy," I said, thinking of the gondola ride and how I felt at this moment in the courtyard. I loved this little corner of Venice and knew I would dream about it as much as I would dream of the gondola ride.

Paulina smiled. "I see you've eaten. Would you like anything else?"

"No thank you," I said. "We plan to explore Burano tomorrow, so we should probably go to bed pretty soon."

She looked surprised. "Not many pilgrims visit that island."

"We thought it would be something different and less crowded," Claire explained.

I understood now why Claire had pitched for us to see all we could on our first day when our adrenaline was running high. She had read on a travel blog that a good way to adjust to the time change as well as see your top highlights was to go full speed the first day and downshift significantly the next.

"May I ask a favor?" Paulina asked.

"Of course." I hoped Claire was getting comfortable with me answering for both of us.

"May I send a gift with you tomorrow? I know someone on Burano who would appreciate a touch of home from my garden."

Claire and I exchanged glances. I waited for her to agree this time. "Sure," she said. "Will it be easy to find their home?"

"I will write it all down in English and Italian. If you need help, show the paper to anyone in one of the shops. They will know. I will have everything ready for you in the morning."

When we were in our beds an hour later, I asked Claire if she minded us making the delivery for Paulina.

"It's a little strange, but after all she's done for us, I don't mind." Claire fluffed up her pillows and slid under the thick comforter. "I love this bedding with only a fitted sheet and the puffy comforter inside the duvet. Did you ever sleep in a bed like this on trips with your mom?"

"Yes, several times. I like it too. How was the bedding when you went to Rome? Do you remember?"

"No." She grew quiet.

"Oh, sorry," I said quickly. "I'm sure bedding is the last thing you noticed or would remember."

"I know everyone has some sort of drama or trauma in their teen years, but . . ." Claire's gaze was fixed on the chandelier. "Let me just say that I didn't have much faith in men until I met Jared. He was so patient with me. He still is. I used to think he developed patience being an electrician. Now I think it's just Jared. He's the calmest, kindest man I've ever known."

"Was your dad patient?" I wasn't sure why I asked that. Claire rarely talked about her parents or her childhood. Maybe the cozy bedding and the feeling that we were having a slumber party made me feel like we should talk about boys and other usually taboo topics.

"My dad was tolerant. Or maybe compliant is a better description."

I knew her father had been in ministry when she was little and then became the principal of a private school for a short time. He ended up teaching at a small college in South Dakota, where he and Claire's mom had lived for the last twenty years of their lives. She hadn't been close to either of them, and their passing only added to the unresolved disconnect in her relationship with them.

"Did I ever tell you what they did to my dad at the high school where he was the principal?" Claire propped herself up on her elbow. "They had a welcome event in the gym, and all the families came to meet the new principal. Our family had to stand in front of all those people and say why we were glad we were there. Then they handed my dad a costume and . . ." Her expression clouded over.

"What kind of costume?"

"A pig costume. Bright pink. Like a big pajama onesie. They told him to put it on, which he did. I still can't believe he went along with it. But it was a new job, and like I said, my father was a compliant person."

"Why in the world did they make him put on a pig costume? That wasn't the school mascot, was it?"

"No, the mascot was an eagle. What they did next was worse. They rolled out a table and told him to climb up on it. Then they put an apple in his mouth and squirted silly string on him while everyone laughed. They said it was his official 'roast,' and now he was part of the faculty family."

"Claire! How could they do that? What kind of dysfunctional faculty 'family' treats their principal like that? That's awful. For all of you."

"It was." She paused again and lay on her back, looking at the ceiling.

"How long did your dad work there?"

"Fourteen months. That was the worst time of my life. Every day someone snorted like a pig at me in the halls."

"Why didn't your dad stop the bullying?"

"I never told my parents."

"How was anyone supposed to have respect for their principal when the staff treated him and his family like that?" I asked.

"I think that was the point. A few key teachers ran the

school. They wanted to put my dad in his place at the start so they could keep up with their . . . their stuff."

"Claire, that's awful. I am so sorry that happened to you."

She sank deeper under the covers and didn't reply.

"Thank you for telling me," I said. "It was wrong on so many levels. I'm sad that your mom and your dad weren't strong enough to take a stand."

"They didn't stand up for themselves, so I knew they wouldn't stand up for me."

Claire turned to her side. I couldn't tell if she was crying or maybe releasing long sighs. It was the first time I remembered her ever sharing such a personal and painful memory with me.

"I don't know why I brought any of that up," she said in a small voice.

"I'm glad you did. I love you, Claire. I hope you dream sweet dreams."

"You too."

I don't know if she fell asleep right away because I was asleep seconds after my head hit the pillow.

The next morning, she was up before me, and any further painful memories had been left behind in the shadows of the night. Claire was energetic and eager to head back to the sidewalk café at first light for another cappuccino and cornetto. I had to scramble to get ready.

We were the first customers of the day at Paulina's café, and the waiter remembered us. He spoke in Italian with a friendly expression while we nodded and kept saying, "Grazie." I don't know why we didn't pull out our translation apps. He seemed to simply be welcoming us back and was satisfied when we smiled and nodded.

"Mmm." Claire brushed the crumbs from the corner of her mouth. "I am going to try making these when we're back home. I think Paulina was right. They are better than croissants."

I half expected to see Paulina show up at the café while we were there. Was it her routine to go to church every morning or only certain weekday mornings? I felt a tug to return to the Frari for morning prayers the way Claire felt the desire to repeat our cappuccino experience.

The plan, however, was set. We were two women on a mission. Although we needed to return to our lodgings first and receive our instructions and whatever item we were delivering from Paulina.

When we arrived, she was waiting for us. "You two are early birds again today."

The trepidation fairy that came with my cordial upbringing hoped Claire wouldn't mention that we had gone for cappuccinos. I didn't want to hurt Paulina's feelings that we didn't invite her. As quickly as I heard that airy voice in my head, I heard another whisper, "Stop worrying about what other people think of you." I tried to brush both voices away.

Paulina handed a woven basket to Claire. It was brimming with fresh vegetables from the garden, two large jars of red sauce, a round loaf of rustic bread, and sprigs of fresh herbs tied with a string. Paulina gave me the written note and repeated instructions about where we were to go.

"Burano is a small island," Paulina reassured us. "You will be able to find the house with no problem." She smiled. "Go in the footsteps of Christ, pilgrims."

I thought her send-off was a little odd. She had written the word "pilgrims" on her welcome note to us as well. We weren't pilgrims or on a pilgrimage, so I couldn't figure out why she said we were to "go in the footsteps of Christ." I guessed the expression was Italian and lost something when translated into English.

"I feel like Little Red Riding Hood," Claire said when we arrived at the stand for the water bus we needed—vaporetto 12. She posed with the basket over her arm and pulled up the hood on her jacket. I pulled out my phone and took her picture.

"That looks heavy. Do you want to take turns?"

"Maybe. I'm okay for now. I can't imagine what it would be like to carry something like this every time I walked to an outdoor market for groceries."

"You know what I understand now? Paulina and women like her are fit even though they live on pasta and gelato because they have to walk everywhere."

"True. She's a lovely woman, isn't she?" Claire said. "I noticed her skin this morning. She hardly has any wrinkles. Just laugh lines by her eyes."

"Must be the fresh air, organic vegetables, lots of exercise, and a thriving spiritual life. Sounds like some of the people you and I know from home."

Loma Linda, the town that borders where Claire and I live, is the only Blue Zone city in the US. In Blue Zones, people live longer than in other places on the planet. The ophthalmologist I worked for had patients from Loma Linda who did not look as old as the date they wrote on their admission forms. When I asked several of them about their youthfulness, they always gave me answers like the four key ingredients I had just listed about Paulina.

"I'd like to think that the reason for her youthfulness," Claire said, "is because of their family motto. Not growing old because you're at the table is a concept I can get excited about. Pass the pasta, please!"

I found it interesting that Claire's reference to the table was linked to her love for food and cooking, whereas my thoughts about being gathered at the table evoked images of communion and the Last Supper.

We validated our tickets and joined the others who were boarding the vaporetto. Our water bus had lots of empty seats inside the cabin, so we settled in toward the middle and each took a window seat. Leaving the canals and entering the lagoon felt as if we had set sail on the high seas. The sky was dotted with big, puffy white clouds that took turns hiding the slanted rays of the sun and turning the water a somber gray. The water wasn't choppy, but our speed was faster than on the canals, and soon we were surrounded by water.

I was captivated by the other boats we passed and the way the sunlight shimmered across the water. It amazed me how flat the lagoon was and how you could see for miles, even on this slightly hazy morning.

Before long, we passed the island of Murano, made famous for their glassblowers who had created beautiful works of art for hundreds of years, including the chandelier in our room. Claire and I had decided the fishing village established on Burano held more interest for us than the artisans of Murano, simply because Burano was more remote.

A light sprinkle began when we disembarked at the dock after our enjoyable forty-minute vaporetto ride. We headed uphill to a wide and almost vacant walkway that led us to the main canal. Small boats with outboard motors were docked in front of each house like a row of cars on a residential street.

The main attraction of Burano was the colorful houses that were visible from our approach via the lagoon and continued as we strolled into the heart of the island. Each one was painted a different color. They lined up like bright, chunky crayons in a giant box. According to tradition, the houses had remained colorful to help wayfaring sailors find their way home even in the densest fog. Most houses were two stories, about the same height, with a front door in the middle, a window on either side of the door, and two windows upstairs. Many had shutters on the windows. A few had flower boxes. Without the colors, I think the uniformity would be depressing, especially on overcast, drizzly days like today.

Claire had her hood up, and I pulled out one of the scarves I had brought along in case we visited any churches and were asked to cover our heads. Even with the light rain, the uniform houses were a bright contrast to the muted and repeated colors we had seen everywhere in Venice.

"You know what this reminds me of?" Claire asked. "The houses look like the long containers that are lined up in a freezer case with all the colorful flavors of gelato."

I laughed. "You're right. Now let's find the pistachio house on this street. On the left side. I think it could be that one."

We stood in front of the door, and I gave a gentle knock.

"You're sure this is it?" Claire asked.

"I think so. The note says his name is Paolo and he lives in the green house on the left." I looked over my shoulder. "Yes. This should be it." I knocked again, this time with more intention.

"Do you think we should leave the basket in front of the door?" Claire asked. "Are there backup instructions?"

I turned the paper over to check. "No."

I knocked again, this time using my fist. If Claire felt like Little Red Riding Hood, I must have sounded like the Big Bad Wolf.

We waited, exchanging wary expressions.

10

> Of all the liars in the world, sometimes the worst are our own fears.
>
> Rudyard Kipling

Claire and I could hear a faint voice from inside the bright green house. The door opened slowly. An elderly man leaned on his cane, eyeing us suspiciously.

"Paolo? Hi. We're friends of Paulina," Claire said.

"Paulina?" His eyes lit up.

"Yes, Paulina." I handed him the note. He briefly glanced at it and looked at us, saying many things we didn't understand.

Claire held out the basket brimming with vegetables as fresh and colorful as the rain-washed houses. "This is for you. From Paulina."

He looked as if he might cry. Opening the door all the way, he motioned for us to come in and spoke rapidly in Italian. Claire pulled out her phone and tapped into the translation app. When he paused, she tried to play back what he had said. Something was not working. The words in English made no sense.

But he knew Paulina, and our role was merely to deliver the gift. That part was understood. Claire placed the basket on a small table to the right of his open door, and the man indicated more enthusiastically that we should come in.

Claire spoke into her phone. Her polite message was translated into Italian for him, saying that we needed to be on our way and that we hoped he had a good day and enjoyed the gift from Paulina's garden. Her app seemed to do its job this time because as the man listened, he nodded and then broke into another string of words that Claire's app was unable to sort out. I wondered if the man had a regional accent or if his missing tooth caused his words to sound different.

We smiled, waved, gave pleasant nods, and headed back the way we had come. I had mixed feelings about our delivery. Had Paulina expected us to stay and help prepare some food for him? She would have included that detail if she'd wanted us to do more than deliver the basket.

As we walked, Claire said, "I realize I didn't ask if you wanted to stay longer."

"No. I think that was the right decision. While we were standing on his doorstep, I was curious if he lived alone and what his small house was like. But I was too nervous to look inside."

"Nervous?"

"You know. Cautious. I didn't want to upset him or offend him."

Claire stopped walking. She looked at me. "You really do worry about those things, don't you?"

"I do. And I've noticed it here more than at home. I caught myself earlier when I was worried that Paulina's feelings might be hurt because we didn't invite her to go for morning coffee."

"Grace."

"I know."

We fell into step again with Claire leading the way to the next stop for us, the Lace Museum. The sprinkles let up as quickly as they had descended, and the sun peeked out from behind the clouds. Claire removed her hood and I took off my scarf. We turned a corner, and I spotted a bell tower rising behind a row of houses. I tilted my head side to side as we got closer.

"Please tell me you're not thinking of going up in that bell tower and trying to convince me to join you," I said. "Because it's leaning. I mean, Leaning-Tower-of-Pisa leaning."

"It sure is. I don't even know if they let visitors go up inside. Don't worry. No bell towers on the list for me today," Claire said.

We took our time to capture an assortment of photos of the pointed tower that looked like a rocket ship headed to the moon. The sunshine made the houses look even more colorful. One of them was purple. Bright purple. And yet, the shade blended sweetly with all the yellows, oranges, reds, and blues of the side-by-side houses. Their vividness made the faded taupe color of the tilted tower stand out even more. Above us, the fleeing clouds unveiled a pastel-blue sky that offered hope for another gorgeous day.

Before we reached the museum, we came upon an older woman who was putting out a rack of lace tablecloths in front of her small shop. She stopped, smiled at us warmly, and said, "Prego," indicating that her shop was now open and we were invited to step inside.

The appeal of being the first to arrive at any location was like honey to us. We couldn't pass up the opportunity.

Another older woman was sitting near the window on a straight-back chair with her feet on a stool. She balanced a round cushion in her lap, and on the cushion, an intricate lace pattern was in process.

Claire and I stood for a long while watching her move the spools of fine white thread and adjust the pins to alter the pattern. Watching her experienced hands was mesmerizing. We didn't speak, and neither did she. I felt like I was watching a ballet performance or a flock of starlings in the evening sky. Each move was intentional and graceful.

A few other shoppers entered and admired the tablecloths, napkins, and handkerchiefs for sale. I looked around for a while, trying to decide if I should buy something. Each piece was a dainty work of art, and unlike books, they would hardly take up any room in my suitcase. But I wasn't sure what lace like this could be used for since it wasn't a modern-day commodity.

"Are you buying something?" I asked Claire. She had a handkerchief in her hand with a lacy letter *B* sewn on one of the corners.

"For Brooke," she said. "I'm going to save it and give it to her on her wedding day. A friend gave me a handkerchief for my wedding day, and I wrapped it around the handle of my bouquet. I didn't need it for tears because I had no reason to cry. But my hands perspired like crazy, and the handkerchief spared many wedding guests from a soggy handshake."

"I love that. Did you see any with an *E*?"

Claire led me to the side table, where she found a hankie with a C and said she was going to purchase it for herself. I found one with a *G* and decided I should buy it. The *E* for Emma required a deeper search and led to my finding one for my mom and also Nathan's mom.

"We picked up half the alphabet," Claire said with a smile

when she handed our purchases to the young woman who took our payment.

She smiled back and asked, "Do you know why the women of Burano perfected the art of lace making?"

"Did it have something to do with fishing?" I asked.

"Everything on our island has something to do with fishing." She smoothed her hair back from her face and said, "The story of the lace started with a fisherman from Burano who sailed the Adriatic Sea to where the mermaids lured men into the water. This particular fisherman, however, held a deep love for his future bride and could not be tempted. The queen of the mermaids heard of this and swam to his boat. She wanted to see the face of innocent love and faithfulness. And when she saw the fisherman, she was not disappointed."

Several other shoppers moved closer to hear the rest of the story.

"Because of his great faithfulness and love for his bride-to-be, the queen of the mermaids gave the fisherman a special gift. She swished her tail against the side of his boat and, in doing so, stirred up a soft globe of sea-foam. Taking the foam in her hands, she turned it into an elegant bridal veil and gave the beautiful gift to the fisherman for his true love."

Claire nudged me and made a cute heart symbol with her fingers. I smiled back.

"The fisherman brought the priceless veil home to Burano. When his bride wore it on their wedding day, she was the most beautiful bride the island had ever seen. Ever since that day, the women of Burano have been trying to re-create the delicate, lacy elegance of the veil that came from the sea. It was the reward of innocence, given to humans by the queen of the mermaids."

"What a charming story," I said.

"Thank you for telling it," Claire added. "I love stories like that."

The woman leaned in as if she was going to tell us a secret. "Stories show us truth, beauty, and hope. Stories are a gift. This is why we must always give others the gift of our stories."

The woman's sage words connected with something inside me. When we stepped out of the shop, I paused and pulled out my phone.

"Just a second," I told Claire. "I want to record what she said about stories. They are a gift, aren't they?"

"Yes. Where would we be without all the books you and I have read over the years?" Claire pulled out her phone and took a photo of the shop. "And here is a sobering thought. Would you and I have ever met if it weren't for our love of books?"

"True."

I remembered Paulina saying at the Frari that St. Francis had influenced artists to tell Bible stories through art. I quickly added that to my note before we started our tour of the Lace Museum.

More insights kept coming to me about the influence of art on our imaginations and how stories impact the way we think. The many lace items on display all seemed to be silently telling stories. I studied the various patterns with new eyes, thinking of the queen of the mermaids.

I had always wanted to come to Venice because I imagined it would be romantic, enchanting, and like no other place on earth. What I didn't expect was the sense that Claire and I kept stepping into living fairy tales. All the people who inhabited these islands over the centuries had left their stories here. Their tales permeated every form of art. I could see the bigger picture of the grand allure of Venice now as I studied the fragile designs created from simple thread. Each piece spoke to me as if it were a miniature, misty echo of the architecture, sculptures, paintings, canals, colors, and music of intriguing Venice. Even the foundation on which this marvelous place had been raised was crafted by clever artisan builders and engineers.

It was all story. All art.

Claire kept strolling through the museum, but I had to pause and try to capture my thoughts. Peering through the top of one of the glass cases, I studied an intricate lace cross. And added another note, dictating softly into my phone. "Hints of God's story are everywhere. I love that at the heart of Venice, embedded in the tiles in the basilica, is the first story. The truest story. His story. Beginning with creation because God is the Creator. We are made in His image, and we are made to create beauty."

I put my phone back in my pouch and stood for a moment, not focusing on anything. I'd never expected to have such a string of insights or such an emotion-stirring experience on Burano, and in a museum of all places. At that moment, the Lord felt very near.

"Did you see these dresses?" Claire asked as I slowly moved across the floor to where she stood by a wedding gown display. "I can see how lace fed the fancies of the wealthy society of Venice back in the day. Look at these lace gloves. Can you imagine having these on when you reach for the handle of your teacup? You would automatically sit up straight and take only tiny sips."

"Stunning." That was the only word I could think of to encompass everything I was thinking and feeling.

The quieting of my heart stayed with me as we left the museum and strolled to a restaurant we had passed on our way to the green house. Our pace that day was the opposite of our quick and sometimes frantic strides the day before. Today we sauntered our way across a short bridge and paused to appreciate the way the full sun caused the brightly colored houses to make curvy, equally colorful reflections on the water.

We entered the restaurant and discovered we were the first to arrive for lunch. The waiters wore crisp white shirts with black bow ties. They spoke English, and one of them told us that even though we were early, we were welcome.

He brought us tall bottles of acqua minerale and included an enthusiastic speech about how this brand was the best water and the only water we should ever drink again. The reason was because it came from that region. We nodded our appreciation. He waited until we had long drinks and nodded again in agreement with his pitch.

"Very good," Claire said generously. To me, it tasted like warm water.

"Molto bene," he echoed, giving his indication of how her praise for the water should be pronounced in his restaurant.

"Molto bene," we repeated with smiles.

After he walked away with our orders, Claire whispered, "If he's that enthusiastic about the water, I can't wait to see what he has to say about the main course."

More diners entered, and our waiter soon became too busy to give us special attention. Our three-course meals were delivered, and the pasta I'd selected was the best I had eaten so far. The menu listed it as pappardelle scampi e ricotta affumicata. The wide, thin noodles were covered with plump shrimp and smoked ricotta cheese. Claire went for spaghetti with clams, but after tasting mine, she agreed that this time I had made the better choice.

"You've been pretty quiet all day. Are you okay?" she asked.

I nodded. "Just thinking a lot."

"What about?"

"The stories we've heard and all the art."

"Oh, good. I was hoping you weren't worried that you had upset someone." Claire paused. "May I tell you something? Because I have some ideas on why you feel so concerned about what people think of you."

"Okay." I leaned back, giving her a chin-dipped, unblinking look. Claire told me once that the chin dip was my Princess Diana look, and when I took that position she knew I was willing to be vulnerable.

I wasn't sure I was ready, though. I struggled enough when I imagined that others were irritated with me. To be told the specifics by my closest friend was not my idea of a good time.

"I have two thoughts," Claire said. "First, I think your concern about how you come across to other people is something you picked up from your mom."

"True."

"That's not to bash your mom," Claire quickly added. "You know I love her. She has a certain high-class way of doing everything, and you learned that from her. It's not a bad thing. It's just that you and Nathan don't live like that or move in those circles. But you're out of your routine here, and I think you're reverting to how you had to be when you traveled with your mom."

"I agree. I thought the same thing earlier."

"Okay, well, good. The second influence is your job. I've watched you become skittish over the past year, ever since you took on more than you should with your boss. He's a perfectionist and too demanding. It doesn't seem like he appreciates your extra efforts because he's critical of everything."

"He is." I put the last bite of pasta in my mouth so I wouldn't say anything negative about my boss. I'd told Claire on the plane that I'd prayed a lot about it and didn't feel released yet from working for him. She said it wasn't a spiritual issue. I didn't try to tell her that for me, everything was a mishmash of spiritual, physical, mental, and emotional. I didn't separate them.

"One last observation." Claire began counting on her fingers. "You're afraid of making mistakes. You're afraid of what people think of you. You're afraid of heights. Or at least, you *were* afraid of heights." She paused and pushed back her bangs. "Grace, I think that just like you faced your fear of heights, you can also overcome being self-conscious. All you have to do is find a way to stop being afraid."

Claire's statement felt like a tiny electrical shock. A small truth zinger. She was right. Fear was at the core of it all. This was a solvable problem. I went to the top of the campanile, didn't I? I could conquer fear.

"Thank you," I said.

Claire tilted her head. "You don't have to thank me. I didn't offer a solution because I don't have any advice on how to conquer fear."

"But you named the root of the problem. I agree. It's fear. Isn't identifying the source the next step in solving a problem, after admitting that something in your life isn't right?"

"I think so."

"That's why I appreciate you telling me," I said.

Our server came to our table and presented us with a small plate of little round cookies as a complimentary dessert. One of them was in the shape of a backward *S* and the other three were shaped like an O.

"Made here. Only here. In Burano." He seemed to be revving up for another lesson on local delicacies. "You must try. Bussola buranello. Bussola is a compass, you see?" He pointed at the O-shaped cookie. "What do you think?"

"Mmm." Claire offered him her best closed-eyes food-appreciation expression and said, "Buttery but with a nice lemon twist. I love it. Do you sell them here?"

"No, not here. At the bakery. I will show you."

Claire added the location on her phone, and we slowly enjoyed the satisfying dessert before splitting the bill. With a round of friendly ciaos from our waiter, we were off on another sauntering expedition. Even though the streets were more crowded than when we first arrived, I appreciated the sense of ease I felt on this colorful island. I was glad that of all the remote islands we could have visited, we had chosen to come here.

The bakery was easy to find and already filled with visitors. The cookies must have been more popular than we realized because we had to wait our turn and ended up buying more bags than we needed. It started with Claire holding one of the bags and saying, "They're small. We better take two."

"I think we should take a bag back to Paulina," I said. "And it would be nice to have enough for another afternoon snack in our room. Actually, based on the way we devoured the cherry tomatoes and apricots yesterday, we should take two bags."

Claire decided she wanted to take a bag home for Jared and Brooke, which meant I better take one for Nathan and Emma.

It got to be kind of silly. In the end, we left the island with ten bags of cookies between us. The first one was open before we even reached our vaporetto.

11

Il dolce far niente.
The art of doing nothing.
Italian saying

"They are different than sugar cookies or shortbread," Claire said once we were in our seats on the vaporetto. "It's the lemon. I love it. Do you think it's lemon juice or zest?"

"You can ask our chef when we take our cooking class."

"I will. Her name is Amelia. I'm really looking forward to our class and staying at the villa." Claire leaned back. "But first, to review our options for the rest of the day. We have three museums on the list, the opera house, and of course, ninety-nine more churches if you want to see more church decor. And we can still go to Murano and see the glassblowers. What would you like to do?"

"Would it be terrible to say that all I want to do is go back to our apartment, eat the rest of this bag of cookies, and read a book?"

"See? This is why you and I are so perfect for each other."

Claire grinned. "Yes, please. Let's do nothing. That's very Italian. I heard someone say that. Who said it? 'The art of doing nothing.'"

"Love that."

"Doing nothing followed, of course, by a scrumptious dinner," Claire added.

"Of course. And I might add a little napini to our afternoon."

"Napini?" Claire repeated. "I thought Paulina called the afternoon rest time a riposo."

I grinned. "Tomato, tow-mah-tow, riposo, napini. Same, same."

Claire held out the open bag of cookies to me. "Take two. They're small."

I laughed. "That was your advice that got us into this overstocked situation. I'm going to wait."

We arrived at our room and went to work carrying out our delicious plan. We figured out how to make tea with the supplies in our kitchenette and took some water, our mugs of tea, and cookies to the chairs under the tree because the afternoon was too nice to stay inside. I could nap as easily with a book in my lap as I could if I were stretched out on a bed.

A small table had been placed between the two chairs and provided enough space for our plate of cookies, water, and mugs of tea. I pulled out my journal and my phone, eager to transfer to the page all the insights I had collected that day.

Claire had smoothed down the first page in her journal. Instead of writing in it, she pulled the bouquet of colored pencils from her bag and began sketching.

"I didn't know you could draw."

"I don't know either. Nobody knows!" Claire chuckled. "That's because I never tried." She squinted and tilted her head, focusing on the walkway that led to the fountain. "I am trying something new."

I turned my chair so I could catch the stream of afternoon light more fully and began writing. I didn't know if I could create an interesting summary of our experiences so far, but like Claire, I wanted to try something new. The last few lines I wrote were about Claire's insight at the restaurant and how I needed to stop being afraid.

Lowering my pen, I realized I didn't want to write more about being afraid. I didn't want to fall into a rabbit hole of overanalyzing. That would be doing something, and the point of us sitting here under the tree was to do nothing. Closing my journal, I reached for another cookie and glanced over at Claire's masterpiece. She had dipped a blue colored pencil into her glass of water and was making slow strokes, filling in the outline of the basin of the fountain with the watery pale shade.

"Pretty," I said.

"Thanks. This is fun. I love having downtime, don't you?" Claire replied. "Let's make sure we have another afternoon like this along the way."

"Agreed."

I gazed at two small birds balanced on the edge of the fountain, taking leisurely sips of the cool water, and whispered a heartfelt "Thank You" for the gift of the moment as I experienced the art of doing nothing in Venice.

Closing my eyes and resting my folded hands on my midriff, I listened to the muffled sounds around us and drifted in and out of a daydream. I couldn't remember the last time I had soaked myself in stillness.

I was roused by Claire's low voice. "Another pilgrim?"

I squinted to see that a young woman had entered our private Eden and was using her fob to open the door to apartment number three. She was close enough for us to see that her only luggage was a backpack dotted with patches from around the globe.

I stretched and wandered over to the raised garden beds. Something in me longed to press my fingers into the soil. I wanted to feel the dirt and see how the tomatoes were progressing. Out of habit, I picked off a few dead leaves and ruffled the frilly tops of the carrots.

Paulina exited her apartment. Riposo was over, and she had come outside prepared to do some gardening. "Would you like to join me?" She held out a basket. "Our chef needs eight of these." She gently pushed back the spiky, full leaves that covered the zucchini, and together we checked for the ripest ones.

"These are beautiful," I said.

"Paolo used to call them naso, which means 'nose.'" She looked up. "How was your visit with him? Did you have any problems finding his cottage?"

"No. He was very appreciative."

"Bene. Good. Was he well?"

"Yes, he seemed to be."

"Paolo is one of my husband's many uncles. He was our chef here at Trattoria da Tommaso for forty-five years. His wife wanted to return to Burano where she grew up so she could spend her last years near her sister. He stayed on after she passed."

I plucked a ripe zucchini and placed it in the basket, wishing I had known that interesting bit of information about Paolo before we called on him.

"I try to get to Burano at least once a month to see him and take a small gift from this garden he started so long ago," Paulina said. "Thank you for being my hands and feet today."

"Of course. You're welcome." I felt humbled and wished

I hadn't been so timid about lingering at his home a little longer and visiting with him, even if our communication wasn't clear.

"Paolo taught me everything about cooking and ospitalità." Paulina put the final green "nose" into her basket and looked at me. She reminded me of one of the brown birds at the fountain by the way she tilted her head. "Do you know the meaning of the word 'hospitality'?"

Before I answered, she told me. "It means showing love to strangers."

It took a moment for her words to settle on me. As I was growing up in a large house filled with expectations, hospitality always felt like a grand production. We had to be on our best behavior, pull out the crystal, and try to impress the important, equally wealthy people who came through the front door. Paulina's description of hospitality was different. She didn't know Claire and me, and yet she had welcomed us into her apartment complex, her garden, and her church.

I was trying to form a reply that described the gratitude I felt at that moment. I wanted to thank her for including us in her life and showing us so many gifts of kindness and love. But I was slow in coming up with adequate words, and our attention was diverted by a middle-aged couple who entered the courtyard, pulling their wheeled suitcases behind them.

Paulina brushed the soil from her hands and went to greet them. I could hear their accents and Paulina saying something about their flight from Oslo, so I guessed they were from Norway.

A few moments later, another pilgrim stepped into the garden. He emerged from apartment number five and reminded me of a mountain climber. His long, curly hair was wet, as if he had just taken a long-awaited shower after many hours of travel.

Claire and I hung back as introductions were made, but Paulina quickly included us. We smiled and shook hands, but the names didn't stick in my brain. I think I was still trying to process what Paulina had said about hospitality and trying to shake off the regret I had about not showing more of that "love to strangers" to Paolo.

"I would like all of you to be my guests at dinner tonight," Paulina said. "Would nine o'clock work for you?"

The others agreed quickly. Claire and I exchanged glances before accepting the invitation. We gathered up our things and returned to our room, relinquishing the chairs under the tree to the Norwegian couple, who had entered a focused conversation with each other in their native language.

"We could bow out of dinner with everyone, if you would like," I said, heading for the bathroom to wash up. "Did you want to eat somewhere else tonight?"

"No. I think it would be nice to eat here again. I heard Paulina telling you about Paolo and her family connections. I feel like she's invited us to be part of that."

"I know. I feel the same way. Showing love to strangers. Did you hear that part?"

Claire didn't answer because someone knocked on the door and she went to answer it. The bathroom door was closed, so I couldn't clearly hear what she was saying. When I exited, Claire was reaching for her jacket.

"The others are going to St. Mark's," she said. "For the sunset. They invited us to go with them. I think it would be fun. Do you want to come? Safety in numbers, if you're worried about running into another Raphael."

A few minutes later our group of six traipsed single file toward "Europe's drawing room," with Claire at the front of the line. I listened as the others visited, getting to know each other. The young woman who had arrived with the backpack was from Canada. Her name was Lexie. She was curious to hear about our travel plans, saying she was gleaning ideas for where to go after Venice.

"We have train tickets to Florence in the morning," Claire said. "We're taking a cooking class at a villa in Tuscany."

"That sounds fun," Lexie said. "Are you both cooks?"

"I'm not," I chimed in. "Claire is. She's a great cook."

I almost added that her skills were born of interest and necessity since she'd grown up on canned spaghetti and microwave popcorn, but I didn't think she would appreciate me sharing that detail about her childhood. I also decided that my story could be equally embarrassing. I never had to learn to cook because my mom had a personal chef who cooked for us. When I married Nathan, he enjoyed making dinner, so I gladly let him take over in the kitchen while I became the dishwasher.

"Do you have a plan for where you're going after Venice?" Claire asked Lexie.

"Not really. I'm meeting friends in Positano in a week. Until then, I'm a vagabond. My meandering starts here and ends here in five weeks. What happens in the middle is a mystery."

"That's a brave way to travel," Claire said. "I don't think I would do well wandering around Italy without some sort of schedule."

"Well, not all who wander are lost, you know."

"Tolkien," Claire said, recognizing the quote from one of his books.

"Yes! Are you a fan?"

"We're readers." Claire included me in her statement. She told Lexie about the Libreria Acqua Alta as well as which gelateria we liked best and how much we enjoyed our gondola ride. By the time we arrived at St. Mark's Square, I dared to say that Claire had helped Lexie formulate a sightseeing plan for Venice, and Lexie didn't seem to mind a bit.

The square seemed transformed from the midday encounter we had experienced the day before. All the restaurants that lined the vast inner courtyard area were now open for business. Crisp white tablecloths were in place and nearly every seat was taken.

The mood in the plaza had shifted. We were no longer viewing the daytime schools-of-fish tourists moving as one across the wide area. In the waning daylight, the view was of sections in front of each restaurant where visitors were sitting, eating, drinking, and talking calmly across the tables.

Even the sky seemed subdued. It had taken on a rich shade of indigo that covered the space like a canopy. The sun was hidden behind the three-story buildings, making the amber lights in the alcoves and restaurants feel like home fires welcoming weary travelers to come closer.

The restaurant directly across from us seemed to have the most outdoor tables set up, and an army of servers moved among them in a well-choreographed evening dance. Diners were being treated to beautiful music performed by a six-piece orchestra. As we stood in our own little unlikely hive taking it all in, several people rose from their chairs and stepped into the open area of the square, where they danced to the waltz.

"Who wants to dance with me?" Lexie asked. The Norwegian man accepted her invitation, and his wife gave him a playful look of shock. The two of them waltzed away. I had never seen anything like it. Two strangers dancing, laughing, and going through the steps impressively, as if they did this every evening. Lexie and her partner made it look easy.

The mountain climber held out his hand to the jilted spouse, and they joined the escapade.

I thought of my wedding and how my dad and I had laughed and cried during the father-daughter dance. He tried so hard not to step on my feet. Nathan was such a good sport for our first dance. We mostly swayed and smiled while looking into each other's eyes. We'd tucked in a few more dances that evening when the music was less formal. I wasn't sure if I'd danced since then.

Claire nudged me. "Come on."

We had to be the silliest couple on the great dance floor. Claire, naturally, wanted to take the lead, but she was learning the steps as we went. My years of dance lessons kicked in, and if I'd had a different partner, I think I might have done pretty well.

The waltz concluded, and Lexie offered a cute curtsy to her partner. Claire and I mimicked her gesture and nearly bumped our heads in the process.

"Not our best skill," she said with a laugh. "But kudos to us for trying."

Our quirky entourage continued our stroll to the end of St. Mark's Square with our spirits high. Claire sidled up next to me when we reached the lagoon and pointed at a gondola returning to the docking area in front of us. From the bow, a small brass lantern swayed gently and shed a romantic, gilded light over the couple cuddled up on the cushioned seat.

"I miss Jared," she said.

"Me too." I quickly corrected my sentiment. "I mean Nathan. I miss my husband too."

The rippled lagoon water had taken on an inky hue, and the waning sun caught one last reflection of herself in the brine. As the others chatted, I watched a large cloud moving through the violet sky like a grand dame headed to a prestigious Venetian event. Her petticoats curved up as she skimmed the horizon, revealing the pinks, oranges, and pale yellows sewn along her hem. She seemed content to float wherever the evening breeze took her.

Maybe humans aren't the only ones who wander. Maybe none of us are ever really lost.

12

Per aspera ad astra.
Through hardships to the stars.
Italian saying

"I could have eaten a bowl of that risotto," I said when we were back in our room that night after our fabulous dinner with Paulina and the pilgrims. "What was in the sauce that gave it so much flavor?"

"Did you hear me ask Paulina the same question?" Claire grinned. "She said it was amore."

"Of course the secret ingredient was love. That seems to be Paulina's secret ingredient to everything in her life."

"I've never had risotto like that. I loved it. Paulina said they use rice that grows nearby so it's fresh. The chef uses Paolo's technique of quick-frying the rice in olive oil first so that the hull is crispy while the inside is still al dente."

I nodded as if I could actually picture how to do that, even though I had never attempted to make risotto, let alone try to fry the rice first to keep it al dente.

"Paulina also said theirs is the best because they mix the butter with the Parmesan first before adding it. She says if it's done correctly, the mixture looks like powder."

Again, I couldn't picture powdered cheese and butter. Shredded, yes. Melted, of course.

"You know," Claire said, "at one point I thought Paulina and some of the others around the table might be in some kind of cult. But the more we talked, they all seemed normal. It was strange."

"Strange in what way?"

"I'm not used to being around people who talk about what they believe and pray before they eat. You always pray, but it's a private thing for you. With her, it was open and as if she assumed everyone wanted to pray with her, because why wouldn't they? Does that make sense?"

"Yes." I finished packing my suitcase and put my pajamas aside. "Childlike faith," I said more to myself than to Claire.

"That's it," Claire agreed. "Her faith is so simple. She's so peaceful. I don't think I've ever met anyone like her." Claire kicked off her shoes and applied a fresh Band-Aid to her blister. "Are you still going to take a shower tonight?"

"Yes. Do you mind if I go first?"

"It's all yours."

I tried to hurry, but it took a while to dry my hair. I hoped the hair dryer wasn't too loud.

When I exited the bathroom, I saw that the noise hadn't bothered Claire because she was snuggled in and already asleep with the lights on. Resting on top of her was the book about St. Francis I had bought at the Libreria Acqua Alta. I thumbed through the first few pages and saw that Claire had circled a paragraph with her purple colored pencil resting on the nightstand.

> The core message of the gospel demonstrated in Francis's life came from the words of Christ to His disciples and is recorded in Mark 12. Francis demonstrated how to love the

Lord with all your heart, soul, strength, and mind and love your neighbor as yourself.

I grinned. Not only because it was one of those "is that odd or is that God?" touches since Claire had circled the verse, but also because the reference was from the Gospel of Mark. Mark, the follower of Jesus. Mark, the writer. Mark, the revered lion of Venice whose bones may or may not be buried in the basilica. I wondered if the coincidence was evident to Claire as well.

I turned off the lights, tucked myself into bed, and said a little prayer. I don't remember even closing my eyes, I was so tired.

Early the next morning we scrambled to get out the door and had to tromp through a chilling drizzle all the way to the train station. The sky wasn't the only thing leaking that morning. I was still misty-eyed when Claire and I took our side-by-side seats on the train.

"You okay?" Claire asked.

"I feel like we're saying a forever goodbye to two friends we barely knew but will never forget."

Claire fiddled with the recline button on her seat. "Two friends?"

"Beautiful Paulina and beautiful Venice."

"They were both wonderful, weren't they? Everything has been so much better than I thought it would be," Claire said. "And just think. The villa awaits us!"

After we had settled in, I pulled out my journal. This would be my chance to capture more memories before too many new adventures crowded them from my thoughts. I balanced the journal on my lap and stared out the large, rain-streaked window as we pulled out of the Santa Lucia station. We picked up speed across the bridge that connected Venice to the mainland, and soon we were moving too rapidly to take in the scenery.

Claire had tucked her jacket over and around her like a blanket. Her eyes were already closed. She had no problem falling asleep anytime, anywhere. It wasn't a gift I shared.

For the next half hour I filled more pages of my journal with slightly wobbly handwriting. I could envision Nathan's gaze resting on me as I told him I danced with Claire in St. Mark's Square. I could picture his grin when I described the taste of the risotto made with love and some secret powder created using butter and Parmesan cheese.

The train pulled into Padua, and Claire looked around, squinting.

"It's just the first stop," I said. "We have at least two more hours before Florence."

She sat up and leaned over to look out the window. "I'm going to find the café car and buy us some cappuccinos. What else would you like?"

"Whatever you pick, I'll take the same thing."

The train began to move again. I finished my journal entry and pulled out my book on St. Francis. I knew very little about the Middle Ages and found the author's explanations helpful. Francis came from a wealthy family and had renounced everything so he could help the poor.

Claire returned with coffee in paper cups and some sort of roll for each of us wrapped in a sealed plastic bag. "Not exactly gourmet," she said. "But we're no longer at the Trattoria da Tommaso."

I gave her an exaggerated pout. "I miss it already." I held up the book. "Looks like you got a running start on me last night while I was in the shower."

"I did. I was trying to find out what his deal was with the birds."

"Did you get to this part where it says that Francis was the first to create a live nativity scene with people and animals? He did that eight hundred years ago!"

Claire swallowed a bite of her breakfast roll. "Here's a question. Do you think your faith is simple?"

"Do you mean simple like only an uneducated person would believe in God? Or simple like not having a lot of rules and rituals connected to worship?"

"Like Paulina. And like what it said in the book about how we're created to basically love God and others. Is it that easy? Is that Christianity to you?"

"I think the foundational piece, the first step, is to repent and surrender everything to Christ."

"The way Francis did."

"Yes. The way millions of people have done over the centuries. Our surrender to God has to happen first, at the heart level, I think. Then we can love God and love others because His Spirit gives us the power to do that."

"The teaching I was immersed in was all about the rules. We couldn't do certain things or say certain things. Girls had to wear dresses to church and not wear makeup or do anything with our hair that made us stand out." Claire put her breakfast roll back in the plastic bag as if she had decided it wasn't worth eating. "No one talked about surrendering to God. Or loving anyone. It was all about obeying and following the church rules."

"I didn't know it was so rigid."

"I don't like to talk about that time in my life." She paused. "But you know that."

"Yes, but . . ." I'm not sure why I leaned in just then and looked at her intently. I wanted to say something meaningful and craft a deeply important sentence on the spot, but no words came to me.

She stared back, her blue eyes slightly hidden behind her bangs. "What? I know you want to say something. Say it."

"I want to say that your friendship is immensely dear to me. I feel like we've gone through so much together ever since we met."

"We have."

"And you know how you told me that I need to figure out how to not be afraid all the time? Well, Claire, I think you need to figure out how to heal from the stuff that was so hurtful in your past."

"And you think Jesus is the answer."

I grinned. "Of course I do."

Claire leaned back and stared straight ahead. The conversation door had just closed.

I hadn't expected her to open up there on the train after all these years of pulling back whenever our conversations moved too close to the part of her that was unhealed. I wasn't a counselor. I never knew what to say. But I cared for her so much. I hoped she saw that in my bumbling words.

Claire returned to her nap under her jacket. I finished reading my book before the train stopped again. More passengers boarded, and every seat was soon taken. The volume of the many conversations went up a level.

When we were about ten minutes outside of the Santa Maria Novella train station in Florence, Claire roused. "I hope the place where we're staying is everything it looked like online. And I really hope the cooking class is as great as all the reviews said it was."

Claire must have been feeling the same qualms I had when we entered Venice, and I had been the one who selected the accommodation and made all the arrangements. I knew very little about the villa except for the lovely photos I'd scrolled through several times and the welcoming letter from the owners, Amelia and her husband, Gio.

Their story would make a great movie. She grew up at the villa but then went to England to help a friend start an Italian restaurant. The endeavor never quite got off the ground. Then she unexpectedly inherited the Tuscan villa, returned to Florence, married, and after three years of renovation, opened a B and B and cooking class in their new home.

Claire and I were captivated by the story, especially the part about how Amelia met Gio in Florence and how they restored the villa together. We knew that was where we wanted to stay and grabbed the three-night opening as soon as Claire found it on the online calendar because it lined up perfectly with our trip.

The train slowed as it came into the station. Claire checked her phone and said, "Ohhh."

"What?"

"Small change in plans. We're supposed to take a taxi to a place called Luogo di Pace. Our host will meet us there to take us to the villa."

I gave her a raised-eyebrow look and said one word. "Claire?"

"We had options," Claire reminded me as the train came to a full stop. "We could have chosen to get ourselves to the villa by renting a car or taking public transportation."

"I know. I'm not questioning our choice to have someone from the villa pick us up. I just wonder why they can't pick us up directly from the train station."

"I don't know."

"Do you know what this place is where the taxi is going to take us?"

"No." Claire gave me a hopeful look.

I reminded myself to be supportive of Claire the way I'd

wanted her to support me when we arrived in Venice. Our budget-friendly transportation had been a mutual choice.

The crush of people both exiting the train and brushing past us as we tried to maneuver our way through the station was horrible. I was grateful once more that we were traveling light. Our first stop was a money-exchange kiosk. We had used all our euros in Venice and decided to exchange more money this time.

After carefully stashing our cash, we made it outside the terminal and found the sign for the taxis. It was only a little after eleven in the morning, but the weather was already much warmer than it had been in Venice. Obviously we were in a major city, which we found a little overwhelming. The buildings seemed huge and modern. I found it strange to see so many cars after a few days of not seeing or hearing any.

The long line of white taxis moved quickly. When it was our turn, the driver assisted with putting our suitcases in the trunk before we got in. Everything seemed to be going at a quick pace.

Claire told the driver the name of where we wanted to go. He looked at us in the rearview mirror and said, "No."

"Here's the address." Claire showed him her phone.

He turned around and looked us over. "No."

"No, it's not a correct address? Or no, you won't take us there?"

"Why?" he asked.

Claire leaned forward and firmly said, "We need to meet someone at this address. Will you take us there, or should we find a different taxi?"

With a dismissive puff, he put on his blinker and pulled away from the curb. I kept shooting glances at Claire, but she was avoiding me the way I had avoided her on the vaporetto in the fog. She studied the map on her phone.

"It's only ten minutes away," Claire mumbled. "I don't know what the problem is."

During those next ten minutes, my prayer life grew exponentially. We drove into a seedy-looking area where graffiti covered the walls. My heart raced, and I was coming up with all kinds of alternate plans to escape what felt like a volatile situation.

Before I could offer any of my fragmented suggestions to Claire, the taxi driver turned sharply down a narrow street and came to a quick stop in front of what looked like an old office building that needed some TLC.

Claire paid him, and he exited the car quickly and opened the trunk. I stayed in the back seat, staring at the building and the two ragged-looking women standing by the door.

Claire opened her car door to get out, but I grabbed her arm. "Claire?"

13

Prima di scegliere l'amico bisogna averci mangiato il sale sette anni.
Before choosing a friend, you must have eaten salt with them for seven years.

Italian saying

Claire looked at me over her shoulder as she was about to exit the taxi, but didn't say anything.

"Claire, I think the driver should take us back to the train station. Or, better yet, let's have him take us to the villa. I'll pay."

She seemed to consider my offer until her gaze fell on our luggage that was now sitting unattended on the uneven pavement. I felt as if our decisions in the next two seconds would affect the rest of our trip. Possibly the rest of our lives.

The driver climbed back into the taxi and said something in Italian that neither of us needed a translator to understand. His meaning was obvious. He wanted to be rid of us so he could leave this neighborhood.

"Ciao! Hello!" A nice-looking man stepped out of the

building just then and was waving at us. Or at the taxi driver. At that point, I didn't know what was going on.

The man came closer, still smiling. "Claire?" He leaned to look into the back seat and pointed to himself. "Gio!"

"Gio! Hi. I'm Claire." She got out and closed her door. "Is Amelia with you?"

"Amelia, no. Gio, sì." He opened the back door for me and reached in to offer me a hand. I was barely out of the taxi when Gio closed the door and the driver took off. If the edge of my blouse had gotten stuck in the closed door, I'm sure it would have gone down the alleyway still attached to the taxi.

Gio had a grip on the handle of both our wheeled bags and was energetically leading us around the corner. I linked my arm with Claire's for sisterly support as well as stability on the uneven pavement. Gio stopped walking when he reached a small truck parked next to an open side door of the unidentified building. The truck looked like something from a children's book because of the rounded front and small shape. In the narrow truck bed was a moped, secured to the sides with bungee cords. Gio tossed our suitcases in the back with the moped and opened the door to the cab for us, still smiling.

The bench seat looked like it could hold two children at best. It reminded me of the old kids' toys at the mall that you put coins in and they would bounce up and down.

"You first," I said to Claire. We both knew I wasn't offering out of my polite upbringing.

The three of us, like proverbial sardines, sat thigh to thigh. I was only halfway on the seat with the other half of my backside pressed against the door. I gripped the handle because I was afraid that if we hit a bump, my thigh would push the handle up and I would tumble out onto the road.

"How far is it to the villa?" I asked once we had jostled

our way onto one of the main thoroughfares leading out of Florence.

Gio answered in Italian. I wondered if I should try to wedge my fingers into my travel bag and dig out my phone so we could use the translator app and find out what was going on. Claire was one step ahead of me. Her phone was in her hand. I wondered if she had held on to it ever since showing the taxi driver the address. Maybe she even had the Italian equivalent of 911 cued up so all she had to do was push a button once we figured out whether we were being kidnapped.

"How long will it take to get to the villa?" Claire asked into her phone. It translated for her and then translated Gio's reply, saying that it was close. Only fifteen minutes. He kept talking and the phone kept translating. He apologized for the inconvenience and said they had a van they used for business but it had a problem, and he was in town to pick up the Vespa so Amelia told him to get us, but he had to make a delivery at Luogo di Pace and . . . He took a breath and said he loved us already.

The man was charming. When we heard his explanation, we both relaxed. The problem was that when we did, gravity took our previously lifted body parts, and we sort of sunk and shifted so that we were sharing our closeness even more.

I glanced at Claire as she tried to operate her phone with both arms pinned back on either side. She resembled a T. rex in one of those funny blow-up costumes. That didn't stop her from asking Gio more questions and trying to hold the phone closer to get his answers. We found out that the other three guests who had booked the cooking class for that afternoon would not be joining us because their flight out of Frankfurt had been canceled. They had rebooked to go directly to Rome. I'm sure Claire felt the same way I did about having Amelia all to ourselves that afternoon. With all the questions Claire would have for her, it was probably a good thing we wouldn't have to share.

My leg was tingling after having the circulation pinched in my squished position. I tried to adjust slightly, but at this point it was an all-or-nothing endeavor. If one person shifted, we all had to shift, and that was going to be difficult with Gio driving.

He turned onto a narrow road that led into the gorgeous green rolling hills Tuscany was known for. I tried to forget about my discomfort and take in the scenery. The Italian cypress trees that lined a road up a hill in the distance reminded me of toy soldiers standing in formation. I scanned the view, hoping to see one of the quintessential fields of bright yellow sunflowers. None appeared. I guessed it was too early in the year for them to be at full height.

Gio suddenly gripped the steering wheel and yelled as the truck swerved to the right and then to the left. We came to an abrupt halt. Gio immediately turned off the engine and checked both of us to make sure we were okay. Claire guessed before I did that we had a flat tire. I thought we had hit something in the road, and maybe we did.

We didn't need a translation to know that we had stopped in a precarious position. Gio wanted us to get out of the cab. Claire and I practically tumbled out as soon as I opened the door. I couldn't feel my foot, and my balance was wobbly on the dismount. Gio unhitched the Vespa from the bed of the truck and at the same time was talking to someone on his phone, which was sticking up out of his top pocket.

"Do you think he's going to go for help and leave us here?" I asked Claire.

She watched him closely, her lips pressed together. I linked my arm in hers and held my breath.

Gio carefully climbed into the back of the truck and pulled a metal ramp from the side. We helped him lower it and held it steady as he cautiously rolled the Vespa down the uneven ramp. I expected him to start up the moped and scoot down the deserted country lane. Instead, he shoved what looked like a large tool chest to the edge of the truck bed, hopped down, and opened the box.

Clearly Gio had done this before. He had everything he needed to patch the tire, reinflate it, and hopefully make it roadworthy. I couldn't help but notice that the other tires looked like they might heave their last gasp at any moment as well.

Since it looked like we were going to be there for a while, Claire pulled her colored pencils and journal out of her bag. She sat down at the edge of the road and began to sketch the rolling countryside. I knew she was tense because she wasn't talking. Perhaps she thought that sketching would help calm her.

I sat down beside her and quietly prayed for our safety. Unexpectedly, a verse I'd memorized years ago came to mind. The words seemed to encircle me like a comforting hug.

For God has not given us a spirit of fear but of power and love and a sound mind.

In that moment, as I gazed at the breathtaking Tuscan countryside, a vivid truth settled into my thoughts. *Fear doesn't come from God.*

Maybe my faith was simple, like Claire was talking about on the train. Maybe it was as easy as loving God and loving others. Maybe the solution to my self-consciousness was to not let fear have a voice in my thoughts. *Because fear doesn't come from God.*

Could it be that simple?

Side by side, Claire and I remained lost in our own swirls

of wonder and paths toward peace. She continued sketching while I fashioned new thoughts and fed them to my previously apprehensive mind.

I reviewed the moments that had caused me to feel anxious over the last month. In each case, I was afraid. Afraid of what might go wrong, and sometimes things did. Afraid of someone becoming upset with me at work, which they were every day. Afraid of losing my job, which I could walk away from if I knew that was what I should do. Afraid of what people thought of me, which really shouldn't matter.

I can't explain how empowered I felt as I looked at the list of what I'd been fearful about and each item seemed emptied of its angst.

What I did next was more important than I realized at the time. I spoke kindly to my timid soul and told her, *Don't be afraid.*

This would be my starting place. A word of courage that I could speak anytime fear tried to shout louder than my logic.

I turned to see Gio wiping his hands on an old towel he'd pulled out from under the seat of the cab. He waved at us and called out, "Andiamo!"

We joined him at the back of the truck. He was pointing at Claire and then at me and went back and forth saying something before pointing at the Vespa that was still on the ground. I concluded that the weight of the scooter would be too much for the patched tire, so one of us needed to ride the Vespa to the villa.

With a burst of newfound confidence, I raised my hand. "Me! I'll do it."

"Do what?" Claire asked.

"The Vespa. I think he needs one of us to drive it to the villa. I want to do it."

Claire's eyes were wide.

"I'm going to try something new." I added my new motto, "Don't be afraid," knowing that I was saying it as much for Claire as for myself.

Gio unlatched the helmet clipped to the handlebars of the Vespa and handed it to me.

I boarded the sleek beauty born of Italian ingenuity and fastened the helmet under my chin. Gio gave me a quick lesson on what to do, all in Italian, and I nodded as if I understood every word, which I didn't. I had never been on a motorcycle or scooter or anything like this before.

Following where he was pointing, I turned the key to start the engine and gave the brake lever on the left handlebar a light squeeze. I pushed another button that Gio pointed to on the right side and balanced myself on the seat. Releasing the bar on the left, I gave the matching lever on the right a squeeze and the scooter lurched forward.

"Grace!" Claire called out.

I quickly grasped the lever on the left side, and to my chagrin, the engine stalled. Gio trotted over, talking, waving his hands, and sounding calmer than I felt. A surge of nervousness marched toward me on familiar paths in my thoughts.

"Don't be afraid," I whispered, and the anxiety army sat down and took a rest back in the shadows.

I went through the steps to start up the little honey again and let her idle contentedly before we took off. The time-to-try-something-new tap dancers were on stage in my thoughts, and they began to do a jig.

Fearless and all smiles, I was already happier than I had been in the truck because I had the whole seat to myself. There might have been enough room to slide slender Claire on the back of the seat, but I was glad my maiden voyage was solo. Nathan would never believe I was doing this. *I* couldn't believe I was doing this!

And, oh, horrors! What would my mother think? I laughed aloud because I didn't care.

Gio and Claire climbed back into the cab of the truck. Claire turned, watching me out the back window, and waved. As soon as Gio was about forty feet down the road, I squeezed the right handle and followed him. Puffs of exhaust wafted into my face every now and then, which was not pleasant, but everything else about the moment was pure delight. I hit a few bumps and had a few wobbles. The first time I needed to turn to the right, I realized I had to keep my lower body stable and make my shoulders and head lean into the direction I wanted to go.

For the next ten minutes I couldn't stop smiling. I pictured all the bugs of Tuscany coming for me and smashing into my teeth the way they crash into a windshield on a summer day. And yet still I couldn't stop smiling. I loved the feel of the wind as it made the sleeves of my blouse flutter.

The farther we went down the road, the more I felt as if I had entered a movie in which rows of vineyards stretched out below great box-shaped, tawny villas with red-tile roofs. They were everywhere. The scenery had to be a dream. It was too pristine to be real. The midday sun seemed to fill the air with golden glitter that dissolved as soon as it touched the deep green rolling earth as far as the eye could see.

The most remarkable part of it all was the noticeable absence of paralyzing fear. I didn't care how silly I looked in the helmet or what might happen if I stalled again or hit a rut and fell off. I felt lusciously alive.

Gio turned down a short road that led to an ornate iron gate guarding the entrance to a villa. Long rows of trees stretched out on both sides. The truck idled roughly, waiting for the slow and gracious motion of the heavy gate as it opened. The movement made me think of two big arms stretching out and welcoming us home.

The silly, slightly wobbly truck puttered into the circular driveway, and the two-story villa came into full view. I drew in a deep breath and sat on the Vespa, letting it idle for a few moments before I followed Gio. I wanted to remember this moment, this view of the open gates, the arched entrance over the front door, and the warm yellow shade of the stone building. A vibrant green vine grew over the entrance, and both windows on the top floor had Juliet balconies from which dainty red flowers cascaded from their planters.

Slowly, I motored inside the gates and stopped behind the truck. As I took off the helmet, Claire stepped over to me with a cute grin and her hands on her hips. "Grace."

I was going to reply with my standard, "Claire." But this time I said nothing. I couldn't stop smiling.

We approached the front door and stopped under the alcove, not sure where Gio had gone and not knowing if we should wait there or go inside. A petite woman opened the front door and pushed up her round glasses. Her curly, peach-colored hair bobbed on the top of her head like a beach ball.

"Oh, hallo! You're here!" Her accent was definitely not Italian. British, maybe. Or Scottish. "Aren't you two the cutest Suitcase Sisters I've ever seen!" she said. "Come in. This way."

"What did she call us?" Claire whispered to me.

"I think she said 'Suitcase Sisters.'"

Claire giggled. "I love that!"

We entered a large, lovely room that had a stone fireplace, two couches, and several armchairs. The walls were a soft sunshine yellow, and a dozen paintings were hung in a harmoniously haphazard manner. A large window provided an inviting view to the back of the villa, where the water in the swimming pool caught the reflection of the sun and seemed to be winking at us.

I will come out there and make your acquaintance soon, I promise.

"Please. Yes. Hallo. Have a seat. Gio will take your luggage to your room. Rest a bit. I'll bring you a little something."

I was surprised at how fast she could speak and how heavy her English accent was.

"You aren't Amelia, are you?" Claire asked.

"Oh! Apologies. No. Should have introduced myself. Rosie. Just in for the mad rush of the busy months ahead. I used to serve at her restaurant and told her that if the day came when she needed to bring on staff at her villa, I would drop everything and come. And here I am! So many new bookings! Very exciting, actually. And you heard, didn't you, that our other guests who were scheduled for this same time had to cancel? Pity for them. Brilliant for you! You have the villa to yourself for three days. Stroke of good fortune, I'd say. Now about your refreshments. Espresso? Wine? Or should I say vino? Everyone here calls it vino. At least from what I've heard. I only arrived ten days ago. Still catching on." She chuckled and paused to take a breath.

"Water would be fine," I said quickly before she could dive in again with more options.

"Right. Okay. Not to worry. Amelia will be here shortly. And if you change your mind about the espresso, I've nearly conquered the machine and can bring you whatever coffee you like. Although not a cappuccino, apparently, because no self-respecting Italian would drink cappuccino after elevenses." Rosie did what looked like half a pirouette and trotted out.

Claire and I leaned to the left so we could watch the bouncing pouf of curls on her head as she turned the corner.

"Not what I expected," Claire said, repressing a smile.

"She's enthusiastic," I added.

"Did you hear what she said about us having this whole place to ourselves?" Claire raised her eyebrows. "And more importantly, did you see the pool?"

"Yes, I did. And I made a solemn promise to visit the pool today."

Claire sat on one of the sofas and spread her arms out. "This is amazing."

I joined her and thought this would be a good time to give her the kudos she'd given me in Venice after we found out how great our room was. "Well done, Claire."

"We seem to have a pattern going," she said. "Did you notice? If the approach and arrival to our accommodations are precarious, the final destination turns out to be lovely."

"We are two for two, aren't we?"

14

L'amore si misura in piatti cucinati.
Love is measured in cooked dishes.

Italian saying

A woman in an apron sailed into the room. Her dark hair was the first feature I noticed. In Amelia's website photo, her hair was long and worn in a thick braid that hung over her shoulder. She now had a short pixie cut with her bangs feathered to the side and cute, narrow bits in front of her ears. Her expressive dark eyes and bright smile echoed her words. "Welcome. Benvenuta!"

We shook hands and exchanged smiles.

"Your home is gorgeous! I'm Claire. This is Grace."

"Rosie is putting together a bite for you. Gio was just updating me on the unconventional pickup and the flat tire. I am so sorry for the inconvenience."

"It was fine," Claire said. "Did he tell you that Grace rode the Vespa the last few miles?"

"We have two available for our guests. Just let us know if you would like to use them. Not this afternoon, though.

We are still planning on your cooking class, even though the other guests won't be joining us."

"I have been looking forward to the class more than you can imagine," Claire said.

Gio entered the room, gave us a big smile, and said something to Amelia in Italian. She replied in Italian, and Gio reached for our suitcases. It was decided that we would follow him to our room and then return for the bite Rosie was preparing.

Gio unlocked the door with a vintage skeleton key and pushed it open so we could enter the small room first. The best feature was the large window and the breathtaking view of the countryside that seemed to roll on endlessly. On a neighboring hill we could view another villa that had only a few cypress trees, but they were as tall as the villa. The warm breeze coming through the open window was delightful. I could easily fall into a pleasant napini right here and right now.

The two beds in the uncluttered room had floral comforters with an extra blanket folded at the foot. On top of the camel-colored blanket was a neatly folded striped bath towel. The rest of the decor consisted of a single watercolor painting of the Tuscan landscape, a square mirror by the door, and a multicolored, hand-braided rug in the center of the room. A small table was placed at an angle in the corner next to the window and was accompanied by one straight-backed chair. Instead of a dresser, two luggage stands were provided.

After the gold trimming and colored-glass chandelier from our room in Venice, this space felt simple. Country. Calm. I liked it.

Gio showed us the bathroom down the hall and demonstrated how the faucets worked. Once again, we were glad we weren't sharing the accommodation with three other guests. He spoke to us with a questioning expression. Claire pulled out her phone and used the translation app to let him know that yes, we liked the room, no, we didn't have any questions, and we would be back downstairs in a few minutes.

Waiting for us in the living room was a tray with a variety of small bites along with two tall glass bottles of water.

"Acqua minerale!" we said in unison, clinking the necks of the familiar bottles. The waiter at the restaurant on Burano had assured us that it was the best, and Amelia must have felt the same way.

Claire had fun evaluating each of the cicchetti before devouring them. She knew more about thinly sliced meats than my brain would ever retain. Her palate seemed to be expanding its ability to recognize new foods because she identified one of the flavors as prosciutto and the other as mortadella. I thought both tasted like ham. But nicer than any ham I had ever eaten.

"I'm still amazed at how filling and satisfying only a few little open-faced sandwiches on a baguette can be," I said.

"Please don't use the words 'sandwiches' or 'baguette' when we start our cooking class," Claire said with a playful stern look. "We must learn what all these wonderful treats are and call them by their proper names."

"Got it," I said. "Are you interested in going exploring? I'm eager to see the pool face-to-face."

We wandered down the main hall and discovered that the kitchen was at the back of the great house. Rosie and Amelia were busily chopping something and talking. They didn't notice us, so we didn't interrupt them and went out the back door that opened onto a large patio area. Four lounge chairs were lined up on the right side, giving the occupants the best view of the neighboring vineyard that rolled down the hill. In the center of the patio the glistening water in the pool called to me.

"How much time do we have before our class?" I asked.

Claire didn't have to check her phone. She knew. "An hour, give or take ten minutes. What do you think? Should we sneak in a quick dip?"

I gave her a mischievous grin and took off at a fast trot, heading for our room.

"I take it that's a yes?" she called out as she tried to keep up.

Our swim was exhilarating. More than exhilarating. It was goose bump–inducing. Neither of us had thought to test the temperature of the water before jumping in. The pool had been in the shade all morning without the afternoon sun to warm it. If it was heated, it wasn't set at the typical temperature of a California pool. For the first few minutes, we didn't care. Paddling around and gazing at the expansive view was enough to keep our minds diverted from the reality that our teeth were chattering.

The lounge chairs awaiting us were in full sun, each of them with a luxuriously thick beach towel folded at the end. We wrapped up like two burritos and stretched out. Drinking in the view and drawing in deep breaths, we waited for our shivers to subside.

"Grace?" Claire said with a sigh.

"I know. We're in Tuscany."

"Yes we are. And by the way, you sure turned into the daring darling of the day with the Vespa. What was that all about? I never would have expected you to volunteer to do that. Way to be brave and try new things."

I smiled at the memory. "You know how you said I needed to figure out how to not be afraid? I think I found a way to do that." I waited for her to ask about my breakthrough. I was eager to tell her the verse about God not giving us a spirit of fear and about my new note to self, "Don't be afraid."

But Claire didn't ask. She was quiet for a few minutes behind her sunglasses before saying, "That's good, Grace. I'm happy for you."

I couldn't tell if she was falling asleep and that was why she didn't want to hear anymore, or if she assumed my breakthrough fell into a spiritual category and didn't want to hear specifics.

Either way, the silence that rested on us felt empty. I was bummed. This was something important and I wanted to share it with her. We had experienced a handful of moments like this in our long friendship when I wanted to exuberantly and openly talk about something God was teaching me. She seemed to sense what I was going to say and always quietly affirmed that she was happy for me but quickly changed the topic.

One time I told her I couldn't wait to share about something I was processing in my spiritual life. She said, "You can tell me if you want, but can I ask a favor? Don't do it if you see me as your prodigal girl project and want me to pick up some kind of message from your experience."

I held back that day. And I held back again today.

"We better get going." Claire popped up, kept the towel around her, and headed up to our room to get ready for our cooking class. I followed, whispering little prayers in her wake, asking that the day would come that Claire would "go in the footsteps of Christ" and we'd both be able to share fully from whatever was on our hearts.

When we were dressed and had our hair pulled back, we reported for duty in the kitchen and donned the aprons Amelia handed us. The refreshing splash in the pool helped keep us cool as we stood at the counter with the warm air coming through the open kitchen windows. The website showed how they had renovated the kitchen by expanding the cozy space while still keeping the original walls. The modern appliances and large island in the center were new. Rosie was conspicuously missing, and I wondered what she was up to.

Amelia started our class by playing a song by her favorite Italian vocalist, Andrea Bocelli. She closed her eyes as he held the long notes at the end. With the cutest smile Amelia said, "I invite you to make space for passion in your life. Be fully alive when you cook and when you love. You were created to experience beauty and love and passion."

For the next few hours, demure Amelia exuded passion as she taught us how to make the same foods her grandmother had taught her to make in this kitchen. Her English was fluent and her accent was distinct. Her inflections carried a touch of British English and a lot of Italian intonations. I loved listening to her.

Claire was elated with all of it.

We started with a Tuscan favorite, pappardelle, a wide, flat noodle made from eggs and finely milled wheat flour that Amelia called semolina. In keeping with her grandmother's recipe, she insisted we add a touch of local extra virgin olive oil. "Only use extra virgin olive oil. Not all olive oil is the same," she said. "You don't need much. Just a bit."

We measured the flour and poured it directly onto the countertop. Then we made a little nest in the center, where the eggs were added. Amelia insisted all we needed was a fork and a bit of wrist action to get the eggs, dash of olive oil, and flour blended perfectly. She skillfully showed us her technique. Hers came together swiftly, looking tidy. I was the slow bunny and managed to make quite a mess.

Claire became an intense student. Her bangs were clipped back, so I could see her concentrated expression clearly. She was loving every snippet of advice and had lots of questions and comments about different types of flour and the color of the yolks in the best organic, free-range eggs. I loved her passion and was learning fascinating details about cooking just watching and listening to the two of them.

I liked the way the dough was rolled out with a long roller into a smooth layer that was then folded and neatly cut. Amelia showed us how to gather a sparse amount of noodles into what looked like a small ball of thick twine. She lined up the pasta clusters on a wooden sideboard for them to dry in the fresh air.

"When we place them in the boiling water later, they will uncurl," Claire explained to me.

Next, we made tagliatelle from the same ingredients but rolled a bit thinner and cut into narrower strips. We laid the strips on several large baking sheets dusted with flour.

"This is another way to let the pasta rest," Amelia said. "This way can sometimes be faster. My nonna always made the clusters with pappardelle, and she always laid out the tagliatelle like this. I have no idea why it makes a difference, but now you know both ways."

I started dreaming of fettuccine Alfredo after we laid out the tagliatelle, and Amelia said we would make a white cream sauce later.

"First, we make pesto," she said.

This process fascinated me. We were given a mortar and pestle that looked like they had first been used during Michelangelo's time. I loved the way the smooth handle of the pestle felt in my hand as we crushed four garlic cloves and a pinch of salt until it looked like paste. Next came the basil, added bit by bit and pounded until the leaves blended into the garlic paste.

The fragrance was divine.

"I only use sweet Genovese basil," Amelia said. "Fresh. Always fresh. Many people don't know this, but you should never cook pesto. It changes the structure and the taste. Make it fresh and enjoy it on almost anything."

"I have a question for the two of you cooks," I said. "How do you manage to wait until the end when you've finished making whatever you're making? My mouth is watering."

Amelia smiled. "The fragrance fuels the passion. For me, it's like a runner focused on the finish line. You must keep going to experience the exhilaration of the victory, when you sit around the table and enjoy the food together."

"I like the process," Claire said. "I love the colors and textures and—"

"The art of the food," I inserted.

"Yes, that's it. The art of the finished dish," Claire said. "But like you, Amelia, I like the feeling when I see others enjoy something I made."

"Then it's gone," Amelia said. "And we need to create something new the next day. Or re-create something we loved and see if we can get it just right once again."

I almost confessed that I had never felt that way about preparing meals. But what a buzzkill it would be if I declared I didn't enjoy the challenge of creating art with vegetables, nor did I ever look forward to preparing even a simple meal.

I did, however, understand the passion Amelia referred to. That fire-in-the-belly feeling came to me in other ways, gardening being one of them. I loved to plant seeds and watch them grow and turn into food. I left it up to Claire and half a dozen other friends and neighbors to figure out what to do when I had an abundance of eggplant or tomatoes. My joy was in tending the seedlings as they reached their full potential.

Amelia checked my mortar and said my basil was well mixed into the garlic. It had taken more than five minutes of dedicated labor, and my hand felt it. Amelia had measured out pine nuts into white ramekins, and bit by bit I added and smashed the pine nuts with a more intentional pounding method than used to decimate the garlic and fresh basil.

"I sometimes add roasted walnuts," Amelia said. "It's too early for fresh walnuts, so we aren't using them today. You'll have to come back in the fall."

"Okay," Claire said without hesitation.

Amelia grinned. "You will love my castagnaccio. My nonna's recipe is the best in the whole region. It's made from chestnut flour and is a favorite dessert around here every fall. The mushrooms are best then too. Please come back. We can go truffle hunting with Tosca and her husband."

I knew Claire wouldn't need to be invited twice. She was faster than I was with the pine nuts and began to add finely grated Parmesan cheese to her pesto in several installments, stirring, pounding, adding more, and repeating the process. She kept at it for the next five minutes. I was weary after two minutes and asked if mine had passed the test yet.

"No tests here," Amelia said. "It's your creation. How do you like your pesto?"

I looked at the lumps and went back to work until I was happy with how it appeared. At last, I added the final ingredient. Yes, extra virgin olive oil.

"This is going to be gone in a flash." I stared at the small harvest of pesto in my mortar. I reached for one of the testing spoons and dipped in for a taste. My eyes opened wide. "Oh, wow. That is delicious. I always liked pesto, but this is really good."

Claire tried hers and agreed. "So good. What are we going to put this on?"

"I have some bread ready for us," Amelia said. "I'll show you the best crostini."

As Amelia and Claire delighted in creating an assortment

of bite-size appetizers that were now becoming familiar, I helped myself to a bottle of acqua minerale and sat for a bit in the corner chair. I enjoyed watching the process more than I liked being one of the creators.

That is, until the crostini assembly was complete and Amelia said we would now make the white sauce for our pasta. I was ready to make the fettuccine magic happen.

We placed local organic butter and heavy cream into our pans on low heat and stirred with a wooden spoon for a few minutes until the combination blended nicely and was barely at a simmer. An assortment of spices was lined up in front of us in small glass bowls.

"Select what you love." Amelia pointed to each bowl. "Salt, pepper, garlic, basil, oregano, rosemary, thyme, and marjoram. And, of course"—she placed the bottle of extra virgin olive oil closer to us—"some cooks, like my nonna, would add a drop of olive oil at this stage."

"Why are we not surprised?" Claire asked with a chuckle.

Aside from salt and a little garlic, I had no idea what other spices would make my Alfredo sauce taste as delicious as I hoped it would. I copied Claire. She fearlessly went for the rosemary first. An interesting choice. Oregano made sense to me, as well as the basil. But I knew nothing about thyme and marjoram. Claire wasn't afraid of them. She also added a good twist of the pepper mill. I stopped after the basil and began to do as Amelia was demonstrating, using a whisk to mix everything together nicely. It turned out that the whisk was also the best way to blend in the Parmesan cheese.

Amelia gave Claire her large block of Parmesan cheese and a grater that was unlike any I had ever seen. Claire efficiently added an unmeasured amount of cheese, whisked away, and smiled at the consistency before Amelia had a chance to praise her.

I was a little less skillful with the cheese grater and asked twice if I should add more. Amelia gave a shrug as if it was up to me. My art. My creation. Rely on my passion.

I added a little more as Amelia continued to explain to Claire how the Parmesan cheese had to be Parmigiano-Reggiano, and according to law in both the EU and US, it could only be produced in certain historical regions of Italy, such as Parma, Reggio, and Bologna.

"It can be expensive," Amelia said, "because it's true Parmesan. Try this sometime on roasted brussels sprouts. You will be amazed."

I secretly hoped brussels sprouts weren't next on the menu.

15

La vita è fatta così.
Life is like that.
Italian saying

Rosie bounded into the kitchen with a crate in her arms. "Mario gave us extra milk and butter because I told him he had friendly eyes, and I think he understood me. Does he understand English?"

"A little," Amelia said.

"He doesn't really have friendly eyes, though, does he? He squints like he doesn't approve of what he sees." She imitated his squint for our benefit.

"I think he has a soft spot for you," Amelia said.

"It's the red hair, isn't it? Enzo started calling me 'fragola.' Isn't that Italian for strawberry?"

"Yes, and the attraction is more than your hair, Rosie. It's you. You're very lovable, you know."

Rosie brushed off Amelia's compliment. "At least we got extra milk and butter as a result of my flattering comment to Mario. And my last gelato was free at Enzo's."

Claire and I exchanged "yes, please" glances at the mention of gelato.

"Tell us more about the gelateria," I said.

"Enzo's gelateria is less than two kilometers," Amelia said. "Our village is tiny and parking is hard to find, but it's worth it."

"The limited parking is why I didn't stop there on my way back," Rosie said. "But I can tell you that Enzo's gelato should not be missed."

Amelia added, "He makes three flavors a week. If we don't like the limited selection, we wait and go the next week."

"Why don't you take the Vespas?" Rosie suggested. "They are easier to park than the delivery van."

"Would that be okay?" I asked Amelia.

"Of course. They are all yours," Amelia said. "We are finished here, if you would like to go now."

"We're finished?" Claire's disappointment was obvious. "Isn't there something else we need to make for dinner?"

I knew she really must want to cook if she so willingly would give up a chance for gelato.

Amelia tilted her head. "What do you two have planned for the morning?"

Claire looked at me. "We have a list of things we would like to see in Florence, but we can do that in the afternoon, if you need help with anything tomorrow morning."

"I host a dinner in Florence every Friday evening. Would you like to help me prepare for the dinner tomorrow morning and then join us around the table tomorrow night?"

"Yes! That would be amazing. Grace?"

"Of course." I thought I should clarify my commitment. "I might skip the cooking part in the morning, though. Unless you really need help."

"That's why she has me," Rosie said cheerfully.

I untied my apron, and since the agenda for tomorrow seemed to be all arranged, I didn't waste another minute before asking, "Where do you keep the Vespas?"

"They will be outside by the front door in ten minutes," Amelia said.

We got ready for our venture into town and found the Vespas right where Amelia said they would be. Claire was surprisingly nervous about turning the key and starting her Vespa after she had her helmet on. "How did you stay balanced?" she asked.

"I don't know. You just lift your feet when you're ready to go. Like with a bicycle." I reviewed the start, stop, fast, and slow directions a second time and thought it was funny that I was the brave one giving instructions.

"Don't be afraid," I told Claire.

"Okay. I got it. I'm ready." She took off with a smooth forward motion that was faster than it needed to be.

"The gate!" I called out. "Stop! Wait till the gate opens."

The entrance gate must have been motion sensitive because the two metal panels were opening their arms as Claire approached. The problem was, they were doing so in slow motion and Claire was still at full speed.

"Claire, stop!" I started my Vespa and hurried toward her.

She must have gripped the lever on the right side instead of engaging the brake on the left because her scooter sped up with a sputter. The gate had only produced a two-foot-wide opening. As I held my breath, Claire squeezed—and I do mean squeezed—through the opening. Her right shoulder tagged the ironwork, and a patch of her T-shirt tore off.

I stopped ten feet away from the gate and watched the swatch of Claire's white T-shirt flutter like a flag of surrender from the old metalwork. She had figured out how to stop and was outside the enclosed villa, sitting precariously and examining her torn shirt.

As soon as the gate was open all the way, I puttered up to the piece of fabric and released it from the clutch of the metal. "I accept your surrender," I said to the gate. "She didn't mean to give you such a fright. Please don't be nervous about opening when we come back."

"Hallo! Are you trying to enter?" Rosie's voice came over the intercom box at the front gate. I could barely hear her, so I pulled closer.

"Rosie, it's Grace. Claire and I are on our way out."

"Right, then. Okay. Ta! Oh, wait. I'm supposed to say ciao now to all our guests. Well, not ciao now, as in ciao now brown cow. Just ciao. So ciao! Oh, and when you return, kindly press the button and one of us will buzz you in."

"I'll do that. Thank you. Ciao, Rosie."

She was still talking as I rode over to my risk-taking companion. Claire was too far from the entrance to hear Rosie's voice over the intercom and asked me, "Who were you talking to?"

I laughed. "I'll tell you that when you tell me where you learned your daredevil skills. Here. The gate was waving this white flag." I handed her the piece of T-shirt.

"I forgot which side was stop and which was go," Claire said. "Don't worry. I've got it figured out now. Ready?"

"I hope so."

She tucked the swatch into her pocket and started her Vespa again. Claire surprised me by motioning that I should go first, as if I were now the designated trailblazer. This was a switch. I wasn't used to having that role, but I kind of liked it. I had a little bit of experience on the Vespa, and Amelia's directions were simple. Turn right out of the villa, go about two kilometers, and we'd be in the village.

The afternoon was warm, which made the breeze feel even better. I loved the gorgeous countryside. Some old trees formed a canopy over us at one patch along the way. The sunlight broke through like golden arrows. I cautiously glanced over my shoulder twice and saw that Claire was having no problem zipping along behind me.

We arrived in the village and slid the Vespas into a narrow space in front of a tiny shop with a weathered sign that said "Enzo." What we noticed first, though, was a vintage cutout of a gelato scoop on top of a pointed cone.

"Buongiorno, principessa!" An older man who we assumed was the famous Enzo was seated on an uncomfortable-looking straight-backed chair by the door of the gelateria. A small dog was curled up at his feet, sleeping. The black-and-white dog looked up when he heard the greeting, then returned his head to the uneven walkway after assessing us and possibly assuming that we hadn't come with treats for him.

"Buongiorno." Claire pointed in the direction we had just come. "We're friends of Gio and Amelia. They said this is the place to come for gelato."

His face lit up. He stood slowly and shuffled into his shop, talking in Italian the whole time. He used his hands excessively, and at one point I was concerned he might topple over due to his limp and how he was using his hands and arms to talk instead of to balance himself.

In the corner was a small chest freezer. He let us peek inside to see the flavors and held up his thumb and first two fingers, indicating the three choices as he said their names.

Claire surprised me by saying, "Tutti, prego."

"Tutti?" Enzo repeated.

"Sì," Claire said, holding up three fingers the same way Enzo had.

I wasn't sure exactly how she knew what to say. Enzo seemed to understand because he leaned toward her with a precarious tilt, and with more words and hand motions he planted a kiss on her cheek.

"What did you tell him?" I whispered.

"I ordered a scoop of all three. Do you want the same?"

"Sure. I don't know if I need the kiss that seems to come with it, though."

Enzo kept talking and went to a cupboard, where he pulled out a canvas bag. He limped back to the freezer, lifted out each of the metal containers of gelato one by one, and placed them one on top of another inside the canvas bag without putting any sort of lid on them.

With a wildly happy grin, he handed the purchase to Claire and waited for payment.

"Oh!" Claire looked at me.

We tried to explain what we really wanted but ended up combining our euros and paying him. I'm not sure we gave him enough, but it was all we'd brought with us. He was elated, so we figured it was all good.

A new challenge was now before us. How were we going to transport our purchase back to the villa? We tried putting the bag in front of me on the narrow seat after I was in place. That was a bad idea. We tried looping the bag over the handles, but it was heavy and the metal containers slipped sideways rather than staying stacked up as a single unit.

We attempted balancing the bag on the floor panel with the intent that one of us would drive with our ankles pressed against the freezing sides to keep it in place. As we tried out that option, I noticed that Enzo and four other people had stopped to watch us try to solve our problem. I'm sure we were entertaining.

Another, older-style Vespa was parked across the narrow

cobblestone road. It had a rack on the back behind the seat. A young man came out of one of the buildings and stopped. His dark hair was slicked back, and he wore a white shirt that had the first five buttons unbuttoned. The sleeves were folded up, and from the perspective of a mother of a preteen, I thought his jeans were too tight.

He seemed to be assessing our situation from across the road before striding over to us. As he talked in Italian, he pointed to the older Vespa and placed his hand on the one I'd ridden into town. He patted the back of the scooter where a rack could go. Then he pointed at the Vespa across the street again.

"Are you saying we can use your rack?" Claire asked. She crossed the street and patted the metal rack and mounting brackets, then pointed to her Vespa and made motions as if she was unfastening the rack and moving it to her scooter.

The man shook his head, talking and waving his hands in a way that made it clear he was saying no, that wasn't his plan. He pressed his palm to his chest, indicating we should entrust our cargo to him. He pantomimed that he would put it on his Vespa and follow us.

I think I was more wary of the plan than Claire. Scanning the expressions of the dozen people now watching us, I tried to gauge if they trusted this guy and thought his suggestion was a good idea. None of the old ladies were giving me a run-for-your-life look.

Claire was already saying "Grazie" to the guy as if it was a done deal. I didn't bring up the possibility that he might rip us off like some sort of notorious Tuscan gelato thief.

Our hero lifted the bag and looked inside. With a wide grin and loud voice, he announced the contents to the audience. A roar of laughter rose. Everyone was looking at Enzo, who was shrugging and grinning. His day had been made.

No one could convince him that we had attempted a different order than the "tutti" we received.

The cargo was quickly secured. Claire stood beside the guy's Vespa, repeating, "Amelia and Gio. That's where we're going. Two kilometers that way."

"Sì, sì, sì," he said. It didn't appear that he had a helmet to wear. Waving to the onlookers, he started up his rickety-looking Vespa and revved the engine as if we were at the starting line of the Grand Prix.

I hopped on my scooter, secured my helmet, and feeling flustered, went through the start-up steps. I hadn't gotten to where I squeezed the right-hand lever yet when he took off, leaving Claire and me in a puff of exhaust.

We exchanged panicked glances. Claire was ready and pulled out in front of me. I brought up the rear and pulled back, going slower on purpose so that I wouldn't gulp so much exhaust. I didn't know how Claire could stand to be so close on his tail.

I admit, I felt relieved when he pulled in at the villa and pushed the intercom button at the closed gate. I pulled up next to Claire and noticed that her helmet was still looped to the handlebar.

The gate opened slowly, and the three of us motored in and parked by the front door.

"Grazie." Claire extended her arm, ready to take the bag and carry it inside.

Our champion wouldn't hear of it. He had brought our gift this far. I presumed his many Italian words were a declaration that he wanted to deliver the goods to Amelia himself.

And he did. He led the way into the kitchen as if he were right at home and gave Amelia a kiss on the cheek. With lots of words, he explained his side of the story. Amelia kept looking over at us. I couldn't imagine what she was thinking.

"I have no idea what he's telling you," Claire said. "But in my defense, the problem was that I told Enzo 'tutti' and—"

"Tutti?" Amelia repeated. "Enzo thought you wanted to buy everything he had."

"Yes," Claire said. "We figured that out. He was so happy, we didn't have the heart to try to go backwards with our negotiation."

"The good news is that dessert is on us," I said with a sheepish grin.

"For a week," Claire added. "At least. Maybe a month."

Amelia had been interpreting what we said, and when she finished, our rescuer laughed warmly. He really was pretty cute the way he communicated with lots of hand motions and expressions.

Amelia pulled a stack of small white bowls off her kitchen shelf and identified the flavors lined up on the counter. "Limone," she said, pointing to the white one.

"I had lemon gelato in Venice and it was yellow," I said.

"No, no. Don't eat yellow gelato. Real limone gelato is white." She pointed to the next one. "Nocciola. Hazelnut. This one is Gio's favorite."

I watched our hero go to the silverware drawer and reach for spoons. His familiarity with Amelia's kitchen surprised me.

"And this one," Amelia said, pointing to the third bin of gelato, "is fragola. Enzo makes it with strawberries from my garden. Rosie just took the first strawberries of the year to him a few days ago. And don't tell her, but I think that's why Enzo kept repeating 'fragola' to her. He was excited about the first batch this year."

"You have a garden?" I couldn't believe I had missed it on our tour.

"Yes. You didn't see it earlier?" Amelia scooped a generous

thank-you-gift serving for our delivery guy. "Who else wants some?"

"I'd love some of the strawberry," Claire said.

"So would I."

Amelia handed us the bowls and scooped a bit of lemon gelato for herself. We stood around the counter, relishing the fresh flavor.

The guy put his empty bowl in the sink, leaned over, and gave Amelia a kiss on both cheeks. He spontaneously stepped over and repeated his farewell brush of a kiss with both Claire and me. With a wave and a "ciao," he was on his way.

Claire and I glanced at each other as if we were freshmen and the captain of the football team had just validated our existence. I knew my face was red.

"Claire," Amelia said, "what happened to your T-shirt?"

I felt a bubble of laughter rising to the surface.

Before Claire could describe the way she had wedged through the front gate, Rosie entered the kitchen with a wide-eyed look. "Did you see that man who just left? Who is he? Where did he come from?"

"Town," Claire said quickly, as if she was eager to change the subject of her torn shirt.

"He followed us home," I added with a grin.

Rosie looked at us and back at Amelia. "Details, please. Who is he?"

"That's Raphael," Amelia said.

"Oh, really?" Claire turned to me and playfully asked, "Does he happen to be a painter?"

"Yes," Amelia said. "How did you know? He did the whole interior of the villa for our renovation."

Claire laughed while I chose to quickly excuse myself and stepped outside. I heard Rosie say, "Why can't he be the local guy giving us free butter and calling me 'fragola'?"

Do few things but do them well, simple joys are holy.

St. Francis of Assisi

I didn't mind if Claire was in the kitchen amusing Rosie and Amelia with the tale of my encounter with the other Raphael. I just didn't want to be the one to tell the story.

Leaning against the low stone wall that enclosed the back side of the villa, I gazed down at the pool. Amelia stepped outside with a tablecloth over her arm and a basketful of votive candles. I didn't ask if she'd heard about the bell tower incident. Knowing Claire, she might have held back, thinking my departure was due to self-consciousness.

A flash of insight came to me: I didn't feel overwhelmed with embarrassment. The level of reluctance I felt over becoming the focus of a humiliating story seemed like a normal amount of hesitation. That was refreshing.

"Did you want to see the garden?" Amelia asked.

"Yes, please. I love gardens."

Her expression lit up. "So that is your passion, is it?"

"Yes. I love to plant seeds and watch them grow."

"Here." Amelia handed the basket and tablecloth to me. "Would you mind leaving these on the table under the trellis? You go down those steps to the left."

"Sure." I took the pathway and the stairs carefully down to the terraced garden. It was lower than the villa and pool, which was why I hadn't discovered it sooner. Unlike Paulina's raised garden beds, Amelia's plants grew out of the rich earth and provided a serendipitous preamble to the vineyard that stretched out beyond the small but efficiently used garden area.

At the top of the terraced garden was a patio covered by a breathtaking pergola. Thick columns held up the four corners, and curling up each column were eager wisteria vines that spread across the top and dripped down between the beams.

"Oh! Hallo! Or, ciao!" Rosie joined me with a stack of colorful blue and yellow plates. "You can leave those on the table. Don't we have the perfect evening for dining alfresco? And isn't this a dreamy spot? This has to be my favorite room in all the villa. If we can call it a room. I think we can. An outdoor dining room, you might say. We rarely have anything like this in England. The weather, you know. But this is the very reason one comes to Tuscany, isn't it?"

Rosie smoothed the cloth over the table and put the plates on both sides while I stood, still mesmerized, under the fragrant canopy of purple blossoms. I drew in their heady scent and gazed at the uneven garden for a few more minutes before going down the next level of stone steps to properly introduce myself to the happy, healthy assortment of growing food.

I decided that when I got home, I was going to revive my garden. It wasn't too late in the year. I could still plant vegetables to harvest in the fall. I'd have to do a lot of work to get the space back in shape, though. When I took on more responsibilities at work, the first thing I'd relinquished was my garden.

Standing in Amelia's garden and thinking back to how I'd felt in Paulina's garden, I realized what a loss I had inflicted on myself when I gave up my time outside with my hands in the earth. It had been a shallow year, and now I knew that was because I hadn't left room in life for my passion. I hadn't pressed any seeds into the earth for the simple joy of watching them grow.

A line from the book about St. Francis came to me: "Simple joys are holy."

That was it. I needed to reclaim and nurture the simple joy of gardening because for me, it was holy. My sweetest times of prayer and meditation always happened in my garden. I missed that time of communion. The challenge was going to be, when would I find time?

I knelt and lifted one of the green leaves in the strawberry patch. Underneath was a ripe, red berry. "Hello, you little beauty."

Right then, a distinct thought rested on me. I was released to leave my job.

It seemed so clear. I could let go of the commitment. The realization went deep, just like the earlier impression that fear doesn't come from God. The two seemed connected.

I remained in my kneeling position and thought about the wide world of options open to me if I wasn't working. Gardening was only one of the benefits. Emma was at the top of my thoughts. I would be free to spend more time with my daughter, which was something I knew had been lacking.

I stood, went over to a bench at the end of the garden, and took in a fresh view of the garden, pergola, and side of the villa. Pulling out my phone, I thought about what I was going to say in my text to Nathan. To my surprise, he had texted me less than an hour earlier, and all he said was to check my email and he'd text me later.

An email from my boss was buried in my inbox. It had been opened, which is what I had asked Nathan to do while I was gone in case anything pressing came through. The short letter had been composed for patients and wasn't specifically for me. The news, however, greatly affected me.

I read the email twice and tried to phone Nathan, even though I knew the rates would be high and he probably wouldn't pick up. My call went to his voicemail, and I kept my message short.

"I saw the email. Wow. So, his last day of practice is June 15. Strange way for him to tell me. But you know what? Fifteen minutes ago I knew that I should leave my job. I just knew. Okay, well, lots to talk about when I get home. I love you so much. Kiss Emma for me and tell her to kiss you for me."

I gazed up at the sky and said, "Thank You." The peace that rested on me in that moment felt like an old friend. An old friend who had not only come back to town but also moved in right next door to me.

I didn't have a chance to tell Claire about my "is that odd or is that God?" news before we gathered around the table under the wisteria at the twilight hour. Gio stood at the head of the table and indicated that the five of us should join hands, which we did. I was closest to Gio. When my hand slipped into his, I felt his calluses and thought of how he'd earned each one of them making the dream of this beautiful place come true as he and Amelia transformed the villa.

Gio then lifted his voice in what had to be a prayer. Even though it was in Italian, the humility and deep gratitude in the tone of his voice came through as he gave thanks to God. Pure gratitude is recognizable in any language.

Gio ended his prayer by singing. The moment felt achingly beautiful. His rich voice rolled over us like the hills that spread out into the fading distance.

Amelia started our meal by having us pass our plates so she could serve generous portions of her nonna's best chicken dish. The recipe incorporated sun-dried tomatoes and spinach along with, I'm sure, a dash of extra virgin olive oil. She pointed out the pesto I'd made, which was in a bowl at the center of a plate of ciabatta. Claire's Alfredo sauce was featured in a large bowl of fresh, hot tagliatelle, and the garden-fresh green beans were sautéed perfectly and sprinkled with breadcrumbs and Parmesan cheese.

We ate slowly under the twinkle lights that lined the pergola and with the glow of the votives that ran the length of the table. No need to rush. Everything tasted delicious, hot or cooled.

Amelia translated Gio's words for Rosie and us. He had lots to say about the food and his love for his wife.

Claire asked questions about the renovations they had made to the villa, and both Amelia and Gio told us stories of crumbling walls, broken water pipes, and people in the community, like Raphael, who helped out.

"I love that we can now share this beautiful place with people from around the world," Amelia said first in English and then in Italian.

Gio pointed at us and said something.

"He loves this too," Amelia translated. "He loves gathering around the table. It's his passion to see people coming together for a feast."

"Our hostess in Venice said that you don't get old at the table," Claire said. "I feel that way tonight."

"It felt that way when Gio and I first met at a dinner." Amelia smiled at her husband.

Gio said something more.

Amelia nodded. "He says we are telling the story of the feast written about in the last chapters of the world's most important book."

I put the clues together and said, "The wedding feast of the Lamb?"

"Yes." Amelia's expression lit up. "Exactly."

"Sì, sì." Gio started talking rapidly.

"My romantic husband sees moments like this, around the table, as an enactment of a holy event that is yet to come. The wedding feast of the Lamb. On that day the Bridegroom will be united with His bride. In a way, we are acting it out every time we gather at the table."

I felt a shiver tickle the back of my neck.

"I think I lost something in the translation," Claire said.

"You know how Jesus refers to Himself as the Bridegroom," Amelia said.

Claire didn't reply.

"Well, at the end of the Bible, in the book of Revelation, is a description of His beautiful bride coming to Him and the great wedding feast."

Claire gave her a wary look. "If you're saying what I think you're saying and the 'bride' is somehow a representation of Christians or anything that has to do with the church, I have a hard time believing 'she' is going to be beautiful by the time she gets to the feast. I mean, she is not exactly attractive from where I'm looking at her. That's just my experience."

Rosie had been surprisingly quiet for most of our dinner. She suddenly had lots to say. "It is a pleasant thought, though, isn't it? Gathering around the table for a feast at the end of all things would be lovely. And to be with humans who actually want to be with each other and be kind would be divine. But I agree with Claire. Religion through the ages has not been attractive. I don't see where a bride is going to come from who could be considered beautiful."

Gio spoke again, and Amelia translated with a smile. "Every bride is beautiful on her day. And you are right. The bride of Christ is not beautiful today. But, you see"—Amelia leaned closer—"today is not her day."

We all paused.

I drew in a deep breath, trying to memorize the scents that surrounded us. I wanted all the fragrances of that evening to attach themselves to my memory of this moment, this conversation.

Amelia's voice echoed in my thoughts. *Today is not her day.*

"Well," Rosie said, stacking the empty plates, "I have a feeling I am more like you, Claire. I don't know if I agree with all the things Gio and Amelia believe about God, but I know that they are the people I want to spend my time with, so perhaps there is something to it."

Amelia reached across the table and gave Rosie's hand a squeeze. "We love you, Rosie."

"Yes, I know you do. You're very good at loving people. It's maddening, really. I keep thinking you'll show your true colors. Yet in the five years I've known you, you have been the same person every single day. And that is a person who cares. A person who is passionate about God. And others." Rosie stood abruptly. "Time to earn my keep."

"No, no. Please leave them," Amelia said. "Stay and talk."

"Thank you, no." Rosie's voice had a catch in it. "I'm going to get this cleared. That's my contribution to the dinner. Would you like me to bring bowls of gelato out here for the rest of you? I'm going to have mine in my room later.

By the way, I'm having one of each flavor, and I think the four of you should do the same." As she headed back to the house she called over her shoulder, "We might just have enough. Barely."

Gio looked confused. He had missed the story of how we ended up with a week's supply of gelato. We told the tale, with Amelia translating. Claire added some flair by acting out how Enzo was so elated he kissed her. And then how people gathered to watch Raphael come to our rescue and deliver the bountiful amount of gelato.

When Gio stopped laughing, he started a string of stories about Enzo while Amelia was kept busy translating. Rosie brought generous portions of all three gelato flavors, and we enjoyed them slowly, evaluating as we dined.

"The lemon is sweeter than what I expected," Claire said. "And yet the bright, citrusy tones are not lost. Very refreshing."

Gio indicated that the hazelnut was the best. His favorite. End of discussion.

"It is velvety, isn't it?" Claire held up her spoon in the candlelight. "Excellent milk-fat ratio."

"No, no, no," I scolded her playfully. "We do not use the word 'f-a-t' or any other related words while on Italian soil, remember?"

"Right. Well then, let me say in conclusion that I'm going to side with Enzo the Magnificent on my vote for the best flavor of the evening. The strawberry is a marvel. My favorite so far of the entire trip."

"That's saying a lot," I said.

"Our splurge quest does not end here," Claire proclaimed. "We have more gelato flavors yet to discover."

I swallowed my last taste of strawberry and had to agree that Enzo's fragola made with Amelia's strawberries was at the top of my list. "What is the growing season for strawberries here?"

"This year the first batch was ready a week ago. That's early for us. We will probably have strawberries through August," Amelia said. "When we moved in, the garden had gone untended for a few years. We had to bring in help to pull all the weeds. They had taken over. It amazes me how abundant the garden is now. Gio poured many hours and much passion into our garden."

He leaned over and placed a kiss on her cheek. She kissed him back on the lips.

When Gio drew back he grinned and said, "Baci alla fragola."

Amelia didn't need to translate. We could guess that he was saying, "Strawberry kisses."

Claire drew in a deep breath. "Is that sweet fragrance coming from the flowers? I thought Rosie had on some lotion or perfume."

"It's the wisteria," Amelia said. "Royal Japanese purple. I helped my nonna plant it when I was young. She always liked it because it's one of the most fragrant wisterias. Isn't it heavenly?"

"It's hypnotic," Claire said. "Everything about your home is stunning."

"Grazie."

Gio stood and cleared dishes.

"Thank you for the gelato," Amelia said. "I might serve it again at breakfast."

"We wouldn't mind," I said.

"Gio and I are going on up to the house, but please stay here as long as you like."

"Sogni d'oro," Gio said.

"Golden dreams," Amelia translated. "Or, as you probably

say, sweet dreams." She gave both of us a hug and followed Gio up the steps. The space felt diminished when they left.

"It's such a beautiful night," Claire said. "If the pool were heated, I would try to talk you into going swimming right now."

"If it were heated, you wouldn't have to talk me into it."

17

Patti chiari, amicizia lunga.
Clear agreements, long friendship.
Italian saying

Claire and I sat in a calm quiet, gazing at the moonlit hillside. Above us, acres of twinkling stars appeared in the deep velvet sky. I didn't want to break the mood, but I also was eager to tell her that I no longer had a job. Before I could break the news, she spoke in a pensive voice.

"Do you really believe?" Claire asked. "In heaven? In a big wedding feast? I mean, truly?"

"Yes, I do."

"How do you know it isn't all just a big story?"

"It is a big story. It's *the story*. God's story."

"It seems to be everywhere here," Claire said. "And told in a variety of art forms."

"I know. I didn't expect that."

Claire stared into the shadowy garden. "I think I should tell you something."

"Okay."

"When we got to Venice and Paulina was saying things like, 'Go in the footsteps of Christ,' I thought you had planned for us to be with her and the other pilgrims that showed up."

"I didn't plan any of that."

"I know. When I booked the reservation for here, I knew that Amelia was religious because on her website she said something about how God opened this door for her to move back and how God brought her and Gio together. I knew she probably would talk about her faith during the cooking class. But she hasn't. And neither did Paulina, very much. She just showed us, the way Amelia is showing us what she's passionate about, which is devotion to God. Somehow, it isn't annoying."

I grinned. "I agree. It's not annoying. For me, the way they live is inspiring." I wanted to say many other things. I didn't. It seemed important that I simply listen.

"You know how Francis pulled away from the opulence of the church in his day and started to do what it said in your book? To just love God and love others?"

I nodded.

"I think Paulina has done that in her own way. And Amelia and Gio have done it in a big way. You've done that too. Like your attitude about your job. I don't understand how someone can feel like they haven't been released from a job. But I've seen you come out on top in the past when you didn't cut corners."

"Well, actually . . ." I told her about the moment of release I had sensed when I was talking to the strawberry, and the email and my voicemail to Nathan. "I felt so close to God when I was in the garden. His timing, you know. It's all falling into place. Not the way I thought it would, but when does anything in our lives ever go the way we think it should?"

"I'm happy for you, Grace. Really happy." Claire leaned forward and pulled one of the candles closer, staring into the amber flame. "Everything you just described is so foreign to me," she said. "I mean, I believe you, but I don't understand it. And the way Gio talked to God tonight with such passion. It should feel fake, but it isn't. I can tell that it's real for him. That was a prayer he offered before dinner, wasn't it? And the song."

"The song was beautiful, wasn't it?"

Claire rose from the table. She slowly moved over to the edge of the landing and reached up to pluck a blossom from one of the hanging wisterias. "There is so much beauty in Italy. Not only the landscape, art, paintings, and the food. It's different from home. I have felt so much love here." She turned to me and seemed to be studying my expression in the soft light. "Do you feel that way too?" she asked. "Like it's easier to think here and evaluate our lives since we're out of our routines?"

I nodded.

"It's as if there is something in the air that makes everything feel so much . . . I don't know the word. Fuller, maybe. Life here feels true at the gut level."

"May I tell you what I really think?" I asked.

"Of course."

"What I've felt, and what I believe you're feeling, is God. It's His love. His Spirit whispering to your bones."

"My bones?"

"Yes. Like you said. True at the gut level. He meets us at the foundational essence of our humanness." I waited to see if she wanted me to go on.

Tilting her head and giving a slight nod, she asked, "Why? Why would He be whispering to any part of me?"

"He's pursuing you. You gave your life to Him long ago.

You told me you meant it. I know something happened that hurt you and pushed you away. But He's still in you and with you and you're still His first love."

She moved a few more steps away from the table and out of the candlelight, so I couldn't see her face. My voice broke as I whispered, "Claire, He wants you back."

She paused with her face toward the garden. I couldn't tell by her posture if she was tensing up or relaxing in response to what I said. I sat alone at the table with the candles flickering and mixing their beeswax fragrance with the heady wisteria. This place had become a cathedral for all my thoughts and senses.

"You've been wanting to say those things to me for a long time, haven't you?" Claire took small steps toward me.

"Yes."

We lingered in a communion of silence that felt like a soothing release for me. Claire's small movements made me think she was restless.

Instead of sitting at the table again, Claire said, "I'm going up. I want to shower tonight because I'll be up early to help Amelia in the kitchen."

"Okay."

She walked away. Surprisingly, the emotion that came over me was anger. I'd thought everything was perfect. This could have been the moment her life turned around. I was mad that she hadn't joined me at the table, bowed her head, and had the come-to-Jesus moment I wanted her to have. I felt it all so deeply. Why hadn't she felt the same nudge?

I stayed behind, calming down, breathing deeply, and asking unspoken questions. I thought of Amelia's response to Rosie when she'd wanted to leave the table. Just love. Lots of love.

My anger melted quickly, and in its place I felt an abiding

love for my friend. She had started our conversation pointing out how she thought I had set up assorted encounters with followers of Christ on our trip. I had nothing to do with them coming into our lives. It wasn't odd. It was God. He was doing something. He was writing Claire's story, and I believed more than ever that He was and would be the Author and Finisher of her faith.

Feeling as if all I could do was turn the page and see what happened next, I blew out the candles and unplugged the string of lights. With only the moon to light my path, I slowly found my way to the back door of the villa and up the stairs to our room.

Claire was already in bed and appeared to be asleep when I entered. If she had taken a shower, it was a quick one. I tried to be quiet, which was difficult in the small space. But the coolness of the room and the fullness I still felt from dinner led to a great night's sleep.

Claire's alarm woke me before the sun had risen. I squinted and pulled up the covers, pretending to be asleep while she dressed and left the room, closing the door quietly behind her. I knew I wouldn't fall back asleep. Not when I could go down to the garden, listen to the birds, and pluck ripe strawberries from the vine at sunrise.

It took me longer to get ready than it had taken Claire. I thought about Amelia's comment that she might offer us gelato for breakfast, and I liked that idea very much.

Instead of gelato, I found a plate of rolls along with butter and jam waiting on the coffee table in the living room. The baked goods were a more rustic option than the scrumptious cornetti we had enjoyed in Venice. I wondered if this was typical for rural Tuscan areas or if it was England's influence on Amelia. I didn't want to eat alone, so I picked up a roll and headed toward the voices of the early-rising cooks.

"Buongiorno," I said as I stepped into the kitchen.

Claire, Amelia, and Rosie all echoed my greeting. Rosie was in the corner chair sipping from a coffee cup and asked if I would like a latte.

The cup and the amount of coffee and hot milk were larger than the cappuccinos we had enjoyed in Venice. The first sip was soothing and creamy, followed by the vibrant kick of the espresso shots.

"I always do three shots," Rosie said. "Hope that's how you like it. I'm headed to the garden to pick what we need for the Bolognese sauce. Would you like to join me?"

I held up my index finger, indicating that I needed a minute before I joined her. I swallowed the bite of roll in my mouth and slid over to Claire. "Everything okay?" I asked quietly.

"Yes, of course. Sorry I conked out last night."

"No problem. Just wanted to make sure . . . you know."

She kept looking at me. Her expression was calm. "Yes. Just lots to think about."

I gave her a nod and an affirming smile. I appreciated that she gave me a touchpoint to understand she was processing our conversation from last night. I hadn't pushed her away, and that was a relief. Downing the last sip of my latte, I headed for the garden.

The sunlight seemed to take the form of glimmering fingers reaching from the sky and gently rousing the world around me. The pool remained in the shadow of the two-story villa. That didn't stop the placid water from inviting me to return. I wasn't sure if or when I'd be able to take another polar bear dip today since we planned to explore Florence that afternoon and had agreed to join Amelia and Gio at their fancy dinner that evening.

Rosie stood with her hands on her hips in the garden, surveying the rows. Her curly hair was pulled back into a fluffy low ponytail. Somewhere between the kitchen and the garden she had acquired a hat. Even with her hair pulled back, the hat seemed to be toppling over, having a hard time staying on her head.

"Where do we begin?" I asked.

"I brought gloves and a few tools, if you would like to use them," she said. "We need carrots and onions, and the strawberries look like they've brightened up in the last three days since I picked some. Which would you like to pick?"

"Strawberries, please."

Rosie handed me a large ceramic bowl with a chip on the rim. As she did, she looked down, and her hat tumbled off her head.

"I give up," she said. "My dear mum sent me to Italy with this hat because she was so concerned my fair skin would blister in the sunshine. The hat simply doesn't fit. Would you like it?"

I tried on the hat, and it fit perfectly. I had no idea how it looked, but I liked having just enough of a brim to shade my eyes. "Thank you. This is a great hat."

"For you, yes. My head is too big, I think. Not too big as in having an inflated ego. That's certainly not my problem. I have other problems, but not that one. The issue is my hair. It's always been my hair. I've never known how to tame it. I do love Amelia's haircut, don't you? She just had it done last week in Florence. I'm thinking of going to the same place and asking them what she asked them."

"What did she ask them?"

"She told them to give her a proper 'Roman Holiday' moment. Only it was in Florence, not Rome, so they put up quite a protest. I wasn't there, but I heard about it. In the end, she got exactly what she wanted. Only they called it a 'Florence Holiday.' I love it, don't you? I need to go there."

I guessed Rosie was referring to the Audrey Hepburn movie *Roman Holiday* and that Amelia had walked into a salon with her hair trailing over her shoulders and walked out with a pixie cut that showed off her eyes and long neck. I took another look at Rosie. I couldn't picture her with a super short haircut.

As I picked strawberries, I considered having my own "Florence Holiday" moment. But my long hair was easy. I could put it up or leave it down. It rarely bothered me and wasn't thick enough to feel hot.

No, I would keep my style for now. And since Rosie insisted, I would keep the hat too.

Rosie delivered the vegetables while I lingered in the garden, letting a few strawberries dissolve in my mouth. I loved drawing in the scent of the fresh earth and the unfamiliar birdsongs. This morning seemed made for prayers and promises. I offered up both before taking the chipped serving bowl to the villa.

An irresistible fragrance wafted from Amelia's kitchen when I entered. Claire had fallen into rhythm with Amelia like an experienced sous chef. She noticed me standing by the kitchen door and smiled at the gorgeous mound of strawberries. "You've been busy," she said.

"So have you. It smells good in here."

"Did you know the center of an onion can cause a bitter taste in Bolognese sauce?" Claire asked me.

"No, I didn't know that."

"Amelia always removes the heart of onions before chopping them up."

"The smaller onions are sweetest," Amelia added. "When you shop, don't reach for the big, fat onion, thinking you'll get more for your money. Buy the smaller ones. Buy for the taste."

"I'll remember that." I took inventory of the number of large pots and pans they were using and had a feeling the dinner in Florence would be a grand affair. I was excited to be part of it and thought it was nice of Amelia to invite us.

"We will let the sauce simmer for exactly three hours and fifteen minutes," Amelia said. "My nonna used to leave hers on the stove for six hours, but she wasn't able to always regulate the heat because her flame would burn out and she would have to relight it. The low heat on this new stove works beautifully. She would have been in ragù heaven if she had this stove."

"Amelia, what would you like me to do with the strawberries?" I asked.

Rosie entered the kitchen with a crate of what looked like folded tablecloths. "These are ready to go. What's next? Oh my, look at how many strawberries you managed to pick! And by the way, that bothersome hat was made for you. It suits you perfectly. I hope you keep it. What do you think, Amelia? Should I zip these strawberries over to Enzo's and zip back to help with the rest of the food after that? I can bring back more gelato, if anyone thinks we're running low. I confess, I did have a generous helping for breakfast." Her robust laughter sounded fluttery that morning. It matched everything else about her.

None of us thought we needed more gelato at the moment, and Amelia had plans for the strawberries in her own kitchen. I slipped upstairs for a quick shower and gathered what I needed for our day of sightseeing. When I returned, Claire and Amelia were discussing our list of places to visit in Florence.

"Start with Piazzale Michelangelo," Amelia said, pointing to the map on Claire's phone. "Then have your driver take you directly to the Uffizi since you have reservations. After that, you can easily walk wherever you want to go. I marked Sophia's on your map if you decide you want a spuntatina."

"Got it." Claire untied her apron and hung it on a hook by the door. "Grace, would you mind setting up our transportation with Amelia? I need to get ready."

Amelia borrowed my phone. "First, I will put the address for our dinner tonight in your calendar. Do you think you can arrive before six o'clock?"

"Sure, no problem." I opened my arms to show the summer dress I was wearing. "Is this okay for tonight?"

Amelia seemed surprised that I asked. She nodded and smiled, which I took to mean that what I had on was nice enough for the dinner. I wondered if it would be similar to last night and if we would sit outside. I had my sweater in my day bag in case I needed it.

Next, she made a call to a local taxi service. "They are reliable," she said. "You Suitcase Sisters don't need any more flat tires or service trucks!"

18

Every now and then a man's mind is stretched by a new idea or sensation, and never shrinks back to its former dimensions.

Oliver Wendell Holmes Sr.

When our driver let us off at Michelangelo Square, I was surprised that the open area wasn't very crowded. It made sense, though, because the best time to visit this hilltop plaza was at sunset. Locals and visitors alike flocked here at twilight to take in the sweeping views and watch the sun slip away behind the city. I'm sure the sunsets were breathtaking. Our morning view was gorgeous too. The rooftops, including the great dome of the Cathedral of Santa Maria del Fiore, were made of red brick. From our elevated distance, the buildings looked like they were all a neutral cream color. The contrast in the morning light evoked the sort of old-world appeal that kept tour and longboat cruise lines in business in Europe.

"If I had brought my journal and we had lots of time," Claire said, "this would be a fun scene to try to sketch. Don't you love how the colors all seem to blend together? It's beautiful."

Behind the old city, the ancient hills were stacked one in front of another with their rounded tops smoothing up against the pale blue sky. In the distance, an uneven row of white clouds lined up and took their time leisurely floating wherever the wind bid them go. The scene was like gazing at an enormous oil painting.

While Claire took pictures she said, "I'm glad we started here. I like Florence better from this view than I did when we exited the train station."

I clicked a few shots and turned to look at the statue of David behind us that was elevated on a concrete pedestal. It was one of several copies of Michelangelo's *David*. The original masterpiece chiseled in marble was on display inside the Accademia Gallery. Previous to that, it had been outside enduring the elements for four hundred years. The replica that loomed above us wasn't carved from marble but was made of bronze and had turned green.

I felt a tinge of regret that we hadn't reserved tickets to tour the Accademia Gallery and see the original David since this one didn't have the wow factor I'd expected. In our research, we'd read reviews about the lines and crowds for the various museums and churches in Florence. Before we left home we decided to make reservations for the Uffizi Gallery, one of the oldest museums in Europe, because it housed room after room of medieval and Renaissance treasures. We hoped to get our fill with only one stop.

Our driver was waiting and took us down the hill and into town to the Uffizi Gallery. It took him less than ten minutes to travel the two miles. At one point we'd thought we would walk the trail that led from the hilltop through a rose garden and into the old city to reach the museum. Amelia's recommendation was wise because we never would have made it in time for our tour.

The line moved quickly, and we were among the first to enter when the museum doors opened. Claire had downloaded an audio tour app on both our phones. We popped in our earpieces and pressed start at the same time so we could be in sync as we sauntered through the enormous building.

The interior walls and ceilings were stunning and offered us a feel for the elegance of historical Florence before we even entered the rooms with the displays. Large windows loomed on either side of the main hallway. One side provided views of the Arno River. I paused to appreciate the domed ceilings that were well lit to show off their gold designs. The interior was not what I expected for a museum that was more than two hundred and fifty years old.

We caught a glimpse of the famous Ponte Vecchio, or Old Bridge, that had crossed the Arno River for hundreds of years. The wide bridge housed rows of shops on the inside, all jewelers. The back side of some of those shops had boxed structures that jutted out over the river. They reminded me of LEGOs because of the straight edges and the way they all looked added on. Most of the additions were painted the same sandstone yellow of the upper covered walkway that ran the length of the bridge.

I noticed the green shutters on either side of many of the uniform windows and zoomed in to take a picture. A few of the units had small terraces on the top floor. I thought I saw a tomato plant growing in a pot on one of the small decks. It fascinated me that world-class jewelers could run a business out of dilapidated-looking buildings. I liked knowing that at least one of them included a tiny garden in the limited space.

We continued room by room through the museum, and I loved everything about our ninety-minute tour. The spaces weren't too crowded with visitors yet. The audio tour was fascinating, and the sculptures were remarkable in their likeness to human figures and movements. I spent a little extra time studying the round painting *Holy Family*, done by Michelangelo in 1505. How could the blues in the painting still be so rich after all these years? The ornate, carved wood frame that circled the image was as much a work of art as the painting.

Claire paused to study the Botticelli painting *The Birth of Venus*. "I've seen this before," she said. "Haven't you? I can't believe I'm looking at the original."

I stood beside Claire, appreciating the feminine interpretation of a pale, unblemished Venus standing at the edge of a large scallop shell. Her long, flowing blond hair curved around her as she looked to the side, her head slightly bent, her expression unruffled and thoughtful.

"Welcome to the world, Venus," I whispered.

"Not exactly what you expected, is it, dear icon of love?" Claire added.

After a while I didn't remember the dates or painters as the works were being described to us on the audio tour. There was so much that happened in this intimate and ancient city. By providing raw materials and gathering artists in guilds, the wealthy patrons gave the gifted men a place to develop their imaginative gifts. Creativity flourished. No wonder Florence was considered the birthplace of the Renaissance. I could see why it was such a romanticized time in history. The artistic beauty overflowed onto the buildings, bridges, and especially in the churches.

We stopped in front of a small painting of St. Francis kneeling. I felt as if I was seeing a picture of a new friend I'd made through social media. Our audio tour guide said Francis was one of the patron saints of Italy and described his upbringing.

Claire motioned for me to pause my recording. "Did you catch that? Francis was from Tuscany. No wonder he's so popular around here."

The next thing the recorded guide said was, "His preaching emphasized the humanity of Christ. At that time, Europe was Christianized and shared a common belief in the Savior's divine nature. Teaching in the church did not encompass Christ's full human nature. Jesus wept. He was tired, hungry, thirsty. In his teaching, St. Francis portrayed a Jesus who was real and approachable. The result was that artists and writers of that day began to portray approachable humanity in their art."

Claire paused her recording again. "The artists he inspired certainly adopted the humanity of anatomy. I have never seen so many . . ."

She didn't finish her sentence because she didn't need to.

We returned to our audio tour and meandered through a few more rooms before exiting the spacious, air-conditioned structure. I felt as if we were going through a wormhole, back into the real world with cars and noise. The weather had warmed, and I was thinking a bench would be a welcome sight right now.

Undaunted and still energetic, Claire led the way on what she assured me was the shortest route on foot through the streets to the Central Market. It felt like we were wandering through the alleys in Venice again except for the many vehicles and wide roads. Shops lined the way, and when we arrived at the impressively large building fifteen minutes later, we found rows of vendor stalls lining the outside of it. The flea market stands appeared to be loaded with every sort of souvenir we could possibly want.

"Food first," I suggested. "Then shopping."

"Agreed," Claire said.

The huge space we entered reminded me of a food court at a mall, only much larger and with items you'd never see in an American mall, such as fishnet bags of big, yellow lemons and strings of dried garlic cloves hanging down like icicles. Fresh produce lined the front of the stalls. Green cucumbers, bright red tomatoes, and shiny purple eggplants. Large slabs of cured pork hung above the counters of stalls that offered scrumptious-looking assortments of meats and cheeses.

The plant and flower booth stood out as friendly as a smile next to a stall with rows of mouthwatering pastries. It was like touring an expedition center, where each vendor did their best to display their goods and make their stall more appealing than the one next to it. I felt caught up in the old-world ambience with every uneven step on the old flooring and every fragrance that wafted our way.

Claire bought spices and sample-size bottles of various olive oils. I slid over to the booth next door to pick up one of the lemon muffins stacked in the case next to the chocolate Nutella muffins. I bought one of each, knowing Claire wouldn't mind if we shared half of both. I paid the older woman with euros and pointed to a sign at the back of the booth that had the words "Buono come il pane."

"Is that the name of your shop?" I guessed that with so many tourists she would understand my English, but she looked confused and looked to where I was pointing.

"Buono come il pane," she said. "Means 'as good as bread.'"

Now I was the one wearing the I-don't-get-it expression. Did it mean her muffins were as good as bread? They looked better than regular bread to me.

"It's what we say of a person with a gold heart," she explained.

"A heart of gold?"

She leaned over the counter, appearing eager for me to understand. "You take bread from the oven. It smell nice. Warm. It's good, sì?"

"Sì," I answered. "Very good."

"This is how we call a person who give to you the feel of warm bread." She pointed her curved finger at me. "You want this friend, sì? You want they are as good as bread."

"Ah, I see." I tried to read the sign with the right pronunciation. "Buono come il pane."

She smiled.

"Grazie."

"Prego." She said something else to me in Italian and turned to help the next customer.

Claire joined me with her purchases, looking content. I opened my paper sack to show her the muffins before breaking one in half and sharing it with her.

"Oh, that's good," she said as we started walking again.

As soon as I swallowed, I tried out my new Italian saying. "And you, my friend, are as good as bread."

"Thanks?" She looked hesitant. "Is that supposed to be a compliment?"

I explained the saying as we headed upstairs to find something more to eat. The area was filled with enough tables and chairs for hundreds of people. It was uncomfortably warm, and the fragrances from the various cooking stations seemed to collide. I didn't like the noise or that the space was so crowded.

"This way," Claire said.

I hoped she had some inside knowledge on where to order a slice of pizza and where to sit. She didn't. Instead, she stopped at the first pizza place we came to and told me she would stand in line while I found a table.

I grabbed a table that had chairs for four. I'd barely sat

down when a middle-aged woman with a backpack plopped next to me and an older man, also wearing a backpack, landed in the chair across from her. His face was red, and the two of them spoke in a sharp tone in a language I didn't recognize. I looked around to see where else we could sit. I saw no other options, so I stayed where I was and put my bag with the remaining muffin in front of Claire's place across from me. Hopefully it would ward off anyone hunting for a place to sit.

The next fifteen minutes had to be the least enjoyable minutes of our trip. Claire arrived with a single slice of pizza for us to share and two cans of lemon soda. We ate quickly, barely paying attention to what was going down our gullets. The couple beside us continued to argue in their mother tongue, getting louder as the noise level around us increased.

The pizza and the remaining muffin were devoured in record time, and the fizzy soda seemed to ride on top of it all in my stomach as we tried to exit. I couldn't tell how any of it tasted.

As soon as we were outside, I pulled Claire away from the main entrance, where people were bumping into each other entering and exiting. I walked far enough away so that we could stand in a fairly uncrowded spot and talk for a minute.

"That was . . ."

"I know," Claire agreed. "Not at all pleasant to be seated with those strangers at that table."

"Do you think we should reevaluate our day-trippin' plans?" I asked. At that moment, all I wanted to do was go back to the villa, take a refreshing swim in the pool, and listen to nature from a leisurely reclined position in the padded lounge chair. But when would we ever be in Florence again? Plus, we had agreed to go to Amelia's dinner that night in Florence.

"I think we should keep going," Claire said. "Stick with the plan for now."

"Okay." I glanced over at the bustling flea market area. "Do you mind if we don't shop there? Unless your heart's desire right now is to purchase a leather jacket to wear the rest of the day."

"No leather jackets for me," Claire said. "How about if we go for a favorite on your list and try to get into one of the largest churches in the world instead?"

"Yes, please."

It took only a few minutes to walk to the Duomo. Anchored at the heart of Florence, the huge church was named for the cathedral's famous dome that was an architectural wonder in the 1400s and still dominated the city today. The Duomo contained several sections, and each required a ticket to enter. However, the main cathedral required no admission fee to walk around, so that was what we planned to do. We were stunned when we found the line for free entry and saw how far it went. We could stand outside for an hour, possibly two, before being admitted.

"It's fine with me if we skip this and venture on to see other parts of Florence," I said.

"Are you sure?" Claire asked.

I nodded. "At one point you wanted to climb to the top of the dome. Do you still want to try to get tickets?"

"No, I'll pass. We saw Florence from the hilltop," Claire said. "I could live without seeing it again from a different direction and being smooshed in a hot and stuffy space. Unless *you* really want to climb to the top?"

I grinned. "The possibility doesn't panic me, but when you said 'smooshed in a hot and stuffy space,' my stomach did a flip."

"Mine too. You know what we need?" Claire checked the map. "Here it is. Perfect. Vivoli's!"

19

Life is either a daring adventure or nothing.

Helen Keller

By any chance, is Vivoli's a gelateria?" I knew the answer already, so I wasn't sure why I asked. I had no objections. "We're coming in low on our splurge-o-meter," I said. "It's past noon and this will be our first gelato of the day."

Claire was already in motion and grinned at me over her shoulder. "Not just any gelateria. This one has been run by the same family for four generations. Amelia said we should go there, but we can't tell Enzo. Vivoli's is her favorite gelateria because they make pear gelato, and Enzo doesn't."

"Pear gelato?" I had fallen in step with Claire and liked the idea of gelato more and more with each step. "My stomach is feeling better already."

We had to take a detour because one of the direct streets was blocked off for some reason. It took us almost half an hour to find the gelateria. I looked at Claire's map with her and realized we were almost back to the Uffizi Gallery near the river. I had heard that Florence was one of the most walkable cities in the world. It seemed we were trying to prove it.

We stepped into the line of customers that trailed out the door of the much-loved gelateria and waited our turn. My selection came in a cup because they didn't sell cones. I went with pear and peach because I could see pieces of peach in the creamy gelato in the case. Peaches were Nathan's favorite fruit. Many times, I had watched him select the best ones from our local Saturday market. Nothing was sweeter than a fresh peach.

Except for fresh peaches in world-class, smooth, rich gelato.

I didn't even know what Claire had along with her pear gelato. My days of gelato envy were over. I was smitten. Peaches and pears at Vivoli's forever.

As we scraped the sides of our cups with our small spoons, Claire looked at me with a pout. "It's over," she said sadly.

"Sorry, Enzo," I said. "Your gelato with Amelia's strawberries is scrumptious. But Vivoli's, you won and will ever remain the standard for the best gelato ever."

"Yes, sorry, but Enzo, really," Claire said as if he were standing there listening to us. "Is it even a fair contest if you aren't willing to at least try creating a version of pear gelato? You could have had a chance. Now we'll never know."

"So? What's next on our self-guided, loop-de-loo walking tour?"

"You know what? I think Sophia's is nearby."

I took our empty cups to a nearby trash can.

Claire followed me with her phone in her hand, studying the map. "It is. Yes, Sophia's is really close." She looked at me with her lips pursed and her eyebrows raised. It took her a moment before she made her declaration. "I'm going to do it."

"Do what?"

"Get a spuntatina."

"Okay." The thought of more food didn't sound appealing since the gourmet gelato flavors were still lingering in my mouth. Why would I dilute such exquisite happiness? But since Claire wanted to get something recommended by Amelia, I knew I should give it a go.

The streets Claire led us down had a variety of signs over their doorways. I saw a bed-and-breakfast place with a planter by the door bursting with amethyst and white phlox. I caught a touch of their scent as we passed, then we continued by a dental office, a leather goods shop, and two small restaurants.

"Here it is." Claire stopped and gave me her apprehensive look again. "What do you think?"

"Sophia's is a hair salon? I thought you were taking us to another place to eat." I studied Claire's expression. "Are you going to do it? Is this your Roman Holiday moment?"

"Florence Holiday," Claire corrected me. She opened the door and stepped inside.

The salon had only two chairs. One was unoccupied. The available stylist greeted us in Italian. Claire stepped closer, saying that we knew Amelia and then held up her phone so the woman could see Amelia's picture.

"Sì, sì, Amelia." More words followed, but we didn't have the translator on our phones ready to give us insights.

"I'd like to get a spuntatina like Amelia's." Claire indicated with her fingers just below her ears. "Short," she said.

The stylist looked her over and said, "Color? More blond?"

Claire nodded.

I took a seat on the narrow bench by the window, sat back, and decided to enjoy every moment of Claire's hair transformation. The stylist chatted with the other stylist and customer in Italian, and I had a pretty good idea they were talking about us.

Claire kept her eyes shut the whole time. As I saw her hair fall to the floor, I thought of the long blond hair that was wrapped around Venus in the Botticelli painting. I wondered what Claire was thinking right now.

I pulled out my journal from my shoulder bag so I could write about our recent escapades. Every now and then I looked up and watched the snipping, the color being applied with a paintbrush, and squares of foil being folded over where the highlights or lowlights were being added.

I finished my journal entry, sent a long message to Nathan and Emma, and checked my email while Claire's hair was being rinsed. She kept her eyes closed during the blow-dry. She continued to keep them closed as the stylist rubbed hair product in her palms and used her adept fingers to gently tug and tuck Claire's short hair until it was just right. Then the stylist turned the chair around to me so I could see the full view from the front.

Claire looked at me with raised eyebrows. "Well?"

I wanted her to see what I saw. "Turn around," I said. "Look in the mirror."

The stylist turned the chair.

Claire stared, expressionless, for a moment. Then she cried.

The stylist seemed alarmed at Claire's tears. She looked to me for interpretation.

I was sure that Claire was crying happy tears, but to verify, I let my honest opinion pour out. "You look adorable! I love it. Don't you? The color is so pretty, and the cut is a great style for you. Claire, look at your eyes!"

She didn't look like the same Claire who had peered at me for years from behind her long bangs. The pixie style put all the emphasis on her clear blue eyes that were now out in the open for the world to see. The lighter blond color was a good choice because it complemented her natural skin tone. The product the stylist used had given her hair a sheen and a smoothness, which was something Claire had often sought with her longer, dandelion hair but had difficulty achieving.

"Please tell me you love it as much as I do," I said.

Claire nodded while dabbing away her tears and clearing her throat. "Bella," she said to the concerned stylist. "Grazie."

The stylist placed her hand on her chest, relieved to hear Claire's verdict.

"You did a beautiful job," I said.

The stylist seemed to understand and nodded. "This is her," she said. She continued in Italian, so I turned on my translation app and nodded as I played the English back for Claire and me. The stylist said it was known that Michelangelo saw figures in slabs of marble, and he said all he had to do was chisel away the pieces that didn't belong. He allowed the statue to be released from the rock. Pointing at Claire, the stylist repeated, "This is her."

"You are a master artist," I said and played it back in Italian for her.

Before we left the salon, Claire paid for her lovely makeover, purchased two bottles of the product the stylist used, and returned the kiss on both cheeks that the stylist gave her. We stepped out into the street, and I felt like I was on an adventure with a different woman. Claire rolled back her shoulders, lifted her chin, and put on her sunglasses as if she was avoiding the paparazzi. I loved the confidence she exuded.

I thought about how I had worn my hair the same way for years and, for a moment, wondered if I should consider going back inside and having my own Florence Holiday moment. The inkling passed as quickly as it came. I already felt that I knew who I was. A new haircut wouldn't change that. For Claire, it seemed to be an essential part of the transformation she had been alluding to since we arrived. Trying her hand at sketching, seeing new things, tasting new foods, and now making a major change to her appearance seemed to be all part of what she needed on a hunt to find her identity.

I hoped she would realize that her true identity came from the Lord and nothing else.

Claire's faithful map app led us to the old bridge we had seen from the window of the Uffizi Gallery. I paused at the wide stone railing along the entrance to Ponte Vecchio and looked out at the Arno River. The pale green water looked calm. Alongside the river on both sides were uniform, boxy buildings with lots of windows looking out on the river. They looked modern to me. Some of them were seven stories high, and many were painted with the warm yellow shade typically associated with Tuscany.

"Tell me everything you know about this bridge," I said to Claire as she took pictures. "I remember reading that the first one washed away in a flood, and this one is something like seven hundred years old."

"I know a covered passageway exists at the top that was built so the wealthy rulers of Florence wouldn't have to traipse across the bridge with the commoners. Originally, the shops were run by merchants who sold leather goods. Messy, but not as stomach turning as the butchers who replaced the tanners and polluted the river with their stinky cow guts."

"No wonder the royalty didn't want to walk across the bridge with everyone else."

"Exactly. The butchers were kicked out by the Medici rulers, and goldsmiths were brought in to set up shop. All the shops are still only jewelers, and they've occupied this space for about five hundred years."

"That still blows my mind," I said. "Looking at paintings, churches, and now a bridge that have endured for half a millennium is hard to fathom."

"I know." Claire turned to saunter across the bridge, adding, "If I find something I can afford in one of the jewelry shops, I'm going to buy it. A necklace, maybe. I rarely wear jewelry, but I would wear something from Florence. Wouldn't you?"

"Absolutely."

Side by side, we wove though the flow of visitors. Most people seemed to take their time, stopping to look in the modern, well-lit display windows of the small, lined-up shops. I felt as if we were walking down a street in an old part of town where ancient and modern had found a way to live harmoniously together. I forgot we were on a bridge until we came to the center section that was open on both sides. We waited for our turn to step over to the waist-high wall and look down on the river. I tried to imagine how many millions of people had stopped in this spot over the centuries.

"This place has a vibe," I said.

"It sure does. Would you mind if we went back to one of the shops before we go the rest of the way?" Claire asked. "I saw some thin gold bands. I want to see how much they cost."

We went inside the small shop and were greeted warmly. The display cases were brimming with fascinating bracelets, necklaces, charms, cameos, and earrings. Claire pointed to a display of thin gold rings in the window, and the attentive salesman presented several to her on a velvet pad. I joined Claire in trying on the dainty rings. I loved how shiny and smooth the gold felt. The prices weren't cheap, but this wasn't a flea market.

"I'm going to buy this one," I announced quietly to Claire. "I think it will always remind me of a little glimmer of all the gold we've seen since we arrived. It feels like a pinch of history that I can take home with me."

Claire tried five more and found one that fit nicely. The one I liked was plain and smooth. Hers had a flat twist that gave it a distinct look on her finger.

"I love this one." She smiled at the shop owner and held it out to him. "It's perfect."

We were still smiling when we exited and continued our stroll to the end of the bridge. I felt young, as if our matching jewelry was a pact that we would be BFFs forever. I wore my dainty gold band on the ring finger of my right hand. Claire wore hers on her index finger, and I noticed it every time she pointed at something she liked in a storefront window as we passed. We took our time and didn't feel rushed or pressed in by crowds as we traversed the old bridge.

"I remember something else about this bridge," Claire said. "It's the only one in Florence that wasn't destroyed during World War II. I saw pictures of the neighborhood after it was bombed, and it was in rubble."

"That's why the buildings look modernish," I said. "I wonder why Ponte Vecchio was spared."

"Apparently a couple of theories exist, but the one I remember is that a homeless man hung out on the bridge and the goldsmiths gave him food. When the Nazis set the charges to blow up the bridge, no one paid attention to the scruffy guy. But he disarmed the charges and saved the bridge."

"I love that."

"I know. Me too."

We had reached the end of the bridge we had started from. I turned to Claire, and for one second I didn't recognize her. I burst out laughing.

"What? Did I miss something?"

"I thought you were somebody else."

"Who?"

"Nobody. I just didn't recognize you for a second. Jared is going to be so surprised when you deplane. Do you want me to take a picture of you now and send it to him? Or do you want to surprise him?"

She thought for a moment. A look of mischief glimmered in her eyes. "I think I'll surprise Jared and Brooke. I heard from them yesterday, and they were going over to your house to have dinner with Nathan and Emma."

"Nathan told me they're having pizza, and when we get home, all of them are counting on us to come up with an amazing full Italian dinner for them. He said it's torture to read my summaries of what we're eating and not be able to taste it too."

"We can let them know that when we are back home, I'm committed to preparing endless Italian dishes, so they better get their appetites ready."

"I don't think that will be a problem." I checked my phone. "Speaking of dinners, I told Amelia we would be there before six o'clock. We should grab a taxi."

"How far away is it?"

I showed her where Amelia had placed a pin on my phone's map. It looked pretty far from where we were. But I wasn't good at judging distances on my phone app the way Claire was.

"I'd rather not walk all the way there. We're not far from the train station," Claire said. "Let's go there. We can see a little more of the city, and we know where to pick up a taxi."

Our route took us past more shops, an art gallery, lots of boutique hotels, and several enticing restaurants. An intriguing church was tucked in between a leather goods shop and a vintage clothing store. We passed a cosmetics store and came out onto a large plaza in front of a grand hotel.

As soon as we were facing the wide intersection and late afternoon traffic, I wanted to go back and wander through the shaded labyrinth and find more narrow streets lined with shops. Our day had gone too quickly. Florence had many small churches we had passed. Michelangelo was buried in one of them, and so was Galileo. I had slipped into an art and history overload at the museum, but if we'd had more time, I would have visited the churches and seen every touch of Renaissance glory that had been added to them hundreds of years ago.

As we stood in line for a taxi, I asked Claire, "What do you think about coming back tomorrow and doing more exploring?"

20

Chi non beve/mangia in compagnia o è un ladro o è una spia.
He who does not drink/eat in company is either a thief or a spy.

Italian saying

Claire looked surprised that I wanted to return to Florence. "What else do you want to see? We experienced a lot today."

"We did. But I know there's more. I'm intrigued by the smaller churches we walked past. And it would be fun to browse a few of the shops we saw."

Claire didn't look convinced that a few churches and shops called for another day of sightseeing. "You know, we will have more shops and churches to visit when we get to Bellagio. I don't know if you heard Amelia say she's making tortelloni tomorrow morning. It's a larger version of tortellini."

"Is she offering another class?"

"No, but she said we could join her. I told her about the cookies from Burano, and she mentioned she has a recipe for them. We could make them tomorrow if we wanted. It's up to you. I can flex."

I didn't want Claire to have to flex on the cooking part of our trip. That was her passion. Maybe Rosie or Gio would have a reason to come back to Florence, and I could catch a ride with them to do a bit more exploring. Or maybe Nathan and I needed to return here and stay for a long visit in one of the cute little B and Bs I had seen.

"Let's stay at the villa tomorrow," I said decisively. "I have a feeling my supply of Burano cookies will disappear as soon as I get home, so I should learn how to make them."

Claire smiled. "Thank you. I feel like I'll never have another chance to spend time with someone like Amelia. I'm so excited to cook with her again."

I knew that staying at the villa tomorrow was the best choice. I also knew that I wouldn't mind spending more time in the garden and by the pool.

The next taxi pulled up in front of us. This time I was the one with the address for our destination. When I showed it to the driver, he did the same thing the taxi driver had done the day before. He turned and looked us over.

I tried Claire's line and said, "We're meeting someone there."

He mumbled and drove to our appointed dinner locale.

Claire leaned over to look at my phone's screen. "Grace, that's the same address. That's where we met Gio yesterday."

"Are you sure?"

She showed me the note on her phone. "Why would they send us there twice? Do you think he's making deliveries again? Of what? Produce?"

"Maybe his mechanic is in that area," I suggested.

"Maybe. But I don't understand why Amelia didn't give you the address to where the dinner is being held." Claire leaned back, resigned. Once again, she looked like a different person with her new short hair.

I put my phone in my lap and looked out the window. "At least it doesn't feel terrifying like it did yesterday. It just seems odd."

This time when the taxi stopped, I paid for our fare and opened the car door without timidity. More scruffy-looking people were hanging out in front of the building. I folded my arm across my travel bag, not caring that I obviously was trying to protect my belongings.

"What time is it?" Claire whispered. "I don't want to pull out my phone here."

"It has to be almost six. Amelia didn't give any specifics on where to meet them."

"Let's look around the corner," Claire suggested. "Gio parked along the side yesterday. Maybe he's there now."

We stayed shoulder to shoulder as we walked away from the front of the building and went around the corner to the narrow alley. Gio's quirky delivery truck was there, parked where it had been yesterday. With a breath of relief, we approached, peering into the cab.

Gio wasn't there.

"Should we get in and wait for him?" I asked.

"I guess so. Is it unlocked?"

I tried the handle and the door opened. The truck was so old and battered, it probably didn't have a working lock. Claire climbed in first and I followed. At least this time we had more room since there wasn't a driver. We closed the door and waited. A few men walked by and glanced at us in the truck. None of them were Gio.

"I'm going to text Amelia." As Claire reached for her phone, I heard someone laughing. It sounded familiar. I looked behind us, in front of us. The laughter was growing louder.

I jumped when I turned and saw Rosie standing next to the passenger side, leaning close to the window and holding a large bouquet of flowers.

"Whatever are the two of you doing?" she called through the rolled-up window. Her exuberant hair was bubbled on top of her head and seemed to be as jovial as Rosie.

I opened the door. "We weren't sure where we were supposed to go, but we recognized the truck."

"This way." She laughed again. "I suppose I had the same reaction when we arrived an hour ago. And your hair is brilliant, Claire. It suits you perfectly. Well done. I am definitely going to get myself to Sophia's one of these days."

She opened a side door to the run-down building, and we followed her inside. In front of us was a large, open area that reminded me of the fellowship hall at the church I'd grown up in. Fifteen rectangular tables filled the space. An older woman in an apron was covering the tables with the linen tablecloths I had seen Rosie carry into the kitchen that morning.

"Wait . . ." Claire looked around. "The dinner is here?"

"Every Friday night. Amelia's been doing this for years. Feeding the least of these. This is where she met Gio."

Rosie walked toward the opening that led into a kitchen. I reached for her arm, trying to make sense of what she had just said. "She met Gio here? They met working together at a soup kitchen?"

With a tilt of her head, Rosie's hair bubble shifted. She smiled softly. "You haven't heard their whole story, have you? Amelia was serving dinner. Gio was here to eat."

Claire and I glanced at each other, dumbfounded.

Rosie lowered her chin and her voice. "The short of it is, Gio had a successful business with a partner who tricked him. Terrible betrayal. The crook took the money and the business. Gio's first wife ended up taking everything else. It's hard to imagine, I know, but for over a year, Gio was homeless. On the streets. He came in here one Friday night. He saw Amelia, she saw him. That was it."

I realized my mouth was open in stunned silence.

Claire leaned closer to Rosie. "Is that true?"

"Every word."

"So, what happened? Did Gio hire a lawyer?" Claire's face turned red over the injustice of Gio's situation. "Did he sue the guy who betrayed him?"

"No. You heard them last night. They are into 'love your neighbor' and 'come to the table.' Gio didn't sue anybody." Rosie adjusted her armful of flowers and moved toward the kitchen.

"What did he do about it?" Claire asked.

"He forgave them."

I couldn't move. My focus rested on the woman preparing the tables. As she lifted the tablecloth and gave it a gentle flap, the linen fabric unfurled and floated above the table like a dove spreading its wings.

"I think I might cry," I said softly before turning to look at Claire.

She stood as still as one of the marble statues we had seen in the museum that morning.

"Grace? Claire?" Amelia called from the kitchen.

We regained our composure and moved to the makeshift kitchen area, where I helped Rosie trim the flowers and put them in glass jars with some water. I placed two bouquets and then set ten places at each table, filling the glasses with water from a beautiful ceramic pitcher that was decorated in the distinctive blue and yellow design of Amelia's dishes at the villa.

Claire put on an apron and went to work next to Amelia.

The fragrances that filled the transformed space became as memory evoking as incense at any altar.

At exactly seven o'clock, Gio opened the doors and warmly, cheerfully welcomed each guest who entered as if they were old friends he held dear. I stood back and watched as a stream of young and old entered and took a place at the tables prepared for them. The ones who seemed to be new were instructed by the others to sit and wait. A few took on the mannerisms of docile children by smoothing down their matted hair or folding their hands and looking down.

Nearly every place was taken when Gio walked into the center of the room and spoke to the hushed guests. Raising both arms, he prayed, or perhaps he was pronouncing a blessing on them and on the meal.

As he had done at our table the night before, Gio concluded by singing a doxology. Half the room joined him and sang along. I had to retreat to the kitchen to find something to wipe away my tears. This was a manner of beauty I had never seen before. Not in my childhood with chef-prepared dinners served on china in my parents' formal dining room. Not during my marriage, where many meals were eaten on the go or in front of the TV.

This was a dinner of passion, intended for communion.

"Here you go." Rosie handed me two plates heaped with steaming pasta covered with Bolognese sauce. I could see bits of carrots that had come from Amelia's garden. "Can you carry a third?"

"I don't think so."

"Never worked as a waitress, then?" Rosie asked. "No matter. Start at the last table by the door. Last shall be first and all that."

My heart pounded as I walked up to the two disheveled women at the last table. They watched my every move. The closer I got, the more I could smell the stench of the street on the guests in the room. I held my breath and placed the gift in front of the women. Amelia was right behind me, balancing four plates with ease. Rosie came along behind her, showing us up by carrying five full plates.

We repeated the trips back and forth to the kitchen, where Claire and Gio were dishing up the plates as quickly as we managed to deliver them. Nearly one hundred and fifty diners were served, and still food was left over in the large serving trays and pots in the kitchen. Amelia handed me an empty plate and indicated that it was my turn to take what I wanted for dinner. Claire followed me and was more generous with her helping than I felt I should be, even though there was plenty.

I looked around for chairs or stools we could pull up to the center counter in the kitchen. There were none.

"This way," Amelia said. Our seats were at the tables, with the guests. Two open seats here, one open place there.

To be honest, this was the most difficult part of the evening for me. I didn't mind being a server. I liked feeling as if I was doing something to help. But I never expected to be treated as an equal of the people in that room. To sit with them and dine with them.

Bits from old Sunday school lessons flitted through my thoughts in fragments.

If you do this to the least of them, you're doing it for Me.

Humble yourself in the sight of the Lord.

In Christ, you are all children of God through faith.

There is neither slave nor free; we are all one in Christ.

I pulled out a chair beside a young woman with large brown eyes. She stared at me and then spoke in Italian.

"Sorry. I only speak English." I didn't have my phone with me to turn on the translator. We had put our purses into one of the empty ice chests in the kitchen that had a lock on it.

"Grazie," the woman said, pointing to her empty plate.

"I didn't have anything to do with the food," I said. "I just helped set the table."

She motioned for me to eat while she kept talking. I think she was telling me how good it was. She was right. The sauce was amazing.

Amelia had taken a seat on the other side of the table, a few places down from where I sat. She picked up on what I had said to the woman and told me, "Grace, you did help with the food. Remember the pasta we made yesterday? We didn't eat it all last night. Some of it went into tonight's dinner."

She then repeated in Italian what she had said to me, and soon she was the interpreter for the table. One man wanted to know where I lived. When I said California, he said he had a brother who had moved to Texas. Another man wanted to know if I had seen the Galleria dell'Accademia because that was where his brother had worked before he passed away. A woman at the end of the table asked how many children I had. I told her, and she said she had two sons who had died, and she had a daughter but didn't know where she was.

What wrecked me was seeing the beauty and the chaos side by side. The beauty in the tablecloths, flowers, gourmet food, and the exquisiteness of the eternal souls hidden inside all of us. The chaos of the many broken lives and painful losses. The interaction was as normal as the dinner conversation under the wisteria and also around the table with Paulina and her other guests our last night in Venice.

I finished my food and leaned back, suddenly immersed in the realization that we were all pilgrims. I saw it now, around this table. All of us were on a journey. Every single life was of immeasurable value. Every soul was loved and sought after by our heavenly Father. Paulina's chef in Burano. Gio and Amelia. The underestimated homeless man who had disarmed the Nazi charges set to blow up Ponte Vecchio. The woman sitting across from me who didn't know where her daughter was. Claire. Rosie. Me.

Even me.

No, the bride was not beautiful. Not yet. But she would be on her day. And today was not her day.

But today felt more like her day than any other day of my life.

21

L'amicizia è come un fiore, ha bisogno di cure e attenzioni per crescere.
Friendship is like a flower; it needs care and attention to grow.

Italian saying

That night I couldn't sleep. I pretended I was for a long while and then finally got up as quietly as I could.

"Grace?"

"Sorry, Claire. I didn't mean to wake you."

"You didn't. I haven't been able to fall asleep. Do you want some gelato?"

I chuckled softly. "You know I'm never going to turn down that offer. Do you think Amelia would mind?"

"No, not at all. Come on. Let's see if any strawberry is left."

We put on our shoes and pulled sweaters over our pj's. Before we tiptoed out of the room like two little girls in a boarding school trying to sneak out, I grabbed the extra blankets at the end of our beds just in case Claire liked the idea formulating in my head. I wanted to cozy up in one of the lounge chairs by the swimming pool and gaze at the reflection of the moon in the still water.

Claire had a different vision, and we went with hers. We carried our bowls of strawberry gelato down the steps to the table under the wisteria. I turned on the café lights that lined the pergola, and with the blankets around our shoulders, we sat side by side, letting each spoonful slowly melt on our tongues.

The night felt alive with the muffled concert of insects in the garden and the chortling chirp and trill of a nearby bird. It sounded like a nightingale. Subtle fragrances of sweet flowers blended with the scent of rich earth recently watered. I felt at home and, at the same time, transported to a haven where I was an outsider, an observer, trying to absorb the elements that were familiar yet outside my scope of experience.

I didn't know if I would be able to say anything. My heart and mind were still trying to meld not only the experience of that evening in Florence but also all the moments in this journey that had led to the dinner being such a defining moment.

Claire finished her gelato and was the first to share her thoughts. "I don't understand."

"Hmm?"

"How could Gio forgive the man who ruined his life? Why? That man should pay for what he did."

"He will," I said.

"How? When?" Claire caught herself. "Oh, you mean at the end of all things, when justice prevails, like you said."

"When did I say that?"

"When we were in St. Mark's Basilica and saw the painting of Christ on a throne. Remember? I said He had a nice journal, and you said that's where He keeps an account. In His book."

I had forgotten about that. It was one of many short conversations, but it had stayed with Claire. Why?

Part of me wanted to answer her and say that yes, the Bible describes the final judgment, when the deeds of all will come to light. But I paused. Of all the things we had seen, heard, and experienced today, Claire was focused on Gio's extraordinary forgiveness. I decided to ask her a question I had tried to ask many times before.

"Claire, I know someone hurt you badly. You've hinted at it many times, but you always pull back before getting it out."

Her lips parted, but no words formed.

"What happened?"

She released a long sigh and pulled the blanket closer around her shoulders. After what felt like a painfully long time, she spoke. "It was the choir director."

Beauty and chaos collided in me for the second time that night. Her willingness to finally confide in me felt beautiful. At the same moment, the thought of a twisted man violating my friend made me sick to my stomach.

"At the school where they treated my dad so horribly."

I waited, and Claire began to slowly, quietly pour out the details. As she did, I kept swallowing and blinking back the tears. I wanted her to stop and no longer dredge up the memory. At the same time, I knew that, like an infected wound, the toxins needed to be released. She needed to let it all drain out.

When the painful account was finished, I put my arm around her and gently rested my head on her shoulder. She was trembling.

"Thank you," I whispered. "Thank you for trusting me with your story. I am so, so sad that happened to you."

She rested her head on mine. We sat in sadness and silence for a pause that was long enough to respect the bravery it took for Claire to confide in me. I affirmed her again.

When we both sat up straight, Claire cried for the first time since we had started talking. She dabbed her eyes with the edge of the blanket. "I told my mother."

"What did she do?" I asked.

"She told me I couldn't say anything because my father might lose his job."

A bolt of lightning shot through me. "Oh, Claire."

Now I was crying. To be assaulted and robbed of innocence was horrible enough. To be denied comfort or protection from her mother was worse. And then to be placed in a position where it was up to her to keep silent so that the whole family could eat and have a roof over their heads was a terrible demand to make of a child. No wonder she struggled with injustice. No wonder she'd had very little contact with her parents after she left home at eighteen. No wonder she didn't want anything to do with the church.

Deep angst welled up in me. My feelings poured out of a reservoir of compassion that had been filling up for my friend ever since I met her. I had seen the shadows, heard hints of the unspoken, and felt the mysterious weight she carried. Now that I knew exactly what it was, it shattered me.

I wept wildly, and Claire didn't know what to do with me.

"Grace?" She waited a moment and repeated, "Grace?"

When I could pull myself together, I wrapped both arms around her. "It hurts me to the core that you went through that and no one was there for you." I let out another burst of tears and tried to stop, but I couldn't.

Claire should not have been the one comforting me, but she was.

We sat under the wisteria for more than an hour. I settled

into a calmness born of emotional exhaustion. The door of Claire's past had been opened all the way, and she seemed to have the freedom to release every grim memory and let it go feral into the night.

She talked about how she had to get on the plane to Rome with the choir director leading their trip and why it hurt so much that the guy she liked wouldn't be there for her or protect her. It made sense why her memories of Rome were so painful.

"I hid from the teacher the whole trip. Nothing happened to me there. After we got home, it came out that he did the same thing to another girl. She told her mom, and her mom blew the whole mess open during the summer. Three other girls came forward. It was awful. The story was reported in the papers, but my name was never connected to any of it. No one but my parents knew, and they wouldn't say anything. I felt like I couldn't say anything either." Claire shifted and adjusted her blanket. "By the end of August, the choir director was fired. My family started the school year as if nothing had happened."

"But Claire, something did happen. Something terrible and wicked and wrong."

"I know."

We sat in silence again. All my tears were spent. She still had a few stragglers.

"Thank you, Grace. Thank you for feeling all of this for me, and with me," Claire said. "I never expected that. I don't know what I expected if I told you. I never wanted to bring it up. I told Jared when we were engaged, and he wanted to track the guy down and make sure he was still in jail."

"Did he go to jail?"

"I don't know. I think so. It was all hush-hush. I wasn't in the group of girls who had gone to court and testified. I never asked, and my parents never said anything. We moved right before the case went to trial. I think my parents figured distance would solve everything. It may have helped my dad in some ways, but it made it worse for me."

"I understand now how you became so strong. And brave. You had to go through all that without any support," I said.

"I tried to move on. I mean, I did. I got married and everything. But how can I forgive? How could Gio forgive the guy who made him homeless? How can he forgive his first wife for abandoning him when he needed her most?" As if she could guess what my answer might be, Claire added, "If Jesus is all about love and justice, He could have stopped what happened to Gio and what happened to me. I was a good little girl. I used to love God and love people. It was simple. Then all that happened. Why didn't God stop it?"

It took me a moment to say the only answer I could give her. "I don't know."

Claire folded her arms on the table and rested her chin on them. "I used to really love God. I told you that. Maybe not as deeply as you do, or Gio, Amelia, or Paulina. But for a young girl, I gave it my all. I trusted Him, and I believed everything the singing vegetables taught me."

I grinned at her "singing vegetables" reference again.

Claire raised her head. "I don't think I can talk about this anymore. My head is pounding, and I feel exhausted all of a sudden. Can we table this?"

"Yes, of course."

As she stood, Claire said, "Thank you, Grace. I mean, really. Thank you for going into the muddy pit of my private horror and allowing yourself to feel it with me, or for me, or whatever it was that came over you. I don't think I've ever cried about it the way you cried for me. Maybe I need to do that."

"Maybe."

"I'm glad I told you," she said. "But in some ways, I wish I hadn't. The whole thing is so repulsive to me."

"It was evil," I said. "All of it was vile. So wrong. It makes me sick too."

"Well, thank you."

I stood and gave her a long hug, wrapping my arms and my blanket around her like two flapping wings of comfort. Silently, we slipped back to our room and found needed comfort in our cozy beds.

The next morning a little after 9:30, I heard a tap on our bedroom door. I rolled over in bed and squinted in the light. "Yes, who is it?"

"It's Rosie. Good morning. Buongiorno! Didn't see you two come down yet. Amelia wondered if you would like to do some cooking. You don't have to, of course. It's only that she said you might want to join her. And don't think I didn't notice the gelato bowls in the sink this morning. A late-night binge, I'm guessing?" She laughed in her robust way.

Claire propped herself up on her elbow. "I'll be down in about twenty minutes."

"I need a little longer than that," I called out. "I hope Amelia isn't waiting for us."

"No. Come down and join in whenever you like. Oh, and did you know the pool man was here yesterday to fix the heater? If you decide to go swimming again, it might be more of a California experience and not the polar-bear plunge it's been since I arrived. I left extra towels on the chairs. Ta for now."

I grinned at Claire. "Well, now you know where I'll be while you're creating torte—whatever it is. But I do want to join in the cookie baking."

She stretched and yawned. "Sounds like a plan."

"How are you feeling?" I asked.

"Like I have a vulnerability hangover."

"Understandable. What you did last night in sharing with me was so, so significant. It was a bold thing to trust me with your story. Thank you."

"No, thank you, for being pretty much the only person in the world I can talk to on such a deep level. Except for Jared. But whenever I tell him about a problem, he wants to fix it right then and there. I love that about him, when the problem is a leaky faucet. But with complex life stuff, it's not a one-and-done kind of fix." She tossed the covers off her and got up. "Mind if I use the bathroom first?"

"All yours." I rose and pulled open the curtains. The sky was periwinkle blue and sprinkled with cotton-ball clouds. If I were a landscape painter, this would be the day to go outside and set up my easel.

Instead, I put on my bathing suit and gathered everything I needed to pursue a different form of art that was beginning to feel as Italian as gelato. I was about to immerse myself in the art of doing nothing, this time by the pool.

22

L'unione fa la forza.
Unity makes strength.
Italian saying

The rest of the morning and into the afternoon, Claire and I were in our happy places, doing exactly what each of us thought was the best way to spend a vacation. She stood in the kitchen for hours next to Amelia, cooking, learning, taste-testing, and talking while I worked in the garden, swam in the gloriously comfortable pool, read, and took a napini.

I was glad I hadn't tried to talk Claire into a second day in Florence. This was exactly what my heart, mind, and soul needed.

Rosie brought me a bowl of the revered tortelloni when the sun was high above. I consumed it with relish. She helped me open one of the umbrellas and let me know that the cookie baking would commence at three o'clock.

At three o'clock exactly, I was showered, dressed, and ready to go. As I entered the kitchen, the lingering fragrances from the previous cooking session rushed to greet me. I put on my apron and said many kind words of praise for the tortelloni.

"I usually only make it in the fall because I can get fresh mushrooms and pumpkins," Amelia said. "Those fillers make the best tortelloni, I think. What we made today was common. Spinach and ricotta."

"With Parmesan cheese," Claire added.

I washed my hands at the kitchen sink. "My taste buds say there was nothing common about your tortelloni. I loved it."

"Wait until you see what we're having for dinner," Rosie chirped. "Gio is going to cook on his outdoor stove. You will love it. I can't wait."

Amelia brought our focus back to everything she had laid out for us on the counter. She was in her teaching mode and reminded me of the English literature teacher I had in high school who introduced me to Jane Austen. She ranked right up there with Amelia in exuding passion for her art.

My teacher used to say that sometimes you have to watch someone do what they love to understand the art form. To demonstrate her theory, she read to us for the last ten minutes of every class and left us hanging when the bell rang. I wasn't the only one who went to the library on a Friday after class so I could check out the book she had been reading and find out over the weekend what happened next.

Thankfully, Amelia wouldn't leave us with bowls of cookie dough. She would see us through to the finished product.

"We are going to make two kinds of cookies. The ones from Burano are called bussola, as you know. My favorite after-dinner cookie is amaretti. We are going to make those too. I have three different recipes for them. They can be hard like cantuccini, or I think you call it biscotti. Those recipes have no butter or oil. For my family, we periodically had cantuccini as an after-dinner biscuit. We always had amaretti morbidi. Morbidi means soft. If you like almond and marzipan, you will love my amaretti morbidi recipe."

"Love it already," Claire said.

Amelia gave us a cute smile. "This is my own recipe. I think it is better than my nonna's recipe because she added extra virgin olive oil."

I grinned. Of course she did.

"My recipe has no oil, and I like how they look when you add what we call zucchero a velo as soon as you remove them from the oven. In England they called it icing sugar. I'm not sure what Americans call it."

"Powdered sugar," Claire said. "Or confectioner's sugar."

"Yes. Okay. Let's begin." Amelia put us to work mixing two different batches of cookies and gave us interesting information on egg yolks. She said the best eggs have the darkest, almost orange yolk. Since the bussola were made from only the yolks and not the egg whites, she made sure the batch I was mixing received the best eggs.

"The yolks will determine the color of the cookies. You want them to be golden yellow. Not pale yellow. It's all in the egg yolk."

The nice balance between the two recipes was that the bussola used only egg yolks and the amaretti used only egg whites. Claire picked up impressive speed as she hand-whipped the egg whites into a froth before adding the almond extract, or as Amelia called it, the almond "essence."

Amelia showed me how she used a small tool to zest the fresh lemon that came from one of their trees. She made a more elegant motion with her hand than I did when I tried to do it. The fragrance was divine, so I didn't mind keeping up with my weak attempts.

"If Gio were here, he would say to add his mother's secret ingredient to this recipe."

"Which is?" Claire asked.

"A spruzzo of rum." Amelia's hand motion indicated just a quick splash of the secret ingredient. "I think she had a different liqueur for everything she made. I prefer when only the lemon takes the credit for the bussola flavor. No rum for us today. But maybe you would like to try it another time."

Claire's dough was already finished and ready to go on the cookie sheet. Amelia recommended that Claire use her hands rather than a small scoop to create the round balls. "How can the biscuits know you love them unless you hold them and shape them before they go into the oven?"

Amelia's poetic words reminded me of her cooking-with-passion intro from our first class. She wiped her hands on her apron and went over to the counter. The kitchen was soon filled with romantic Italian music.

I loved the way I felt right then with these two women, surrounded by delicious fragrances and classical music. After the depth and breadth of emotions I had experienced yesterday, today was restorative.

As dusk spread her calm over the villa that evening, we gathered again at the table under the wisteria. The menu featured Gio's pride and joy, an unbelievable piece of beef. I referred to it as a porterhouse when I saw it on the grill. Gio called it bistecca alla Fiorentina, and Amelia explained that it was famous in this region because the meat came from a Chianina cow, which is a breed found only in Tuscany.

Along with the steak we had a salad made of fresh greens from the garden, small red potatoes, and cannellini beans, another local traditional side. Amelia paired our meal with an incredible local red wine that opened up the flavor of the tender meat even more with each bite. I had never in my life eaten such a delicious piece of meat. Ever.

"I don't want to leave," Claire said after her last bite.

"You can't leave the table because I haven't served our bussola and amaretti yet."

Rosie took Amelia's comment as her cue and popped up to clear dishes, then brought out our baked treats. I liked the lemon flavor in the bussola, but I told Amelia I had to agree with her. The soft amaretti melted in my mouth, and with the honeyed apricot wine, they were my favorite too.

"Both batches turned out scrumptious," I said. "How could they not? They were made with love. So much love and passion."

Amelia glowed at the compliment. I had taken a photo of her well-used recipe card and had a feeling I would always keep the photo on my phone to remind me of our afternoon in Amelia's kitchen.

The five of us lingered in the silky evening for another hour, sipping the amber dessert wine and nibbling on the cookies.

"I don't want to leave," Claire said again.

"As you said," Rosie teased. "But now we've truly run out of courses."

"I meant I don't want to leave this place. I don't want to leave you guys. I learned so much about cooking, and everything we talked about this morning gave me a lot to think about," Claire said, turning her gaze to Gio.

"It's been our pleasure," Amelia said.

"We are so grateful," I added. "I feel like we've been here for a month, not just a few days. Amelia, what you and Gio have created here is a sacred space."

"That's what we hoped it would become," Amelia said.

Since I was seated next to our radiant hostess, I surprised myself by leaning over and giving her an Italian-style brush of a kiss on both cheeks. She smiled warmly.

Claire added, "This place is special and the three of you are very special. Thank you for letting us invade your lives."

"Invade?" Amelia repeated. "No. You were welcomed in, and I hope you know you are always welcome in our home and at our table. I want you to come back and stay longer."

"Be careful!" Rosie teased. "She said those same words to me, and here I am for the summer!"

"And hopefully longer," Amelia added.

Gio reached across the dishes and gave Claire's wrist a squeeze. He looked her in the eye and said something in Italian. Amelia didn't translate. Apparently she didn't need to because Claire seemed to understand and nodded.

I glanced at Rosie. Her expression told me that she knew what this was about.

"I must have missed something significant while I was having my swim and napini," I said.

"Napini!" Rosie echoed. "Perfect. Yes. I love that. I'm going to use that. It's not a real word, is it? It's not really Italian."

Amelia grinned. "It's not Italian for taking a nap, but it is the word for the flowering bud on a kale plant. I have a recipe for sautéed napini. I've never tried it. When you two come back, Claire and I will try my napini recipe."

"And if you want to know where I am," Rosie said, "I'll be with Grace, trying *her* napini recipe by the pool."

Once we were back in our room, I asked Claire what her conversation with Gio had been about while I was at the pool.

"Forgiveness and other assorted mysteries."

I waited for her to say more, but she didn't. Both of us were in somber moods as we packed and made sure we had everything ready for our departure from the villa the next morning. Ours was the sleep of the well-fed and grateful.

The alarm sounded at five thirty, and we went into a

scramble before we whooshed out the door. The whoosh was a good thing, because without it we would have had space for all our big emotions. It would have been easy for us to cancel the rest of our travel plans and stay in the intimate lull of life at the villa. It was better that we didn't have time to think about all we were leaving behind.

Amelia had arranged our ride with the local taxi driver, and he was waiting shortly after dawn. Amelia stood under the beautiful arched entrance, offering quick hugs as our suitcases were loaded into the trunk. Her buoyant "ciao" felt more like a "see you later" than a "goodbye forever" parting.

We didn't speak all the way to the train station.

I thought about how we hadn't factored in much wiggle room in case we encountered a delay on our way to Florence. Once again, in our attempt to save money, we'd prepurchased tickets to Milan that had no flexibility or refund value. If we didn't use them for the exact time we booked, we would have to shift our schedule. That would cause further problems because we had to change trains in Milan to reach Lake Lugano, where we had a reservation for a rental car.

Before my anxious thoughts could reach a pinnacle, the reminder "Don't be afraid" seemed to ruffle the air around me. I looked out the window, and with slow breaths I whispered my melancholy farewell to the achingly beautiful Tuscan scenery tinted with soft greens by the shy morning light.

We arrived in Florence with time to spare. The station was busy but not as crowded as it had been when we arrived. I wondered if traveling on a Sunday morning contributed to the lower flow of travelers. As the train pulled from the station, Claire went on a hunt to find us some coffee to go with the generous supply of amaretti and bussola Amelia had wrapped up for us.

Our departure from Florence seemed slower at first than

the fast train out of Venice. I hoped we would continue at that pace for a little while because the views were so pretty. However, the train picked up speed, and soon we were whizzing along.

"Here you go." Claire returned with two coffees and settled into her aisle seat. "It's not very hot, I'm afraid."

"That's fine. Thanks for getting it. I think it's my turn to treat next time." I wanted to take the lid off my "not very hot" coffee and dunk my cookie, but that was a luxury that would have to wait until we got to our hotel in San Mamete. The train had too much sway to venture a dunk. It didn't matter because the cookies and the coffee were delicious.

"I was wondering what it would have been like to take this route fifty years ago or even a hundred years ago," I said.

"It would have taken a lot longer, that's for sure."

"But at a slower pace, you could take in the scenery. It's so beautiful."

"There is a train that takes five hours to reach Milan," Claire said briskly. "This one takes about two hours because it's direct. I thought we would want to spend more time at Lake Lugano than on a train."

"I'm not complaining. But I am glad we're renting a car in Lake Lugano. We can travel at our own pace."

Claire looked annoyed. "We had to rent a car because the hotel we agreed on is in a small village and the transportation is—"

"Claire, I'm not complaining!" My retort came out more abrupt than I'd intended.

She leaned back and stared at the back of the train seat in front of her. "It's a big unknown."

"I know. I felt the same way with Venice. I'm sure our hotel in San Mamete will be fine. Venice and the villa were better than fine. They were beyond our expectations."

"Doesn't mean we'll be three for three." She took a sip of coffee.

Both of us went into a slightly tense hibernation mode for the rest of the way to Milan. Neither of us had sisters, but when Claire and I fell into these places where we were short-tempered or on the defensive, I thought it was normal for people who spent so much time together. I didn't know if Claire felt the same way, but I decided I'd ask her. That is, after she got over being so grumpy.

We had to change trains at Milano Centrale and did so with minimum conversation. Once we were in our seats and headed to Lake Lugano, we kept to ourselves and fell into our previous pattern on planes and trains during this trip. Claire slept and I read or looked out the window.

At our arrival at the Italian-Swiss border town of Chiasso, I had to wake Claire because a conductor was coming through the cabin to check our passports before we could enter Switzerland. As soon as we were cleared and the train began to move, Claire said, "I'm going to find the restroom."

"Good. I'm going with you." I didn't add that I'd been waiting for the opportunity to get out of my window seat for a while but didn't want to wake her. "I think we only have about a half hour to go," I said as we waited our turn for the restrooms.

Claire nodded. "Sorry I was snappy earlier."

"Me too."

I could tell that the issue was resolved. Not a big deal. I appreciated that about Claire. When she let go of things, she didn't look back. That realization made me wish she could resolve the hurt from her past. I knew she would feel free once she let it go.

When we were back in our seats, Claire showed me the map on her phone. I remembered from our earlier planning conversations that the Swiss and Italian borders both meandered through Lake Lugano. We were in Switzerland now and the train station we would arrive at was in Switzerland, but our hotel was a fifteen-minute drive that would take us back across the border into Italy.

"We're staying here," Claire said, putting a pin in San Mamete. "And Bellagio is over here. We're on Lake Lugano, but Bellagio is on Lake Como."

I brought up something I'd been thinking about that morning. "I know I added a lot of gardens to my list of things to see. But honestly, I would be content if we visited only one. And if you don't want to do a tour, I'm fine going by myself."

"Grace." She gave me a serious look, which came off looking innocent with her new haircut. "You jumped in with both feet on my cooking classes."

"And they were great," I said quickly.

"Exactly. Your gardens tours will be great too. We can visit as many as you want."

I smiled, knowing that we were back to being the best versions of ourselves.

23

Piantare un giardino è credere nel domani.
To plant a garden is to believe in tomorrow.

Italian saying

Before our train pulled into the station at Lake Lugano, we went through the list of garden tours and agreed that Villa Melzi would be our first destination when we toured Bellagio later that afternoon. Claire liked that the villa was only a ten-minute walk from where we disembarked from the ferry. I liked that they raised exotic and rare plants.

"It intrigues me," I said, "that the area we're going to is at the base of the Alps and yet has a Mediterranean climate. They have palm and citrus trees as well as cacti and calla lilies. And hydrangea. It's hard to imagine what kind of climate and soil would allow for that."

Claire grinned. "You really are a flora and fauna nerd, aren't you?"

"That is a label I will proudly wear," I said. "I'm far from an expert on any of it. I just love gardening and want to learn more."

"Same as my love for cooking. I'm looking forward to this."

I sat back and smiled. A friend who knows what makes your heart happy is a true treasure. Claire and I were good at being that kind of friend to each other.

We arrived in the town of Lugano and were back in rhythm. Claire efficiently led the way to the car rental desk and had all the required documents ready. It still took an inexplicably long time for us to be handed the keys to our compact car. When we pulled our suitcases out on the lot and discovered which car was ours, we burst out laughing.

"It's so cute!" Claire patted the roof of our bumblebee-yellow, two-door Fiat.

"There's no trunk, is there?" I observed. "Do you think our luggage will fit in the back seat?"

"Look," Claire said from the back of the car. "It has a luggage rack. We can strap one on here. Or we could look around for another Raphael and see if he can follow us home with our luggage."

"No more Raphaels, please. How about if we try to wedge one of the suitcases in the back, and I'll hold the other one on my lap?"

We squished and adjusted and laughed and shifted some more.

"Ready?" Claire started the car and pushed a few buttons to find the map mode on the tiny screen on the dashboard. She checked the address on her phone and typed it in. As she drove forward, the directions were spoken in Italian.

"How do we switch this to English?" She tapped the screen, and a voice came on speaking French. "No, English," she said.

Two more attempts failed.

"Deutsch," I said, just to see what would happen. The voice spoke to us in German, and we cracked up again.

"Change to English," Claire spouted, emphasizing "English."

The system reverted to Italian.

"Here." She handed me her phone. "Just read the directions to me. Which way do we turn to get onto the road highlighted on the map?"

"Take Riva Giocondo Albertolli to Viale Carlo Cattaneo." My accent was terrible.

"Grace, please. Just tell me either right or left," Claire said. "In English."

We ended up going both right and left and then left and right and around a block before managing to find the correct main road to San Mamete. Claire managed the narrow, twisting road with more expertise than I think I would have. She wedged our little honeybee into the last spot in a lot at the north end of the village, and we walked to the hotel with our luggage.

Our hotel was charming inside and out, and we were right on the lake. Our room was small, but I loved that we had a balcony overlooking Lake Lugano. The two of us stood on the balcony breathing in the sweet, fresh air and drinking in the view.

"So gorgeous," I murmured. "You did it, Claire. You found us another gem. Well done!"

She leaned on the railing and let out a sigh of relief.

We settled in a bit but didn't allow ourselves to completely downshift. Our plan was to tour Bellagio, so we gathered what we needed for the rest of the day and popped into the panetteria across the street. We made the pleasant discovery that the shop was more of a mini market than just a bakery.

"Acqua minerale," Claire sang out as she held up two bottles she'd found.

"Molto bene," I said, remembering our polite support of the waiter who'd introduced us to his favorite and best local water. We gathered an assortment of picnic goodies and nibbled on them during our almost hour-long drive around the northern end of Lake Lugano. We reached Menaggio on the shore of Lake Como in time to catch the next ferry leaving in five minutes.

Clouds had gathered overhead in long, frilly shapes, and the temperature felt cool coming off the water. Claire and I had the same idea. We didn't enter the covered area on the large ferry. Instead, we took the stairs up to the next level and stood on the deck during the twenty-minute ride. The snow-covered mountains in the distance sent a brisk wind over the water.

In front of us, lining the docking area, were four-story buildings painted the color of fresh butter with red-tile roofs. Each building had the uniform rectangular windows we had seen on most structures in Italy. I loved the colors of Bellagio and had fun trying to spot balconies where the residents were growing flowers and even tomatoes in terra-cotta-colored planters.

"Which one of those do you think is the hotel where your parents stayed?" Claire asked.

"I don't know. The nicest one, whichever that is. And Claire, you know how my mom gave us a list of her favorite shops and restaurants? There's only one that I'd like to go to."

"Only one? Are you sure?"

I nodded. "I want this to be our trip, not a replica of hers. She listed a silk shop I'd like to visit. I have the address."

"Sounds good." Claire smiled. "Congratulations, by the way."

"Congratulations for what?"

"For not being afraid of what your mom might think when we recap our trip for her."

"I let go of that fear the minute I hopped on the Vespa and followed you and Gio to the villa."

"That really was a defining moment for you, wasn't it?"

I loved that Claire noticed my newfound confidence, because I felt it.

Our exploration of Bellagio began with Claire striking out in her pathfinder mode. I had become accustomed to following her swinging ponytail through the crowds in Venice. Today her cute new short hair was my guide. I wore the hat Rosie gave me, which Claire said later that day had made it easy for her to spot me when we dipped into a sea of visitors.

Her goal was to find the gardens of the Villa Melzi, and the route was along a wide walkway skirting the lake. We strolled under well-cared-for oleanders pruned to be small trees rather than bushes. They were just beginning to show their magenta flowers. Every few yards along the promenade a bench appeared, facing the lake and inviting strollers to rest and reflect. Planters were abundant along the walk and on the railing that separated the path from the lake.

"Do you know what kind of flowers these are?" Claire stopped by a planter spilling over with a delicate-looking flower that was a pale purple color with a star shape.

"Those are vinca," I said. "They're also called periwinkle. In folklore they were referred to as the flower of death because they're toxic. But years ago, a drug was created from the flower that is used to treat leukemia."

"How do you know that?"

"I was going to plant some vinca when Emma was little, but I asked at the nursery, and the guy who worked there told me to buy impatiens instead. They look similar. He's been my go-to flower guy ever since."

"I never knew you had a flower guy," Claire teased. "What are those?" She pointed to a planter of deep purple flowers.

"Petunias. But you knew that, right?"

"I get petunias and pansies mixed up."

"Well, I get mozzarella mixed up with mortadella, as you observed at the villa."

Claire stopped walking and gave me an incredulous look. "Mozzarella is a cheese. Mortadella is a meat."

I shrugged. "Petunias are annuals and pansies are perennials." With a playful I-know-something-you-don't-know voice, I added, "Except in mild climates. Petunias can be winter hardy in Zones 9 through 11. We live in Zone 9b, which is why orange trees grow so well there."

"I'm kind of afraid of you right now," Claire teased. "You really are a flora and fauna nerd *and* you make a mean pesto. I think I better plant some seeds when we get home just to keep balance in our friendship universe."

"If you're serious about planting seeds, try carrots. They like our climate. Get Nantes. They're sweet and crisp, but they don't last as long as Danvers."

"Keep talking," Claire said. "I'm seriously interested in this because I would love to grow my own carrots for Bolognese sauce, like Amelia does."

We continued our cooking and gardening exchange as we walked through the gardens at Villa Melzi. Much of the path was shaded with a variety of trees that were still dressed up in their shimmering spring-green leaves. Claire loved the Japanese pond with the bright orange koi fish. I was delighted to see so many colorful rhododendron bushes in bloom. Both of us were entranced by the lily pond that faced the lake.

Claire asked lots of questions about the variety of plants and flowers and acted impressed that I knew almost every answer. I thought everyone knew what an aloe plant looked like and that there were more than a dozen kinds of palm trees that grew in different climates.

"Thanks for letting me go on about the flowers. I've been thinking a lot about reviving my garden when I get home. Or, well, after June 15."

"Did your boss ever send you anything that officially notified you that your job is ending?"

"No."

"Doesn't he have to do that, legally?"

"Of course. But guess what? He has no idea how to do that. I'm going to have to write my own notice of termination and calculate my severance package. I'll be busy before June 15. But then the gardening will begin, along with many other simple joys."

"I kind of want to quit now too," Claire said. "Not that we could afford it, but I have so many things I'd like to do. Take a watercolor class and cook delicious new recipes are at the top of the list."

Our hour in the immaculately manicured gardens was like honey to me. I loved walking with Claire and dreaming together aloud. We took pictures of the elegantly crafted footbridge over the reflective waters, and I saw for the first time a tall Australia fern tree. A fun surprise was the California redwood tree that appeared to be thriving. The giant dogwoods took my breath away, and then a short distance down the path were African palm trees.

"That was fun," Claire said as we exited and picked up the pace, heading toward the main part of the old town. We hadn't gone far when she said, "Look, Vespas! Come on."

A gelato cart was parked to the right side of the promenade.

On the left side were two Vespas with a sign on the front saying "20 Euros w/ Gelato."

"We have to do this," Claire said. "We didn't take any good pictures of us posing on the scooters at the villa. Let's do it here."

A man was propping up an umbrella over the cart, and one of the two young women with him saw our interest. She briskly stepped over and made it clear that we needed to buy the gelato first, and photos were twenty euros each. Claire didn't hesitate. She bought gelato cones for both of us without asking what I wanted because the cart had only one flavor. The woman took Claire's phone while her companion reached for both our travel bags and told us to hurry and get on the Vespas. Claire sat on the seat and leaned into the handlebar as if this were a magazine shoot. I wasn't sure how to get on and balance the cone at the same time, so I leaned against the yellow moped, feeling a sense of intimidation returning.

Claire seemed to catch my hesitation. "Pretend you're posing for Raphael."

I broke into a loud laugh, and the woman took the shot with Claire's phone.

"Off," the woman said.

"Wait!" Claire said. "I wasn't looking at the camera."

"Twenty euros." The woman held out her hand. "Each."

"I already paid," Claire said.

"Another photo? Twenty euros. Each."

"No," Claire said, grabbing her phone. "No!"

Another couple was already waiting their turn, and a line had formed at the gelato cart. I was more concerned about collecting our travel bags and sweaters than I was about paying for another quick photo. I made sure we retrieved all our belongings while Claire held my cone and tried to keep it from dripping.

"What flavor is this?" I asked as we walked away from the crowd that was forming.

"I don't know. Pomegranate, maybe?"

"Not at the top of the list for me." I took a few steps over to a trash can and covertly tossed my cone. Claire saw what I did and tossed hers as well.

"Just to make sure," I said, "I want to check my bag."

We went over to one of the benches facing the lake and sat close, opening our travel bags and taking inventory. All our documents and wallets were still there, which was a relief.

"That could've been a disaster," Claire said. "They lured me with gelato and a Vespa. What an American I am."

"Let's see the picture."

She turned her phone, and we leaned close to see the single shot.

"It's cute," I said. "Even if you're not facing the camera, it's still a fun picture. I was worried for a moment that she may have taken a picture of only our feet."

"They definitely knew where the best location was to get the lake and Bellagio in the background. But their gelato could use some improvement."

"Listen to us!" I said. "We've officially become gelato snobs." I looked back at the crowd that had formed around the gelato cart. "I sure hope their setup is legit and we didn't just break some Italian law about paying unlicensed street vendors."

"Let's go," Claire said.

We didn't stop our brisk pace until we came to Salita Serbelloni, which was more like an alleyway than a street, with hundreds of low steps made of pebbles. It had to be centuries old by the way the path had been worn smooth.

We kept climbing. I wished we had thought of bringing an extra bottle of acqua minerale with us.

Claire turned around at the top, smiling as if we had conquered the Matterhorn. "Totally worth the climb," she said. "This is just like the picture in my coworker's office with the sliver of the lake and the mountains in the background. And look at the street lantern on the fancy hook. Isn't it adorable? Could you take my picture?"

"For you . . ." I paused as if contemplating her request. "For you, ten euros."

"What a deal."

I took a dozen shots, at no extra charge, from different angles. I captured the highlights Claire wanted as well as a rich green vine dangling from a balcony on the right side of the shot.

With her goal completed, Claire and I began our descent and found the silk shop. The pieces were lovely, and it was easy to make a choice for my mom. She adored red accessories at Christmastime, and the shop carried her shade of "blue red" in a silk scarf.

"Is that what you're going to buy for your mom?" Claire asked.

"Yes. Are you going to buy anything?"

"No, but could I split the cost with you on the scarf? Would you mind if it was a gift from both of us? She supported us so generously. I wanted to find a way to thank her."

"You don't have to do that."

"I know. But I want to."

"My mom would love knowing this scarf was from both of us."

A saleswoman stepped over with a gentle smile. She spoke to us in English, and I realized she had understood our conversation. The woman held up a pretty pale blue scarf to

Claire and said, "Perhaps your mother needs a small gift as well."

My throat tightened. I wanted to intervene, but words didn't surface quickly enough.

In a quiet voice Claire said, "My mother doesn't wear silk scarves."

24

> The question is not what you look at, but what you see.
>
> Henry David Thoreau

I leaned closer to Claire as the saleswoman wrapped the silk scarf for my mom. "Are you okay?"

She nodded, almost convincing me that the woman's comment about her mother had not pierced her like an arrow. Our midnight talk at the villa still felt fresh and raw to me. I knew it had to be at the surface for my friend too. Claire appeared composed and calm. I wondered if she was shutting down as a familiar tactic when this part of her life simply hurt too much.

Once we were outside the shop, Claire asked, "Anything else you want to see here?"

"I think we should catch the ferry back to our car," I suggested. All afternoon I had been watching the sky, captivated by the soft blue color and the wispy clouds. Claire had said earlier that her weather app predicted rain, but so far it hadn't come our way.

I loved the ferry ride. It reminded me again of childhood

summers on my grandfather's boat. Our family had a cabin at Lake Arrowhead in the Southern California mountains, and I'd spent many happy hours there and on the lake. I looked at some of the private boats scooting around on Lake Lugano and wondered how many of them held little girls who were like me and were being spoiled by their grandparents.

When we docked, instead of going to our car, we decided to do a little meandering through the town. Menaggio looked as old and charming as Bellagio and also had a tree-lined promenade along the shore. We gravitated toward the walkway rather than the shops and stopped to look at the long row of docked sailboats.

Claire took a selfie with the boats as her background. "Can you imagine spending your summer here? Staying in a villa on the hill and coming down to take your sailboat out on a perfect morning?"

What she described was not much different from the summers I'd experienced with my family at Lake Arrowhead. I realized again how different my childhood was from hers and how different our mothers were.

We strolled into a large plaza where a small band was setting up. The air had cooled, and the sunlight on the water was making long, wavy, pale yellow streaks like submerged veins of gold. In the corner of the square was an outdoor restaurant with large blue-and-white-striped umbrellas over the tables. The café was the ideal place for us to sit and finally have a real meal after a day of snacks on the go.

"At last," I said, pointing to the word "lasagna" listed on the menu. "My taste buds have been waiting patiently for authentic Italian lasagna since Venice."

"I'm going for the fettuccini," Claire said. "That's my secret comfort food at home."

Both of us were more than pleased with our choices. My authentic lasagna was worth the wait. The layers of pasta were thin, and I thought the meat and sauce were seasoned in a way that rivaled Amelia's Bolognese sauce. Claire tried a bite and declared that Amelia's was better.

While we ate, the band played. Surprisingly, their music choice was pop songs from twenty years ago. We exchanged humored looks and mouthed the words to one of the tunes that had been popular during our college years.

A small group formed in the open area as the music continued. The audience was made up of grandmas with toddlers on little tricycles and young couples standing with their arms around each other, swaying to the music. The grandmas looked like they had lots of gossip to catch up on while the toddlers rode circles around them on their trikes.

Three teen girls who I presumed were locals stood close to the band and giggled a lot. One of them tried a few dance moves, and her friends broke into laughter and mimicked her, initiating even more laughter. I took a couple pictures, thinking about how Emma could be one of those girls if we lived here. She and her friends loved to dance, and they especially loved to laugh.

A secret dream waltzed into my heart right then. I hadn't thought much about the possibility before, but I wondered if one day Emma and I might go somewhere thrilling together. Just the two of us. I think I'd never given space to the thought because I didn't want to subject her to the expectations and stretches of boredom I'd had when traveling with my mom.

"This trip has been so good for so many reasons," I told Claire.

She nodded and playfully slurped up the final fettuccini noodles.

I leaned back and folded my hands over my lasagna-filled

belly. The idea of going on a trip with Emma filled me in another way. It gave me hope for the future and something exciting to look forward to. No fear was attached to the possibility. It had been a long time since I'd felt that. The key, it seemed, was to be patient and wait until the prospect of traveling together was Emma's idea as much as it was mine.

I could wait. I had a sweet sense that when the time was right, the Lord would make it happen.

As we settled into our after-dinner contentment, more people of all ages gathered, filling the plaza with smiles, conversations, and children. We had seen people strolling along the walkway for the traditional evening passeggiata. Here, more than in Venice, the long-standing Italian tradition of talking a leisurely walk in the cool of the evening was still alive. The central piazza seemed to be their final destination.

A young girl arrived with her father and blew soap bubbles into the air. The dad looked pleased, as if he had treated her to a bottle of bubbles and his simple gift was a hit. I grinned at the little ones who raced over and jumped up to try to pop the bubbles before they floated away.

"Can you believe this?" Claire asked. "I didn't think places like this existed in real life."

I had turned my gaze to the view of the lake, where the water had turned a deep gray. The clouds that had bunched up over the Alps were heading toward us like a lumpy carpet being unfurled. "We might get that rain you predicted," I said.

"We should probably drive back to our hotel," Claire said. "I hate to leave here. I know I keep saying that about every place we've been to, but it's true. Our trip is going too quickly. I feel like we could have spent more time at almost every place we visited."

I felt the same melancholy. It was going to be hard to leave.

"Italy feels like a mama to me," I told Claire. "She's like a smiling, warm Mama Mia wearing an apron and opening her arms to welcome in any who would come and eat and share their passion in equal measure to the passion she pours out."

"Be sure to write that in your journal," Claire said. "Because I want to remember what you just said. I feel the same way."

Twenty minutes later, as Claire leaned over the steering wheel trying to see the road with the wipers set on high speed, she said, "This is a true downpour."

"Should we pull over and see if it passes?" I asked.

"No. I think we're okay if I keep going slow. The roads aren't too crowded. Am I making you nervous?"

"Yes." I laughed. "What about you? How are you doing?"

A car suddenly passed us, causing Claire to hit the brakes. We swerved to the right before she managed to steer us straight again. A second car passed us, and this time Claire remained focused and steady.

"If you feel like praying the way you do," Claire said, "this would be the time to do it."

We had two more slosh-and-slip moments on the wet road. I prayed all the way back to our parking space in San Mamete. To our surprise the rain had stopped.

"This is crazy," Claire said. "I expected it to still be pouring here too."

Night encircled the small village, and the scent of jasmine lingered in the air. We locked the car, headed toward our hotel, and saw that an old-fashioned fire truck was blocking the narrow road. We had to walk past the hubbub to reach our hotel.

"I hope no one had an accident," Claire said.

At least two dozen residents of San Mamete were standing in the street looking up. When we came around the corner we saw what they were staring at. A young man who couldn't have been more than twenty years old was balanced on a ladder that extended from the fire truck. The rusty ladder leaned against the cracked wall of an old building. The daredevil was not dressed for a fire. He was wearing jeans and a polo shirt. It appeared that his objective was to attach the end of a banner to a hook on the side of the building.

Claire and I slid into the bunch of observers and watched along with them. Another man, also young and in casual clothes, seemed to be controlling the ladder from his equally precarious position on the vintage fire truck. The ladder, still supporting the polo-shirt guy, slowly swung to the other side of the street. An older man in a bright orange safety vest held a light that was strong enough to illuminate the whole operation.

As the ladder moved, people around us provided commentary. Loudly. They all acted as if it was up to them to direct the man in the fire truck as well as the man clinging to the ladder. I imagined their Italian phrases were along the lines of, "Go slow! Be careful! Don't drop the banner!"

However, as the audience grew, the volume rose and wild hand motions began. It sounded like the people were saying, "Hold on for dear life! He's trying to kill you! Where did you learn to operate that thing? You're doing it all wrong!"

I wanted to laugh at the exuberance of it all. It was after ten o'clock, and it appeared that this was the most exciting thing the locals had seen in a long time. When the man on the ladder reached his intended destination of the building on the other side of the road, the comments quieted. Everyone watched to see him complete his mission.

But instead of attaching the end of the banner to the waiting hook, he motioned for his accomplice to extend the ladder farther down the building. The bright light was adjusted, and his new target was revealed. Two young women in scoop-neck tops were leaning out of their second-story window, waving and smiling at the hero.

The cheers and jeers of the townsfolk changed in tone and volume. It reminded me of a reenactment of a medieval passion play I had gone to with my parents on one of our trips to Europe. The actors in Germany were trained to evoke emotions in the audience.

These Italian guys were upstaging those professional actors without knowing it. Our growing audience reacted as one. Would the brave knight reach the damsels? Would he be rewarded for his grand gesture? The word "baci" rose from the crowd, and I recognized the Italian word for "kiss." Shamelessly, I joined in the chant.

Without warning, the ladder wobbled dangerously. Claire grabbed my arm, and we gasped along with the rest of the party. The women changed their signals from "come hither" to shouts and motions that clearly meant "Save yourself!"

Two more significant shimmies of the ladder had us gasping again before the rickety device was maneuvered back to stability and the brave knight was realigned with the hook. He made quick work of attaching the banner. The crowd erupted in wild applause and cheers as if he had just won an Olympic event.

If anyone within five blocks had been trying to sleep, it would have been pointless. Although it was hard to believe anyone in town was still in their homes. The crowd had grown and now included old women wearing nightgowns with shawls and a few little ones in pajamas riding on their fathers' shoulders and rubbing their eyes.

We clapped along with the other fans and let our laughter mix with their cheers. The ladder slowly retracted, and the Cirque du Soleil performance came to an end. The women in the window blew kisses to everyone below. A man next to Claire gave her a friendly nudge with his elbow and started talking in Italian. His expression made it seem like he was raving about the great performance. Claire went with the flow and kept saying, "Sì, sì."

As soon as the hook-and-ladder man was back on Mother Earth, he gave his adoring fans all the gestures and bows of a conquering hero while the applause continued. We hung around with the others until the fire truck was on its way down the road. Our hero leaned out the passenger-side window, waving vigorously as if this was his final curtain call.

The crowd dispersed, still discussing, still elbowing each other. A few raindrops splattered on us as we set off on our walk to the hotel. Neither of us could stop smiling and unleashing spontaneous, sporadic giggles, just like the teen girls in the piazza.

"What was the banner for?" Claire asked.

"It looked like an announcement for a concert because it had dates and musical notes in the corner."

"I think you're right. That was hilarious. I will never forget that." As she unlocked the door to our room, Claire added, "I will never forget any of this. I'm so glad we came."

"Me too."

Once we were in our warm beds, I said, "I don't want to think about this, but tomorrow is our last full day. How do you want to spend it?"

"You know how you managed to take some downtime at the pool at the villa? I want to do that here tomorrow. I know there's lots we could see, but it's like I said earlier today. I want to sit and take some time to absorb all this and enjoy it without needing to dash off."

"Good. I was hoping you felt that way."

"I want to try some sketching." Claire turned off the light. "And I have some thinking to do."

"Anything you want to talk about?" I asked.

"Tomorrow. Let's save it all for tomorrow. I want to fall asleep with the image of the fire truck escapade playing over and over in my dreams. That had to be one of the funniest and cutest things I've ever seen. I wish I had thought to pull out my camera and record it all."

I smiled, closed my eyes, and let the entertaining memory roll me into a dream in which everyone was speaking in Italian.

I woke to the sound of heavy footsteps in the hallway and people speaking in what sounded like a Slavic language. Claire heard it too and turned over with a groan. "What time is it?"

"Almost ten. I can't believe we slept so long! We needed that." I stood and pulled back the curtains. Our balcony glistened with raindrops clinging to the metal railing. The sun seemed determined to take center stage while the clouds kept trying to steal the show. "Looks like we had more rain last night. I hope it didn't soak the banner."

"The banner." Claire sat up and grinned. "I want to be here when the boys come back in the fire truck to take it down."

I chuckled and opened the glass doors to the balcony. I couldn't tell if the sun would grace us fully or if it would be a game of hide-and-seek with her all day. The delight of the fresh air and the sound of the birds rushed to greet me. I saw one of the birds in a treetop. He was shaking his wings and hopping from branch to branch as if trying to find a dry spot.

Our leisurely day began with us taking our time to get ready and enjoying the balcony. By the time we ventured from our room, the outdoor restaurant was open, and we were among the first to be taken to the dried-off chairs under a covering of mature, healthy vines. I noted that the nearly tree-size vines sprouted from half a dozen spots and intertwined themselves above us. The pink flowers that curled up and throughout the long trellis were a variety of climbing roses that clearly adored this climate.

I loved that the air was so fresh. The only things that separated us from the view of the rocky edge of the shore below were wooden planters hung on the metal railing that ran the length of the restaurant. I felt as if I were sitting in a flower bed, and my heart was so happy I could hardly stand it.

"I need a pergola," I declared before we even looked at the menus. "You can help us figure out all the regulations and permits, right?"

"It's what I do every day," Claire said. "That is, every day in my other life back in California. Today, in my life in Northern Italy, I am about to eat something delicious."

"I want to have a cement slab poured in our backyard," I continued. "Then have a pergola built over it. I think it will be more permanent that way. I'll string some lights and plant the right climbing rose that grows well in our zone. Or wisteria. Oh, wouldn't I love my own pergola with dripping wisteria!"

Claire nodded her agreement while she studied the lunch menu. "This is going to cost more than I expected, but I can tell you right now, it is going to be worth it. I am so hungry."

I pushed my menu aside without looking at it. "Would you order for me?"

"Are you serious?" Claire looked as if her dearest wish had just come true. "Okay, yes. You don't mind eating rabbit, do you? They also have dishes with wild boar and deer. I'm so excited."

At first I didn't think she was serious, but she was. She

had been spot-on before when it came to food selections, and she was right again. Our multicourse meal was incredible. I'm not sure exactly what everything was, and I didn't ask because it seemed better not to picture a fluffy little bunny while I was chewing.

25

Draw near to God and He will draw near to you.

James 4:8

We took our time, watching boats skim across the water and listening to the lulling accent of the four people at the table behind us who were speaking French. The sun was prevailing over the flocks of clouds that frolicked in their field of blue. I was glad I had worn my sweater, though.

Neither of us had room for dessert, even though I'm sure anything we tried would have been as delicious as the rest of our meal. We walked through the small garden connected to the outdoor dining area and found a gate that opened to cement steps. The steps led down to a rowboat bobbing in the lake water. I felt like we had stumbled into a place that combined the peaceful haven of the villa with the appealing lure of water at your doorstep from Venice.

"Aha!" Claire said. "This is what I want to try to sketch." She had come prepared and took a seat on a bench in the sunshine, pulling out her journal and pencils.

"I'm going to explore around town a little," I told her.

"Have fun," Claire said over her shoulder. "And please try to avoid all impostors of famous Renaissance artists."

I put my hand on my hip. "I'd almost forgotten about him."

"That's why you have me in your life." Claire turned and gave me a grin. "You can count on me never to forget that moment on your behalf."

I shook my head. "What would I do without you, my friend?"

"I don't plan on you ever having to find out," she said.

I left her to her creativity and stopped at the front desk, where I collected all the information I needed about the chapels in the area. The desk clerk convinced me that the one at the top of the hill, known as Chiesa di San Martino, was the best church to visit. He referred to it as the "Little Sistine Chapel" because of the frescoes painted on the ceiling. Even though it was possible to take a pathway up the hill and walk through the village to the chapel, I thought it would be best to see if Claire wanted to go later because driving there would be easier.

I headed for the spot along the road where we'd enjoyed the late-night entertainment and was glad to see that the banner had weathered the rainy night. I stopped in a small shop that had an assortment of this and that, the way a thrift store would at home. I found a small pottery creamer that had the word "Bellagio" hand-painted on the side. It looked like a souvenir from a century ago, and I knew it wanted to come home with me.

I spotted two small glass vases that reminded me of the pieces we'd seen in shop windows in Venice and Florence that were labeled "Murano Glass." If these blue vases had originated in Murano, I was certain they were a fraction of their value in this shop. I bought both, knowing I would let Claire have first pick of which one she wanted.

When I returned to the grassy area, she was finishing up what had turned out to be a good sketch of the lake and the rowboat.

"For us," I said, showing her the blue vases. "Which one do you like?"

She chose the smaller one, which was so like her. I told Claire about the church we could drive to at the top of the hill, and she was up for the adventure. We made sure we had what we needed before walking back to where our little scoot-about car was parked.

Claire took the narrow road slowly as we wound up the hill. I had to get out and direct her as she squeezed into a narrow parking space next to a large van. How the van had made it up the steep and winding road, I couldn't imagine. But then, a lot of skilled drivers had negotiated narrow spots when we were in Florence.

"Is there a map or signs for the church?" Claire asked.

"I don't think so. The hotel clerk said we walk through the village to the chapel. Maybe it will be easy to spot because it's uphill."

We took what we thought was the main thoroughfare for walking into the town and discovered that the pathway was made of small pebbles with grass sprouting up between the cracks. The houses were mostly two stories with chipped paint in orange and yellow. Many of them had front doors painted bright colors, such as lapis blue, cherry red, or emerald. Clay pots with mixes of pansies and violets popped up everywhere on stone walls and by pebble-filled steps that led to another level of houses. The experience was incredible. We saw only two people: a woman holding the hand of a young boy as they headed under an archway. They seemed to barely notice us.

Our combined efforts got us to the front of the church. We heard singing coming from inside. I recognized the worship song but didn't recognize the language. It didn't sound like Italian.

Claire went over to the rock wall around the edge of the flat property to take pictures. I paused long enough to gaze with her. I realized that I had walked right up to the wall and wasn't standing three feet back. The expansive view made me feel a little wobbly, but I wasn't fearful as I would have been in the past.

"Look at you," Claire said. "No fear, girl. I'm impressed. This was a good call. I can soak up this beautiful view, and you can explore another church, complete with a choir." Her slightly flippant tone changed, and she looked at me with clear eyes. "I miss music like that." Her voice lowered. "That was one of the only things I loved about going to church and being in a choir. Music like that isn't like other music, is it?"

"It's worship music," I said. "It's expressing love in a simple but beautiful way."

Claire nodded. I was thrilled that she agreed with me and didn't turn away when I was trying to express my spiritual view on something. I thought of other things to say, but the singing stopped, and I couldn't contain my curiosity. I went over to the open door to peek inside.

To my surprise, the choir was a group of teenagers. They were exiting, so I quickly stepped out of the way. The teens gravitated to the wall for photos, and one of them struck up a conversation with Claire. She nodded and took their phones one at a time to take some group photos of them.

A middle-aged couple stepped outside. I guessed they were the leaders, and that they all were the group with the van.

The woman looked at me and said something in what I

guessed was German. When I didn't respond, she tried again in English.

"Do you have coins?" she asked.

"Coins?"

Claire had joined me and heard the question. In a sharp voice she said, "Don't tell me you're soliciting funds."

The woman looked confused.

Claire tried again. "Are you asking us for a donation? For your choir?"

"No," the man said. "For the box inside. You must insert coins for the lights to stay on."

"Oh," Claire said.

"I think we have some coins," I said.

"Here. For you." The woman handed Claire three euros.

"You don't have to . . ." Claire's face was turning rosy from embarrassment over her assumption.

"It's a gift. Please. Receive it." The woman slipped her arm through her husband's and politely said, "I hope you have a good worship in the chapel."

I felt stunned by the transaction. Touches of the eternal seemed to be the theme of our trip. God kept connecting us with believers. I couldn't remember anything like that ever happening on trips with my parents. It rarely happened at home. I felt a shiver thinking that God was doing something. We were on the edge.

I entered the chapel first, feeling reverent and expectant. I quickly understood the need to turn on a light. A few windows at the top of the arched ceiling provided enough illumination to look for the coin box but not enough light to see the paintings. Claire entered the shadowed place of worship and put the money she had just received into the box. The space was transformed.

"Wow" was all we could say.

The colors in the centuries-old frescoes were vivid, and the scenes were dynamic. The figures appeared to be three-dimensional. When the hotel clerk called it the "Little Sistine Chapel," I had wondered if this ceiling would also have an image like the famous reach of God's finger to touch Adam's. Instead, at the center of the cupola in this chapel was a painting of Christ, the triumphant victor, coming in the clouds. The image took my breath away.

I walked toward the altar and took a seat on the pew in the first row, eager to take it all in. We were surrounded by masterpiece images of timeless stories of redemption. God's stories. His love poured out, His victory over sin and death, His people, flawed and funny, all of them invited to the table. And above the tangle of humanity, Christ, the Lord of all.

Claire sat down next to me. "So, they were a youth choir. Did you catch that?"

"No."

"They're from a church in Munich." She paused before adding, "Is that odd?"

I couldn't hold back this time. I had to say it.

"Or is that God?"

Claire sat a moment in silence. At the end of a long sigh, she said, "It's God, isn't it?"

With a sense of wild hope, I turned to her. "Yes, it's God."

In a voice as still as a single raindrop, Claire said, "It's always been God, hasn't it?"

"Yes." I reached over and gave her hand a squeeze. We sat side by side. Silence with Claire never bothered me. I waited.

"You know when you asked about my conversation with Amelia and Gio while you were at the pool, and I said we talked about forgiveness and other mysteries?"

"Yes." I let go of her hand and turned so I could see her fully revealed face.

"I asked Amelia and Gio why they thought bad things happen to good people. They said the same thing you did. They didn't know. But Gio said the only way he could be free to live inside the mystery of never knowing the answer was if he chose to forgive. Then Amelia said forgiveness was a process and that God's kindness led her to repentance."

"Do you mean led Gio to repentance? You said led *her* to repentance."

"No, I meant Amelia. She told me her story. It's rough. Her mom wasn't involved in her life at all. That's why she grew up at the villa and why she learned all her cooking from her nonna."

"I never would have guessed," I said. "She's so whole. So confident."

"I know. She told me she gave her life to God when she was in England. Then she met Gio, and while they were working on the villa he told her God was renovating her heart and that a big wall needed to come down."

"A big wall?"

"She needed to forgive her mom for abandoning her. Her unforgiveness of her mom had become like the main load-bearing wall in her life. I get that. Gio told her the cross needed to become the support beam that replaced the wall. I'm still thinking about that." Claire looked down at her hands. "I didn't tell Amelia any of the things I told you, but she seemed to know. She told me there was someone I needed to forgive. A wall I needed to tear down." She wove her fingers together in a position of prayer but seemed stifled, as if she couldn't form the words she wanted to say. "Grace?" she whispered.

I knew what she was asking. "Yes, I would love to pray with you."

I looked up at the fresco of Jesus coming in the clouds,

ruler of all. I prayed aloud for my friend, asking as I had many times that our heavenly Father would draw her close to Himself. That she would be released from all the pain in her past.

"Lord," I added, "will you show Claire how to forgive so that she can release those who caused such painful injury to her soul? Tear down the wall. Release her. Set her free so she can start a fresh new chapter in her life. I ask this in Jesus' name."

"Yes," Claire whispered. "Please, God. Amen."

I tried to read her body language. This moment felt big. This prayer seemed important. Was this the plot shift I'd longed to see happen in her life?

She gave me a wavering smile. "Thank you. You said exactly what I wanted to say, but I wanted to watch an expert do it."

I wasn't sure I was an expert at praying, but I understood what she meant. She'd searched for a cooking class when we began planning this trip because she wanted an expert to teach her how to make true Italian pasta.

Claire sat up straight and pressed her palms flat on her knees. "Lots to process. But this feels like a first step."

"It's a beautiful first step." I gave her a chummy nudge and indicated she should look up.

She followed my gaze and took in the epic painting of Christ, vibrant and victorious, descending from the heavens, coming to make all things right.

"One day," I said. "Until then . . ." As soon as I said "then," the meter box by the door clicked and all the lights went off, hiding all the gorgeous paintings of the old-as-time stories and leaving us in the dense shadows.

"Subtle," Claire said.

26

Il primo amore non si scorda mai.
The first love is never forgotten.

Italian saying

After we left the church, we decided to go for a short drive since the weather was so nice. We pulled into a campground on the lake, but instead of getting out, we chose to get back on the road so we could drive along the lake.

"Can I tell you something else Amelia told me?" Claire asked after she'd been driving for about fifteen minutes.

"Yes, please."

"It's from a verse in Psalm 23. I had to memorize that chapter when I was a kid. I never understood the line about how He prepares a table before me in the presence of my enemies. Do you know that verse?"

"Yes."

"Of course you do. Well, Amelia said that's another one of the ancient mysteries of life. God provides us with everything we need. He prepares a table for us. And yet our enemies are still right there. They don't go away. That's life. Reality. Both Gio and Amelia said that wonderful things happen and God is with us. Horrible things happen and God is with us."

I nodded slowly, not quite sure where she was going with this.

"I guess I feel like I've been living with my back turned to the table. I've only focused on the enemies lined up beyond the table. The world is full of enemies. And it's full of pilgrims around the table, apparently, because we've certainly met a lot of them on this trip."

I grinned. "True."

"I don't know what I think of all this yet, but when we were in the chapel and the lights went out, I thought about what she said and how there is a lot of darkness in the world."

I was ready for her to express the next part of what I longed for her to see and experience. She was on the brink of a significant breakthrough in her life. An abundance of analogies was at her fingertips. Walls and support beams, the invitation to come to the table, darkness and light.

However, in typical Claire fashion, she changed the subject. "How hungry are you?"

I had to make a shift in my thoughts before saying, "Not very."

"Would you be open to trying a café a little farther down the road?"

"Do you have one already picked out?" I asked.

"No, I thought you could find one for us. We're almost back to Switzerland, and I thought it would be fun to have dinner in a different country tonight."

I searched for restaurants on my phone. I wasn't as adept as Claire, but I found one that was listed as being small, family owned, and on the lake. We crossed the border, found the restaurant, and were glad they could seat us without a reservation. The decor was Swiss Alpine style, and although the menu was in Italian and German, I recognized many of the names of the Italian dishes. They also provided enough Swiss-inspired options to make Claire slightly giddy.

"Älplermagronen," she said, putting down her menu. "That's what I'm having. What about you?"

"I'll have the same."

When our plates arrived, I looked at the fancy-sounding dish and then back at Claire. "Macaroni and cheese? With a side of applesauce?"

"It's a famous blending of the Swiss and Italian influences in this region." Claire used her fork to move the ingredients around as she identified them. "Macaroni from Italy with Swiss cheese, potatoes, caramelized onions, and bacon."

I picked up my fork and Claire said, "Do you want to say grace, Grace?" Her question struck her funny bone, and she tried to swallow her laughter but it spilled out. Just as quickly as her giggle escaped, she composed herself and bowed her head. "I'm serious," she said without looking up. "You can pray aloud if you want."

My prayer was short, sweet, and heartfelt. I loved that she wanted to share in my life rhythm of always bowing and thanking God before I ate. It felt like a small dream come true that I was able to pray out loud at this table with her and she was the one who had invited me to do so.

I took a bite of the melt-in-your-mouth scrumptiousness and gave a proper "Mmm."

"Now that is Swiss cheese," Claire said. "Wow."

We didn't talk much while we ate. As usual, I had lots of thoughts running around in my mind like tigers escaped from the zoo. I didn't want those thoughts to pounce on Claire, but at the same time, I didn't want to keep silent if there was anything important I should say. I tried a work-around approach to see if it would lead us back into the conversation I was longing to continue.

"Thanks for telling me about your talk with Amelia and Gio. Was there anything else they said that stuck with you?"

Claire thought for a minute. "Amelia said that when they decided to marry, she still wanted Gio to press charges, but he told her he wasn't going to do that. He said he wanted to be remembered for the things he did and not for the things that were done to him." Claire pushed her empty plate away. "I thought that was profound."

"I do too."

"I think both of them are doing that by the way they live and with their Friday night dinners."

I nodded, and our discussion ended there. As we drove back to our hotel, I thought about how I'd told Claire that Jesus was pursuing her. Now I needed to believe my own words and stop feeling like it was up to me to say something profound the way Gio had or to pelt her with more questions. What was it that Amelia had said about how God's kindness led her to repentance? Maybe the best thing I could do was watch the eternal expert in kindness do what He did best and learn from Him.

The next morning, we started the day early. We knew we couldn't leave San Mamete without one last memory-sealing moment on our balcony, slowly drawing in deep breaths and releasing them over the lake. In that way, we said our farewell to another part of beautiful Italy that had woven itself into our hearts.

As we moved through the hotel lobby one more time with our faithful wheelies, I tried hard not to feel the departure melancholy that had followed me out of Venice and the villa.

It may have helped that our first stop was the little bakery-market across the street that had just opened its doors. We selected from the assortment of scrumptious-looking pastries as well as some cheese, fresh cherry tomatoes, and a small round loaf of some kind of bread that looked like it was made from rustic grains and had a nice, thick crust. We added a bar of Swiss chocolate and four bottles of our beloved acqua minerale. Our plan was to have a breakfast picnic along the way before getting to Lugano, where we had to turn in our rental car and take the train to the Milan airport.

Claire turned into the campground. "This could be a good place for our picnic. What do you think?"

"Great."

The grounds manager was kind to us because it was a weekday and family vacation season hadn't fully begun yet. The campground didn't offer an entrance pass for day use, but he let us come in for our breakfast picnic at half the overnight rate. Parking was close to a large grassy area on the lake that was dotted with lovely shade trees as well as benches. Only three other people were out enjoying the view from the green area. Two of them were feeding the ducks that waddled up from the water. I felt as if we had slipped into a painting. The bench we went to was perfect for quiet observation.

"This is picturesque," Claire observed. "I wish we had time for me to draw it."

We gazed together at the placid lake and bit into our pastries. A man who had gone for a quick dip emerged from the water, reached for his towel, and wrapped it around his shoulders. I imagined the water was colder than our first swim at the villa. Even so, I found it exhilarating to imagine how refreshing an early morning swim would feel.

From behind us, we could hear cheerful voices that were louder than they probably should have been. The laughter from one of the girls seemed especially boisterous. We glanced over our shoulders at the group of teenagers gathering on the grass about ten feet from where we were sitting. Both of us laughed.

"Of course it's the youth choir," Claire said. "God sure likes to get His point across."

The director's wife recognized us and came over with a couple of towels over her arm. "Hello!"

"Good morning. Planning a morning swim?" I asked.

"Two students want to be baptized."

"Here?" Claire asked. "Now?"

"Yes. You're welcome to come over and join us if you'd like." She caught her husband's wave and trotted over to their little flock.

"Were you ever baptized?" Claire asked me.

"Nathan and I both were, soon after we met."

"What is it supposed to mean?"

"For us, after we both surrendered our lives to the Lord, we knew that baptism is the outward expression of what happens on the inside. So we wanted to publicly make that declaration."

She kept looking at the students. "Those kids are so respectful and focused. My experience was nothing like theirs."

"Fresh starts," I said. "The next generation walking in the footsteps of Christ. It's so beautiful."

We watched as the first student, a petite girl with curly hair, stepped into the chilly lake water along with the director and his wife. We could hear their muffled "Eeees!" as they waded out to about waist deep. The leaders asked the girl something. She replied, plugged her nose, leaned back, and the two leaders gently dipped her all the way under. She came up giggling.

The group erupted into cheers and applause, and I felt tears running down my cheeks. I couldn't help it. I always cried at baptisms. This moment was so pristine in its simplicity and yet so ancient and universal.

Once again, God was revealing the elemental essentials of the Christian faith, as we had heard and seen since arriving. This living demonstration of denouncing the old, dead life and being reborn into eternal life felt as sacred to me as the enactment around the table of the wedding feast of the Lamb seemed to feel to Gio.

I had become so wrapped up in my thoughts, I didn't catch something Claire said. My focus was fixed on the next student, a tall boy, who received a round of cheers before he even stepped into the water. He called out something to his friends, and I recognized "Jesus" in his tumble of words. I choked up even more. Hearing a teenager shout the name of Jesus was powerful.

"I'm sorry," Claire said.

I turned to look at her, not understanding what she would be apologizing to me for in such a moment as this. Her eyes were closed and tears streamed down her face.

"I was wrong, Father God. I blamed You and my parents and that horrible man. But I don't want to look at my enemies any longer. Please set a place for me at Your table. Please forgive me. I want You. I want to forgive those who hurt me."

"Yes," I murmured under my breath. "Yes and amen."

All of a sudden, Claire stood up.

I held my breath as she walked toward the group.

Jumping up, I instinctively grabbed our bags and joined her as the teen boy popped up from the water and shook his long hair. The droplets scattered like crystals in the streaming light of the new day. Again, the group burst into cheerful applause.

Claire kept walking.

She didn't look back. She didn't look at me. Her gaze was fixed on the couple whose kindness had been one of many pieces that led Claire to repentance. When they saw her, they stopped. Claire slipped out of her shoes and took nimble steps to the water's edge.

The group fell silent. I walked closer to the shore, my heart pounding wildly. My hand rose to cover my mouth. This was Claire's moment. Her declaration. Here. Now.

The wife held out her hands to welcome Claire farther out into the waist-high water. I could hear the choir director asking her name, then he said, "Claire, do you believe Jesus is the Christ, the only Son of God?"

"Yes."

"Do you promise to love God and walk with Him the rest of your life?"

"I do."

"In the name of the Father, the Son, and the Holy Spirit, I baptize you."

Claire closed her eyes, leaned back, and was submerged in the clear water. She rose like the morning sun, her smile radiant, her eyes blinking.

The wife hugged her, and the three of them quickly exited the shimmering water. That was when I noticed that the applause of the group was as welcoming and jubilant as it had been for the others.

Claire was beaming as she scurried up to me with her arms crossed and shivering from the chill. I wished I had a towel for her. Instead, I hugged her and held her, letting her joy soak into me along with the lake water. Together we wept and laughed and wept and laughed some more.

Then the most extraordinary sound rose as the youth choir began to sing an ancient, sacred hymn in four-part harmony. The world around us seemed to stand still as the notes floated in the air, covering us and blessing us, before scattering out across the lake like a benediction.

27

> Twenty years from now you will be more disappointed by the things you didn't do than by the ones you did do. So throw off the bowlines. Sail away from the safe harbor. Catch the trade winds in your sails. Explore. Dream. Discover.
>
> H. Jackson Brown Jr.

Claire and I never recovered from our visit to Italy. We didn't want to.

Nathan saw a change in me immediately. So did Emma. He said my love for him and Emma and especially my love for God seemed bigger. Fuller. Claire's love for God and others was unmistakable. She looked and acted like a different woman. Her new haircut played an interesting part in her renewed life because her bangs no longer fell forward and hid her expressive eyes. Jared loved everything about her transformation. On most Sundays our families sat together in church and then had lunch, gathered around a table at a restaurant or in one of our homes.

As the weeks unfolded, I followed the footsteps of Christ into a brand-new pace of life. I closed out the longtime ophthalmology practice of my boss. Even on the very last day, he didn't have any words of thanks or appreciation for what I'd done over the years. So I chose to thank him for the job and for the experience I'd gained as well as the valuable lessons I'd learned. Somehow, I thought that was what Paulina would have done.

On the Saturday morning after my final day, I took Emma to the coffee shop where Claire and I met, and the two of us sat at a corner table. "Now that I'm not working," I told her, "I want you to know that I'm available."

"Available for what?" Emma asked.

"For you. For us. For more time to do fun things."

Emma gave me a hesitant look. I realized she had spent far too many years hearing about how stressed I was and how busy I was. She didn't know how to respond to me attempting to tell her that I valued her and I wanted to spend time with her. I knew now that girls need their moms in some seasons more than others. Claire had taught me that.

"This is what I want to say to you, adorable Emma." I leaned closer so that I wouldn't embarrass her by anyone else hearing us. "I am sorry that I let my job take over so much of my energy the past few years. Please forgive me for not making time to give you more attention."

"Mom." She glanced left and right, clearly embarrassed.

"Just know that I love you and I'm available." I leaned back, leaving my declaration on the table. "Oh," I added with a sincere, dipped-chin gaze, "and I love you."

"You said that." Emma's slightly repressed grin told me that my words had planted a seed. I felt a sweet and fervent passion for the opportunity that was now before me. I couldn't wait to watch our mother-daughter friendship grow.

My dad was so intrigued with my vision of cleaning up and expanding my garden, he came over with some of his lawn maintenance guys. They brought rented equipment, and the expert workers turned the soil and prepared a large area of our big backyard for planting. I was going to have the biggest garden I had ever planted. I wasn't home the day they made the earth ready and was grateful for that, because the scent of fertilizer lingered for a couple days.

Several fellow gardeners from church joined me on planting day, and we became a sort of club. I found out that one of the women served at the local soup kitchen.

"Do you think I could donate vegetables this fall?" I asked. "I'd love to help serve meals too. On Fridays, maybe?"

She set everything up, and starting in early July, both Nathan and I served at the soup kitchen every Friday night. I loved that he shared that with me. Best of all, Emma and her giggling girlfriends came one Friday night and provided dinner music. Nathan was their bodyguard and hogged the mic at the end of their five-song set so he could tell his best dad jokes.

Nathan was also on board from the beginning with the plans for a pergola. His answer to everything was "No, larger." I didn't expect his vision to exceed mine, but he was an outdoors guy. This was a dream he'd never dared to bring up because we'd spent so much time and money renovating the inside of our house.

Claire efficiently moved through all the clearances for building permits with the city, and the patio and pergola were finished the day before Nathan's birthday, September 21. Of course we had to have a grand party.

I invited my new gardeners group and their spouses. Emma invited five of her girlfriends. Nathan invited everyone from his physical therapy office. Claire, Jared, and Brooke brought two families from their neighborhood with their kids, and my mom and dad surprised us and brought a DJ with his traveling sound system.

My mom wore her new red silk scarf that Claire and I got for her in Bellagio. As the evening cooled, she fashionably draped it across her shoulders, and in the filtered light, she looked as beautiful as any of the women whose portraits hung in the museums of Florence. I felt more love and appreciation for my mother in that moment than I ever had in my life. She had given me so much. She was my Paulina, and I'd never realized it.

We ate an abundance of fabulous Italian food under the twinkle lights of our brand-new pergola. I pointed out to several people where the vines would be planted.

"I haven't decided yet if I'm going with wisteria or honeysuckle." I asked my gardener friends, "Any suggestions?"

By the end of the evening, honeysuckle had won by popular opinion.

Since we didn't have a table yet, it was easy to clear the chairs and have our dance floor ready. The birthday boy walked over to me and held out his hand.

"May I have the honor of the first dance?" he asked me.

You know what? I didn't care one bit that all those people, friends, family, and strangers were watching Nathan and me as we swayed and smiled and tried not to step on each other's feet. I felt as in love with him as I did the last time we'd danced like this at our wedding reception.

When the song ended, our DJ started a tune that brought all the children and teens out on the dance floor, where they thoroughly entertained us. As the California summer sky mellowed to a lovely shade of sienna orange, I kept thinking, *Simple joys are holy.*

Claire sidled up to me. "I wonder, do you think there will be dancing at the wedding feast of the Lamb?"

"I hope so," I said.

She had been making the rounds with a plate of cookies,

serving everyone, and now held out the round, compass-shaped bussola to me. "Take two. They're small."

We laughed and gave each other hugs.

That night, after all the guests were gone, I went into Emma's room to check on her because her light was still on.

"You okay?" I asked.

She patted the side of her bed, inviting me to sit down. "Tonight was fun," she said.

"Yes, it was."

"I wondered, Mom . . ."

"Yes?"

"Do you think maybe sometime you and I could go somewhere? Like on a trip the way you and Claire did?"

My heart melted. "Yes. Absolutely. I would love to go anywhere in this wide world with you, Emma."

She sat up and wrapped her arms around me in a hug. I thought of Paulina's note about the two gifts that come from traveling and smiled. This moment was a wish that had been on hold in my heart.

I embraced my daughter a little longer and smoothed her silky hair as if it were a veil spun from sea-foam by the queen of the mermaids.

Bussola Buranello Cookies

2 cups all-purpose flour
½ cup granulated sugar
½ cup cold butter, cut into pieces
4 egg yolks
1½ teaspoons vanilla extract
1 teaspoon finely grated lemon zest

In a large bowl, stir together flour and sugar.
Use a pastry cutter, fork, or food processor to cut butter into the flour mixture until crumbly.
In a separate small bowl, combine egg yolks, vanilla, and lemon zest.
Add the egg yolk mixture to the flour and sugar mixture and mix until the dough comes together. You will have to get in there with your hands toward the end of mixing to make sure the dough holds together.
Turn out of the bowl, shape into a foot-long cylinder, and wrap well in plastic wrap. Let the dough rest in the refrigerator for at least an hour.
Line two baking sheets with parchment paper.
Divide the dough in half, then divide each half into ten pieces. Roll each piece into a rope 6 to 7 inches long and shape into a backward *S* or a circle.
Place shaped cookies on prepared baking sheets two inches apart and refrigerate for 30 minutes.
Preheat oven to 350°F and bake cookies for 13 to 15 minutes or until just beginning to brown on the bottom. Cool completely before removing from cookie sheet.
Store in an airtight container.

Amaretti Cookies

3 egg whites
pinch of salt
2½ cups almond flour
¾ cup granulated sugar
1 teaspoon almond extract
1 teaspoon vanilla extract
granulated sugar in a bowl, for dipping
powdered sugar in a bowl, for dipping

Preheat oven to 325°F.
In a large bowl, beat egg whites and salt until stiff peaks form.
In a separate bowl, blend almond flour and granulated sugar well. Fold ⅓ of the mixture into the egg whites with a light hand.
Add almond and vanilla and mix well.
Add the rest of the almond mixture in two more parts, mixing well after each addition.
Roll dough into 20 balls.
Dip each ball first in granulated sugar, then in powdered sugar.
Place on cookie sheet lined with parchment paper and press each cookie gently to flatten halfway.
Bake for 20 to 25 minutes until they are golden brown and slightly cracked on top. Exact time will vary based on the size of the balls.
Check the cookies frequently to avoid overbaking, as they should remain slightly soft when pressed. Allow to cool on the cookie sheet before removing.

Discussion Questions

1. Why do you think it was a good idea for Grace and Claire to go on a trip to Italy?

2. If you have been to Italy, share about where you went and your experiences. If you would like to go to Italy, what areas would you like to visit?

3. Grace and Claire planned their trip thoroughly, but when they arrived in Venice, they were nervous because it appeared that nothing was the way they thought it would be. Have you ever found yourself in a situation like that? How did it turn out?

4. What is one historical piece of information you learned from the story?

5. Why do you think Claire felt more comfortable being the leader?

6. Are you more comfortable expressing yourself in words the way Grace did in her journal, or are you more like Claire, preferring to capture the moment with an artistic approach like sketching?

7. Why do you think Grace was able to overcome some of her fears on this trip? Can you share about a time when you found that telling yourself the truth changed the way you felt in an uncomfortable situation?

8. If you were with Grace and Claire at the villa, how would you spend your free time? In the kitchen? In the garden? At the pool? On a Vespa? Why?

9. Do you have a friend who is close enough for you to trust with the deepest thoughts and feelings of your heart? What do you think is needed for a friendship to grow that close?

10. Do you think Grace and Claire ever returned to Italy? What do you think a return trip might be like for them?

Dear Beautiful Reader,

I wish you could have the pleasure of knowing all the people who came alongside and left their fingerprints on this story.

I'm grateful that Vicki Crumpton reached out to my dear friend and agent, Janet Grant, and planted the seed that grew into the Suitcase Sisters collection.

Rachel McRae is a fiction editor extraordinaire. When she and I had the pleasure of meeting face-to-face, it was one of those moments in which it felt as if we'd already been pals for ages. Every writer needs a cheerleader, and Rachel excels at the position.

The Dream Team at Revell went above and beyond to get these stories into the hands and hearts of readers around the world. Jessica English, as my senior editor, did not need to taste-test the recipes at the end of my books, but she did! Erin Bartels, senior copywriter, got the back cover copy just right, and I loved the way Laura Klynstra, senior art director, listened to all my suggestions and created dreamy covers along with the illustrator, Art of Nora.

As soon as it was time to start letting people know about the new stories in the series, I was in good hands with Brianne Dekker and Raela Schoenherr, my two marketing maestros. It's a gift to work with creative people who support your marketing ideas.

For many weeks, my publicity manager, Karen Steele, and I kept our email strings nice and long as she set up a wide variety of interviews and updated me on reviews. Joyce Perez and Lindsay Schubert, associate marketing managers, kept up with loads of behind-the-scenes promotional details. Thank you!

The hard workers at Baker Book House did a remarkable job getting preorder copies ready and shipped. Thank you for such encouraging support.

The comments shared by you beautiful readers have been a gift. Thank you. Your words fuel my imagination and keep me going on slow writing days.

Several of my friends made this book extra special. Hourik Kazarian, my favorite food blogger, created the Italian recipes and shared details on her Instagram. Rachel Schwartz created cute Book Club Hostess boxes and crafted lovely reels and posts for social media.

Paula Gamble-Grant at MySoulRefresh.com made space, as she does, to have a long conversation about Italy, where she hosts reFresh retreats. I'm glad book writing coach Mary Pero and I live close enough to meet for lunch so we can talk through tricky scenes. My critique partner and award-winning author, Tessa Afshar, has taught me so much during our monthly video calls. Every woman should have a friend like Marlene Rice, who has spent years praying for me and championing everything I write.

My first trip to Italy was with the best Suitcase Sisters anyone could ask for—Luanne, Loraine, Carol, and Laurie. What an adventure! And yes, as Carol said, we'll always have Vivoli's.

I am blessed every day by the abundant support and love from my husband, Ross. My agent, Janet, has been the source of endless brainstorming, advice, editing, laughing sessions, and tearful conversations. What a gift she is! My daughter, Rachel, is the clever author whisperer who inspires me to go deeper into understanding and caring for my characters. Every Christmas, my son, Ross, fuels my research for upcoming novels by going through my wish list and gifting me with the resource books I need. I could not do what I've done all these years without the continual encouragement from my family.

Above all, I'm grateful to the Lord for the privilege and delight of being created to be a storyteller.

Read on for an excerpt from
Robin Jones Gunn's

Tea with Elephants

Available now wherever books are sold.

Prologue

Learn to be a faithful friend to your soul.

Hildegard of Bingen

Some mornings I wake up thinking I've just heard the chittering call of the cheeky monkey that watched Lily and me from his loquat tree. I'm certain I can smell the spicy-sweet fragrance of a steaming cup of masala chai placed on the nightstand.

Then I squint in the half-light and see that I am in my own bed, with the soft glow of the hallway nightlight sliding under the door. I am not with my closest friend, back in the place of gentle mystery, of emerald tea fields, stampeding wildebeests, elegant giraffes, and an unobstructed view of a singular baobab tree silhouetted against an amber horizon.

I am home, nestled under my thick comforter, settled into my once-again ordinary life.

Nothing, however, is the same as it was two years ago when Lily called me in the middle of a stressful workday. Her unexpected and exuberant announcement stirred in me the long-dormant embers of a wish we had whispered to each other twenty years earlier. We had big hopes back then. Back when we were starry-eyed teenagers who had just experienced our first taste of another corner of the globe. We dreamed of traveling together and were naive enough to believe anything was possible.

Then we grew up and went nowhere.

Lily's surprise announcement broke the stalemate of our unfulfilled wishes. Her father-in-law had given her a gift. An African safari for two. She said I had to go with her. Simply had to. Her husband didn't want to go. He thought I should. If Lily and I did not use the all-inclusive package, it would be lost.

I resisted.

She insisted.

The trip was impractical. It made no sense. Not when things at work were so intense. I was the senior fiction editor for a publishing house and fully aware that our sales numbers for the last two years had been less than stellar. I couldn't possibly request more vacation time until next year.

Lily persisted.

Again, I resisted.

She pleaded with me in that winsome way of hers, reminding me that this had been our dream. Our sincere and eager wish to go somewhere exciting, back when we could still fit into our skinny jeans.

I softened.

She asked if I remembered.

Of course I remembered. How could I forget the summer she and I met while volunteering at a Christian conference center in Costa Rica? Our prayer of surrender at the final campfire had marked both of us. We meant it when we turned our faces to the heavens and told the Maker of the stars that we were His. We wanted to serve Him the rest of our lives, wherever that might be. Two girls, ready for anything.

Returning to our cabin, we whispered late into the night. Would spending our lives doing what God created us to do involve travel? Yes, Lord, please! Where would He send us? Europe. England. Ireland. Brazil. Or even . . . Lily had whispered the name of the mysterious continent with panache. "*Ahh-free-kaa.*"

Now I smiled at my desk when she said it again on the phone, and it brought back all the feelings of adventures that awaited us.

"*Ahh-free-kaa!* Think of it! We've been given a free trip. I forbid you to say you won't come with me. We've waited too long for a chance to go somewhere together again." Lily lowered her voice and asked the question that melted my resistance. "If not now, when?"

Without thinking, I answered, "You're right. Yes, we have to go. We need to do this."

I had no idea how I'd pull it off. With some careful planning, it might be doable next summer. Possibly in the spring.

Then Lily included a few minor details. The dates of the tour package could not be changed. We were leaving in three weeks, on November 7. Oh, and by the way, she had an aunt and uncle who lived outside Nairobi. They were expecting us.

Before I could alter my impulsive reply, she hung up.

My pulse throbbed like a beating drum. I sat back and blinked. I felt like Lily had burst into my cubicle and popped a cardboard tube of glitter, and shimmering possibilities were floating all around me. How could I put the invisible glitter back in the tube? I couldn't bring myself to call her and insist that my yes had been too hasty. Yet I knew I couldn't go. Not in three weeks. It wasn't possible.

And then, sadly, sweetly, unexpectedly, it was possible.

Three weeks later, I was on a plane headed to Africa.

Ever since our remarkable trip I have not stopped thinking of *her*—of Africa. Every glimpse of her remarkable beauty made me want to see more. Every vivid image and unique sound, every fragrance and new taste invited me to absorb the wonder.

In a small way, I caught the feeling behind these words in the book *Out of Africa*:

> If I know a song of Africa . . . of the giraffe and the African new moon lying on her back . . . does Africa know a song of me?

Lily and I spent only a week in Kenya, and yet, I'd like to think we heard a bit of her song. A low, unmistakable, contented hum. It caused me to wonder what the great gentlewoman thought of us.

In those first days, when my affection for Africa was forming, I remember feeling shy, the way one does in a new relationship when you fear your deep fondness might be embarrassingly one-sided. But then I felt enfolded in Kenya's womanly presence, and I was sure I could hear more than her hum. I could hear the rhythm of her heartbeat as she presented her large self to us and drew us closer.

Lily and I arrived in such a flurry that neither of us fully realized we had brought with us great lumps of hurt in our punched and kneaded souls. We had kept our folded-in feelings and fears hidden even from each other until we arrived on Kenya's doorstep.

When we were welcomed in without hesitation, we calmed ourselves and saw why we'd really come all that way. I smile now to think of the gentle, maternal manner in which Africa scolded us, and how she took us in and covered us. She gave us a place to rise, to prove, like a loaf of my own mother's best sourdough bread.

And rise we did. All the way to the top of Mount Kenya, where my best friend and I gazed contentedly upon the hushed arrival of the golden hour and calmly sipped tea with elephants. Two women, ready for anything.

Robin Jones Gunn is the bestselling author of over one hundred books, including the Sisterchicks series and the Christy Miller series for teen girls. Her books have sold more than 6.5 million copies. Robin and her husband have two grown children and four grandchildren and live in Southern California, where she cohosts the *Women Worth Knowing* podcast. Learn more at RobinGunn.com.

A Note from the Publisher

Dear Reader,

Thank you for selecting a Revell novel! We're so happy to be part of your reading life through this work. Our mission here at Revell is to publish stories that reach the heart. Through friendship, romance, suspense, or a travel back in time, we bring stories that will entertain, inspire, and encourage you. We believe in the power of stories to change our lives and are grateful for the privilege of sharing these stories with you.

We believe in building lasting relationships with readers, and we'd love to get to know you better. If you have any feedback, questions, or just want to chat about your experience reading this book, please email us directly at publisher@revellbooks.com. Your insights are incredibly important to us, and it would be our pleasure to hear how we can better serve you.

We look forward to hearing from you and having the chance to enhance your experience with Revell Books.

The Publishing Team at Revell Books
A Division of Baker Publishing Group
publisher@revellbooks.com

Connect with Robin

Visit Robin's website to sign up for her newsletter, browse her online shop, listen to her podcast, and more.

RobinGunn.com

AuthorRobinJonesGunn

RobinGunn

RobinGunn